Undersea Odyssey

Undersea Odyssey

by
Captain Danrit

translated by
Frederick Lawton

A Black Coat Press Book

Acknowledgements: I should like to thank Georges T. Dodds and Jean-Luc Rivera for providing valuable materials and offering advice and support in the preparation of this text.

Translated into English by Frederick Lawton and first published in England by Grant Richards in 1910 under the title of *The Sunken Submarine*.

Visit our website at www.blackcoatpress.com

TABLE OF CONTENTS

Introduction

Undersea Odyssey is the translation of *Robinsons Sous-Marins* (*Robinsons Under The Sea*), published in France in 1908, and not, as indicated in some catalogs, a translation of Volume 2 of *La Guerre Fatale*, a.k.a. *En Sous-Marin* or *Les Exploits d'un Sous-Marin*. It was translated into English by Frederick Lawton and first published in England by Grant Richards in 1910 under the title of *The Sunken Submarine*, then in America by Little Brown & Co in 1911. The term "Robinsons" was often used in French popular literature as a synonym for "adventurers" following the success of *Robinson Crusoe*.

Emile Auguste Cyprien Driant (a.k.a. "Capitaine Danrit") was born on September 11, 1855 in the town of Neuf-

7

chatel, located in the French department of the Aisne in Northern France. His father was a magistrate and a public notary who wanted his son to follow in his footsteps; however, young Emile was deeply affected by the humiliating defeat of France in the Franco-Prussian War in 1871, and decided to embrace a military career instead. After studying the Law, he entered the prestigious military academy of Saint-Cyr in 1875. Four years later, he earned the rank of Under-Lieutenant in the French infantry. In 1884, Driant served in Africa under the controversial General Boulanger, a charismatic and ultra-conservative *revanchard* (meaning, one who sought revenge against Germany), who went into politics and was made Minister of War in 1886. The following year, Driant married the General's daughter. The timing was less than fortuitous, career-wise, as his then-popular father-in-law was considering a coup d'état. But, the General missed his opportunity and ended up disgraced. He had to flee France or face arrest, and eventually committed suicide in Belgium in 1881. Such an infamous family connection hurt Driant, who shared his father-in-law's strong, militaristic convictions.

In 1889, Driant resolved to rekindle what he thought was a waning patriotic flame in the breasts of the younger generation, and embarked on writing lengthy military sagas, depicting "near-future" wars, under the anagrammatic pen name of "Danrit."

In 1896, and again in 1899, Driant was promoted by the Army, which posted him to Troyes, in the Champagne region, and placed a growing number of men under his command. He turned these battalions into an elite troop of great renown.

French politics were, at the time, strongly divided between an ultra-conservative right-wing comprised of Royalists, Bonapartists, the Catholic Church, and various ultra-nationalist, *revanchards*, anti-Republican and anti-Socialist factions on the one hand, and Socialists, Freemasons, Republicans, pacifists and internationalists on the other. The former faction was represented by politicians such as Paul Déroulède and Maurice Barrès; the latter by Aristide Briand and Jean

Jaurès. Control of the Army was, of course, of strategic importance in this political battle, which raged during the first decade of the 20th century. It turned out that secret files were kept on each officer, indicating his political and religious leanings; the discovery quickly mushroomed into a political scandal.

Driant took an active part in this ideological battle by creating an anti-Masonic society of officers sharing his views, but was exposed in the summer 1905. After refusing to back down, and loudly and publicly proclaiming his opposition, Driant was forced to resign from the Army at the end of 1905.

This, however, did not put an end to his political life; on the contrary, he continued championing his ideas, which now included the promotion of a new war against Germany, through his writings. In 1910, he was elected as Representative for the district of Nancy, and reelected in 1914.

When World War I was declared in August 1914, Driant rejoined the Army and, despite his age, which would have guaranteed him a desk position, insisted on serving at the front. He was made Lieutenant-Colonel of the 56th and 59th Infantry Brigades. He was killed by the Germans on February 22, 1916 at a copse nears Caures, in a skirmish that was a prelude to the battle of Verdun, the bloodiest in all the war. He died a hero, being shot as he had stopped to assist a wounded soldier under his command.

Unsurprisingly, his death was used in the most blatant propagandistic way to further bolster patriotic fervor and anti-German sentiments.

With Louis Boussenard and Paul d'Ivoi (also a notoriously ultra-patriotic writer), "Capitaine Danrit" became one of the most popular contributors of the famous *Journal des Voyages*, a best-selling illustrated magazine started in 1877, which published serialized novels and stories by some of the most famous authors in the Jules Verne tradition.

Danrit's work mostly consisted in describing in great technical detail and melodramatic style "near-future" wars, intending to raise the alert and make his readers aware of the various factions threatening to destroy France—unless, of course, the French took action first. In that respect, Danrit was, in modern-day parlance, a "neo-conservative." His understanding of military tactics and technology, in terms of knowing what existed, and what might exist in the near-future, and how it could best be used in the battlefield, as well as his forward-thinking mind, gave his work a prophetic and chilling effect.

Danrit's first work in the genre was the three volume *La Guerre de Demain* (*The War of Tomorrow*) (1889-92),[1] aptly sub-titled "A great patriotic and military tale." In it, Danrit basically retold the story of the 1870 Franco-Prussian War, but with new technology and better French leadership, eventually resulting in a victory for France. Combatants from both sides were shown to be brave, patriotic men, but the Germans naturally did not fear resorting to the most heinous spying and dirty tricks. Danrit introduced machine guns, sea fortresses, balloons and dirigibles into his fictional theater of war, but nevertheless relied on great infantry and cavalry charges to keep the war going. More interestingly from a science fictionesque standpoint was the concept of giant, electric-powered airships (as tried by Giffard in 1862) which ended up giving France her victory. In this alternate version of history, the Kaiser died on the battlefield. Danrit's final words made his manifesto very clear; he concluded the book by addressing the reader as follows: "Wherever you go, remember the flag that sheltered you, and when you are called on to defend it, soon perhaps, when the war of tomorrow comes, soon I hope, go with trust, little soldier."

In 1895, in *L'Invasion Noire* (*The Black Invasion*), dedicated to Jules Verne, Danrit imagined that a charismatic Muslim Turkish Sultan, robbed of his lands by the Western Powers, declared a Holy War against Europe (today, we would use

---

[1] A fourth volume, published four years later, added the fictional diary of a German officer recounting his version of the same events described in the earlier three volumes from a French viewpoint.

the word *jihad*). The Sultan enlisted not only the Islamic world of North Africa and India (i.e.: Pakistan), but also several nations of Africa which had been converted to Islam. The lack of unity amongst the European nations first led to the successful invasion of the Balkan Peninsula, then Spain, by the Muslim forces, after some terribly bloody battles. Danrit describes the enemy forces as composed of bloodthirsty, mindless fanatics, and even cannibals (!). However, the Europeans' superior technology enabled them to mount a counterattack and, ultimately, prevail, just as the enemy was marching onto Paris. In the book, Danrit painted a dark and yet prophetic picture of France on the verge of defeat, in total disarray, where civilian authorities had no choice but to resign and transfer all power into the hands of an enlightened Marshall, said to be a descendent of Joan of Arc. He was the supreme leader sent by Providence to rescue the country, with the help of an elderly, brilliant scientist. The Sultan and his son chose to commit suicide rather than surrender.

L'Invasion Noire contained some brilliant, if frightening, technical predictions, such as automated batteries, armored battle trains, bacteriological and deadly gas, the rather eerie depiction of a flying saucer-like metal airship (perhaps inspired by designs from aeronaut Capazza?) and even a proto-television using telescopic mirrors. The war was shown to have been won through a combination of air-power and gas attacks, a somber but accurate prediction of World War I.

In *L'Invasion Noire*, Danrit had stigmatized England, which had caused the war. His anti-British prejudice blossomed in his next saga, *La Guerre Fatale, France-Angleterre* (*The Fatal War, France vs. England*) (1901), which focused mostly on new and futuristic technologies, and was remarkable for its Tom Clancyesque description of advanced types of submarines, which eventually led to the defeat of the British and the destruction of London.

Danrit's next genre work was *Evasion d'Empereur* (*The Emperor's Escape*) (1903), a uchronic tale in which Napoleon escaped from Saint Helena aboard a submarine, but died be-

11

fore he could reshape the world, *à la* Louis Geoffroy's *Napoleon et la Conquête du Monde* (1836).

Danrit returned to global warfare with *L'Invasion Jaune* (*The Yellow Invasion*) (1905). In it, the Japanese led the Chinese and other Asian nations to attack the West. There were few striking technological predictions in this book, but quite a number of prophetic pages regarding the war in the Pacific, including the use of kamikazes. Surprisingly, Danrit showed the European armies united under the command of not a French General, but the Kaiser. Equally surprising, at the end of the book, the Asians have won the war and their troops march on the Champs-Elysées. (However, the Japanese general is shot by a resistant.)

Robinsons de l'Air (*The Robinsons of the Air*) (1907) was a less bellicose, Vernian story of the exploration of the Arctic by a joint French American expedition, using a super dirigible inspired by those of Krebs, Renard and Santos-Dumont. It was followed by *Robinsons Sous-Marins* (1908), presented here, which followed the same template.

L'Aviateur du Pacifique (*The Aviator of the Pacific*) (1909) was intended to be a celebration of aviation in which a French engineer who has invented a revolutionary "helico-aeroplane" using a special fuel, flies across the Pacific; but Danrit could not let such an opportunity go to waste. He described how, when his protagonist reaches Midway, he discovers that the Japanese are preparing to launch a sneak attack against the American Pacific Fleet anchored in Hawaii. Unable to radio his information because of a fleet of Japanese scrambling ships, our stalwart Frenchman has no choice but to fly across the Pacific to the mainland U.S. to alert America. Again, the prophetic value of the novel was boosted by Danrit's brilliant understanding of the strategic analysis of a Japanese-American conflict.

Robinsons Sous-Marins (*Robinsons Under The Sea*), presented here as *Undersea Odyssey*, followed in 1908, returning to Danrit's Vernian roots, but never neglecting the military applications of the technology depicted in the book.

Danrit, who had already railed against freemasons, free-thinkers, radicals and socialists in his novels, decided to make them the enemy in his next novel, *La Révolution de Demain* (*The Revolution of Tomorrow*) (1909) which, curiously, was written in collaboration with Arnould Galopin, the author of *Doctor Omega*.[2] In it, Danrit whipped up his readers' fears of the Red Menace by showing mobs of communist-inspired Parisian *communards* taking over the capital and attacking the Army and dynamiting the Eiffel Tower.

In *L'Alerte* (*The Alert*) (1910), Danrit pitted again France against Germany using the context of their geo-political rivalries in Morocco; the book emphasized that science's only value was to serve the Nation. *Au-Dessus du Continent Noir* (*Above the Black Continent*) (1912) was another Vernian take on Africa, seen through the prism of a French Colonial Empire threatened both from inside and outside. Finally, *Robinsons Souterrains* (*Underground Robinsons*) (1913), later retitled *La Guerre Souterraine* (*The Underground War*) to capitalize on Danrit's marketable association with War, explored interesting possibilities in terms of new, earth-boring technologies.

Driant also wrote several purely historical novels devoted to military history and families which are not relevant to this article.

The key to understanding Driant's work, and indeed his life, is to understand how, at age 16, he was deeply traumatized by the French defeat of 1871, a blow far, far worse than 9/11, with dramatic consequences for France, including the humiliating loss of Alsace and Lorraine to Germany. Driant saw that defeat, not incorrectly, as the first knell of doom for his beloved Imperial France, and spent all his life trying to stop what he believed to be the impending destruction of his country.

---

[2] Available in a Black Coat Press edition, translated and retold by Jean-Marc & Randy Lofficier, ISBN 978-1-0-9740711-1-4, 2003.

Driant's fiction was not rooted in imperialism, colonialism, exploration or conquest, like some of its English or American counterparts; it was rooted in fear.

Where Verne playfully explored all the continents, Driant saw a catalog of enemies ready to attack; where Verne imagined new machines and technology for the joys of science and discovery, Driant put them to the only good use he knew: military applications. He was single-purposed and obsessed in his view of a world he feared.

Driant was interested in science fiction only to the extent that it served his ability to predict advances in military technology and strategy, and sound the alert by making his novels more believable. To that extent, with hindsight, he was indeed very successful. His predictions of the roles of the *blitzkrieg* and air support proved frighteningly accurate, even though they were derided by his colleagues and critics at the time. Like Verne, Driant relied on solid documentation to predict technological advances in wireless transmissions, submarines, tanks, airplanes and even information gathering methods; he included maps and schematics in his books, but it was all in the service of his cause.

Not surprisingly, Driant was at his worst in his political predictions, because of his personal prejudices. His chauvinism and fierce isolationism seem incredibly naive today and have aged horribly. His obsession with fear and decline, and his paranoid view of a world where France is under constant threat of invasion, is pathetic. Characteristically, Driant was all too ready to identify the enemy inside the Nation: socialists, journalists, freemasons, freethinkers, all those preparing to stab the Army in the back. That ineluctably led him to favoring an enlightened military dictatorship over democracy, because the Army and the Church were, after all, the only ones who could protect the Nation. From there to Pétain, Franco, Pinochet, and other military dictators, is but a small step, which Driant would have crossed enthusiastically.

As we wrote, had Driant been born in the later part of the 20th century in America, he would undoubtedly have been a "neo-conservative" and shared the same paranoid vision of a world where America is under constant threat. However, unlike many modern-day war propagandists, Driant was not a hypocrite: he lived in accordance with his convictions, leading his men in battle, and died a hero like one of his characters.

And for that, despite his misguided ideas, he deserves our respect.

Jean-Marc Lofficier

UNDERSEA ODYSSEY

CHAPTER ONE
IN THE *DRAGONFLY*

In beginning this story, I don't know whether I shall have the courage to finish it!

To live through those six days again, six centuries, during which I suffered the worst mental and physical torture, shut up in the steel shell of a submarine, would be a task beyond my strength if, when in the depths of despair, I had not promised...

I fulfill a vow in once more going over this period of my life, in exposing the sad frailty of a man who had fancied he was inured to adversity, proof against pain, and who, on the threshold of the unseen, found himself the weakest of creatures...

I dedicate these lines to skeptics, to those who boast of having their thoughts free, to the new generations, in particular, who are no longer willing to believe in aught but present enjoyments, and who deny eternity. I advise them merely to place themselves in imagination, for a few moments, in the tomb from which I have just returned!

I am only a landsman; and the technical setting forth of facts which have so recently excited the country, naval circles especially, would have been far more interesting, had it come from the pen of a naval officer.

However, chance willed that I, an army officer, should be in a submarine which was wrecked in 30 fathoms of water, although outsiders like myself are strictly forbidden to enter these mysterious boats.

The public inquiry instituted by the Minister of Marine, an inquiry demanded by public opinion at the time of each submarine disaster, but invariably forgotten a month afterwards, will involve the Port Admiral of Bizerte.[3]

How came this Admiral to authorize an officer having no connection with the Navy to make a descent into the sea in a submarine, notwithstanding specific, ministerial orders to the contrary?

How came an army officer to be on board a submarine, when a naval officer was not allowed to go on the same boat, not even the naval lieutenant who had been in command of her the day before?

There is no need for the Committee of Inquiry to investigate, nor yet to incriminate any one. The only persons to blame are first myself, who had long dreamed of carrying out the plan, and next, poor d'Elbée, the naval lieutenant in command of the *Dragonfly,* whom I discovered clad in a diver's dress, drowned in his conning-tower, amidst the tragic obscurity of sub-ocean night; Jacques d'Elbée, who, before dying, had done everything required by professional duty, but who, after the fatal accident, was powerless, since the essential machinery of his boat refused to act.

This last revelation should astonish no one. In spite of what optimists say, every one now knows that the same mishap occurred to the *Farfadet,* whose crew succumbed in four fathoms of water only, in the lake of Bizerte; and that, notably, in the disaster of the *Lutin,* from which no one escaped, the safety-leads could not be cast off, because the ratchets stuck.[4]

Everyone knows this, just as one knows that the unstable condition of our powder caused the explosion on board the *Jena;* that the projectiles of our ironclads' big guns burst as

---

[3] Bizerte is a harbor city in Northern Tunisia. (Ed.)

[4] *Farfadet* was a French submarine launched with the *Lutin* in 1901. It is remembered chiefly for the accident of July 6, 1905, off the coast of Tunisia, which killed all 14 of its crew. The details of the catastrophe, once released by the press, horrified France and drew national attention to the dangers of submarines.

soon as they are shot; and that our Navy cannot practice meli-nite-firing [5] in time of peace, because the howitzer fuses are too sensitive.

These things one learns, and much besides, by listening to the disheartening confidences of ships' officers. The Navy is in the throes of a crisis, and the foreigner is as well aware of the fact as ourselves, perhaps better.

The crisis is especially one of material, and has been brought on by those who are at the head of the Department. Lower down, among the admirable body of naval officers, as also among the valiant crews of our fleet, we know that there are reserves of courage and energy capable of repairing the mistakes of incompetent politicians and of doing violence to fate.

And we are still full of assurance, which is in itself a force, because we have history to remind us that, from the middle of the *Directoire*,[6] issued the radiant, matchless *épopée* of the Grand Army.

I will, therefore, forbear recrimination, which could not produce more impression than the melancholy facts alone. But, since chance cast us twain into this tragedy of the *Dragonfly*, which lasted six days, and since Providence, in whom I believe, permitted us to be delivered, I will relate, in simple words, our hourly anguish and suffering, our efforts and our hopes, our weakness likewise, during this long ocean night.

I had submitted the old friendship of Jacques d'Elbée to a severe test when I asked that I might accompany him in a sea-descent.

For a long while, he refused. His first answers were fierce, indignant negatives:

"You ask me what is impossible," he said. "More than anyone, you ought to realize the imperative nature of an order, since, like me, you are an officer in command..."

---

[5] A high explosive made of picric acid. (Ed.)
[6] Last stage of the French Revolution, following the Convention, and preceding Napoleon's Consulate.

"Granted; and yet I insist. I am bent on going down into the sea, deep even... Seriously, Jacques, what danger can you fear for the national security?"

"That is not the question: *the thing is forbidden.*"

He pronounced the last word with an emphasis on each syllable, and I looked at him and laughed.

"Forbidden! How about the newspaper men who descended in the *Narval* with the President of the Republic? And the English officers who went over the Cherbourg arsenal from one end to the other? And the Japanese naval attaché who had his private view of the port of Brest last year? And the young attachés of the Admiralty who, not so long ago, went down into the sea for a trip with their Minister?"

"They had permission."

"Well! You shall give me permission; aren't you master on board your boat, next to the Deity?"

"For you to go and analyze your impressions in a new novel, relate what you have seen, and betray some secret without suspecting it..."

"Ah! So that's what you are afraid of! But secrets in the construction of submarines! Would you have me believe that such still exist?"

"Certainly. Compared with certain navies, our own is five years ahead."

"Of the Swiss navy, perhaps. Bah! Don't try to impose on me with your mysterious airs! Do you think I don't know that the American Navy, for instance, is better equipped than our own as regards submarines?"

"You are joking! The *Hollands,* you mean?"

"Yes, the *Hollands,* in which at least one can breathe, since there is a surplus supply of oxygen on board; the *Hollands,* in which our own unfortunate seamen of the *Farfadet* might have lived several days while waiting to be towed back into the basin, since in them has been installed the apparatus necessary for the crew to be able to breathe."

"The *Hollands* does not have our rapidity of movement under water, our stability, our dexterity in maneuvering, our..."

"Nonsense. They have machines we don't possess; explosion motors which derive their detonating gas from oxylith,[7] and restore to the water soluble carbonic acid, so that there is no gurgling and bubbling at the surface..."

It was now Jacques' turn to interrupt me:

"You seem well up in these matters," he remarked.

"Because I happen to know Jaubert and his marvelous invention, and also because I am in love with your calling. I ought to have entered the *Borda,* as you did, instead of going to Saint Cyr.[8] How often I have yearned for the sailor's life, with its ups and downs of poetry and peril!"

"And of solitude, too, remember... How would you like to spend three-fourths of your youth and ripe age 1000 leagues away from those you love—your wife, your children?"

"If I had entered the Navy, I should have arranged my existence differently... but that's not the moot point at present: will you let me make a descent into the sea or won't you?"

"No."

"Only one?"

"No."

"A short one?"

"No, I say..."

At last, I gave up all hope of getting my wish gratified; for, if Jacques refused me thus bluntly, where else could I meet with a submarine officer who would be more pliable?

As a matter of fact, Jacques d'Elbée had been my friend from my early childhood. Our families, being intimate, had placed us together in the old Lycée at Rheims, of which we always spoke afterwards with pleasure, because the Lycée of those times was not the Lycée of today. We often met, espe-

---

[7] A substance, containing sodium peroxide and other salts, which releases oxygen upon contact with water. (Ed.)

[8] The topmost French Military Academy. (Ed.)

cially at the annual Alumni banquet, or *Bonorum Puerorum,* as the ancient University inscription we were proud of called them.

Once I had spent three days with him on board the *Amiral-Duperre,* during the naval maneuvers in the Mediterranean; he had managed to get a permission for me from the Admiral in command.

I was, therefore, justified in counting on him, and on him alone, if my dream were to be realized.

A dive in a submarine! It had been long in my mind.

What novel sensations one must experience in this long, spindle-shaped vessel, poising in the silent depths of ocean! What tranquility close to the restless surface! What fascinating power must be that of the master who with a mere twist of the hand makes it rise again to the surface, glide hither and thither, then dip and plunge once more into the watery gloom!

And what an uncanny emotion when daylight melts away in the denser liquid strata! And, *in fine,* what anguish when a difficulty in steering occurs, and, on the face of him in command, is read the fleeting fear of remaining a prisoner below!

I had taken part in motor-races of speed, had traveled on express locomotives, and had acted the jockey's role.

I had been overtaken by severe storms in the Mediterranean, and had plodded through the long, sandy solitudes of the Tunisian Sahara, seeking for water, or pursuing Djichs.[9]

I had made a dozen balloon ascents, and felt the strange excitement of departure, when the ground seemed to fall away beneath the car. But all that had been in the open air, in the sunlight. A fall from a balloon, which is the accident from which one has the least likelihood of escaping with unbroken limbs, is nothing to be compared with the dreadful agony of human beings shut up in a shipwrecked submarine. A fall from a balloon is the affair of an instant, as the formula we learnt at

---

[9] Berber tribe from the desert region of Bir Bouiret ed Djich on the Algerian-Tunisian border. (Ed.)

school informed us; in about the time one might take to repeat it, the Earth is reached and the victim is out of his misery.

In a submarine, it would be possible to live for hours and days, buried in the bottom of the sea, far from all human aid… and the thought of this sufficed alone to connect with a submarine excursion all sorts of shuddering anticipations that were not without their charm.

I had resigned myself to ignorance of these latter, and had given up trying to persuade my friend, when one morning I met him, in Paris, in the Rue Royale.[10]

His face wore a look of suppressed anger, which was evidently ready to burst forth; he had scarcely shaken hands with me before he wheeled half round and exclaimed as his eyes fell on the building at the end of the street:

"What a hole!"

"The Admiralty?"

"Yes. It is not enough to leave applications waiting six and eight months for an answer, to dispatch unseaworthy transports, to order boilers unsuitable for the vessels that have been wanting them for more than a year. Even now, after disasters like that of the *Latin,* not one of the improvements proposed by the Commission of Inquiry can be obtained."

"You are astonished! Do you fancy such questions have any interest for our masters? Do you think that beyond the care of picking up the millions needed to deliver them from their political Bohemia they have a single other preoccupation?"

"But, gosh! The lives of our men have some little significance. Even if I have to resign for it, I must give vent to my indignation. Just to quote you an example, they not only delay constructing a floating crane capable of raising a submarine from shallow water, but they neglect to provide our boats with outside accessories that would permit of chains being attached, and of towing operations—a precious saving of time in case of accident."

---

[10] Address of the French Admiralty in Paris. (Ed.)

"And the method of air-renewal which is practiced near-ly everywhere?..."

"Exactly! That is why I am so annoyed now. I have just come from the Minister's offices. You probably know I was appointed secretary to the Commission of Inquiry after the last mishap. Well, I had gone to the Minister with a message from the Chairman of the Commission, Admiral Marchal, urging him to fit up our boats with the Jaubert apparatus. And the young snob I found waiting at the Department to receive me contented himself with the barest politeness."

"What did he reply?"

"In so many words this—that the matter was not one of immediate importance, and that they must wait for the results of experiments at present being carried out."

"Ah, yes! Wait, and wait, until the Ministry falls, with the same inertia in those that follow."[11]

There was a pause. D'Elbée reflected, then suddenly ex-claimed:

"You told me the other day, if I remember rightly, that you are acquainted with Jaubert?"

"Yes; a man in the first vigor of youth, a first-class fel-low."

"Disinterested?"

"He can't be otherwise, since he has put up with all the exigencies of the Rue Royale, experiments at his own pecu-niary risks, contracts allowed to remain in abeyance, tergiver-sations without number... If the Americans had not adopted his invention, he would have been ruined long ago."

"Do you think he would be willing to install one of his oxylith apparatuses on board my boat? A sort of semi-official experiment, I mean, that I alone should be the judge of?"

"Perhaps. Would you like me to speak to him?"

---

[11] A heartfelt expression of Danrit's own feelings regarding the stub-born lack of will towards modernization of the French army and navy. (Ed.)

"I should be only too glad if you would. But there would have to be absolute discretion on his part."

"I will guarantee it—but on one condition."

"And what is that?"

An idea had occurred to me, suggested to me by my still unextinguished longing.

"My condition is that I shall be permitted, when the installation is complete, to share in the trial that will be made of it."

"Ah! So you are as obstinate as ever."

"Obstinate, if you choose to call me so; but there's my bargain. You are free to accept it or to refuse."

Our conversation went no further on that day; however, shortly after I received a letter from Jacques, who, writing from the *Dragonfly*, said:

My Dear Friend,

I am so exasperated by the negligence of the Rue Royale authorities, and so tired of asking in vain for the thing I mentioned to you when we last met, that I have decided to act on my own initiative. To the winds with orders and red-tapism, when the lives of a crew are at stake! Experience has shown that, despite all precautions, a submarine may be compelled to stay at the bottom of the water for several days, waiting till its saviors are ready to raise it. In order to be able to wait, one must be able to live, and to live, one must breathe. I have just been designated to command the new Dragonfly, *which was launched at Rochefort last month. It is a submarine of 600 tons. I know the boat now from top to bottom. She is superior to anything that has hitherto left the ways. In particular, there are water-tight compartments in sufficiently large number for a part of the crew to escape drowning, in case of accident. Will you get me four oxylith apparatuses for four of these compartments? There are still workmen enough in the arsenal for the presence of the person installing them to be unnoticed. As for any remarks that may be made by the Visiting Committee, I will take the responsibility. And, since you stipulate it, I*

will let you accompany us in one of the trial submersions.
Hurry up with the work, and provide yourself with a suit of
waterproof leather, a cap to match, and hold yourself ready to
embark as soon as you get a wire. Kindest regards.

D'Elbée.

On receipt of this letter, which was dated from Rochefort, I hastened to Jaubert's works. Most obligingly, and with
the fullest particulars, the inventor explained to me how his
oxylith was produced, and how the apparatuses acted. He consented also to send a foreman and some mechanics to Rochefort with the four apparatuses required.

Then, I waited week after week, and two months went by
without the invitation I was expecting. At last, I was about to
write to my friend when a second letter from him announced
that he had been ordered to Bizerte to take part in the Defense
Mobilization.

He would be better able to keep his promise there, he
said, and hoped to see me by the next steamer.

This news made a lugubrious impression on me.

The names of the *Farfadet* and the *Lutin* have cast a sort
of funeral pall over our great African military port. The penury
of salvage appliances in which the metropolis had left it, and
the humiliating necessity to which our Navy had been reduced
of then accepting succor from the English, the Germans, the
Danes even, were so many unpleasant reminiscences attached
to Bizerte; and I should have preferred to undergo my first
experience of a submarine in a French port.

But my disagreeable foreboding did not last. The next
morning I reached Marseilles, and, 30 hours later, the *Ville
d'Alger* transatlantic, on which I had taken my passage,
doubled Cape Carthage, and the panorama of the hills on
which the rival of Rome once stood was displayed before my
eyes.

However, the sight was a familiar one to me, for I had
spent 12 years of my soldier's life in the 4th Zouaves Regi-

ment, garrisoned in Tunis.[12] I knew nearly all the posts of this magnificent country; and many a time, while reading the chapters of *Salammbô*,[13] I had wandered about the ruins of Carthage, from the heights of Bou-Saïd, where Hamilcar's gardens had spread in tiers, down to the *Toenia*, a narrow strip of land separating the Gulf from the Lake of Tunis.

But, still, on arriving by the steamer, at dawn, I took pleasure in gazing at the jagged hills and mossy fringes with which the Mediterranean girt the ancient quays of the Punic city hated by old Cato.[14]

When the steamer passed abreast of where the ancient harbors had been, I said to myself that beneath the ship's beam, 20 or 25 yards down, were buried the hundreds of triremes which besieged Carthage had built with the wood of her houses, and roped with the hair of her women; that on this fleet now sunken had been made the great city's supreme effort as she writhed under the blows of Scipio.[15]

And no one would ever go and visit these antique debris. A submarine alone would be able to break into their sepulcher.

Ah! If anyone had told me then…!

On the hill of Byrsa, whose slopes, riddled with black holes, showed the excavations of Père Delattre,[16] rose Cardinal Lavigerie's cathedral of Moorish style.

---

[12] The Zouaves were first recruited in Algeria in the 1830s, initially from the Zouaoua Berber tribe, hence their name. They eventually consisted of a number of light infantry regiments serving in French North Africa. (Ed.)

[13] Gustave Flaubert's famous 1862 novel which tells the story of a mercenary revolt in Carthage in the Third Century BC. (Ed.)

[14] Cato the Elder, Roman politician credited with the quote *Carthago delenda est* (Carthage nust be destroyed). (Ed.)

[15] Scipio Africanus, a Roman General in the Second Punic War, who defeated Hannibal. (Ed.)

[16] Alfred Louis Delattre (1850-1932). French missionary and archeologist who spent 50 years excavating the ruins of Carthage. (Ed.)

At the edge of the slope stood a small white marble-pillared villa amidst a grove of verdure. It had been built since my last voyage, and I remarked it for the first time.

As we went by, the sight of it left but a fugitive impression on my mind; but the tragedy which was imminent brought it back and fixed it indelibly in my memory.

I was intending to take the early morning train from Tunis to Bizerte, when the following telegram was handed to me at the Grand Hotel, where I had spent the night:

Wait for me tomorrow at the port of Tunis ; shall be there at 5 p.m. Can start together for Bizerte. Remember promise. Jacques.

My promise was that I would speak to no one of the excursion I was about to make.

Now I was so strict in keeping it that I had not even taken into my confidence she to whom I told everything.

I had quitted Saint Cyr, where I was teaching, with captain's rank, just at the moment when the holidays were commencing, and had merely said that I was going to Tunis on business of a private nature which would not detain me long. My absence, I added, would scarcely last longer than a week.

However, even if I had not promised Jacques, I should have concealed the motive of the journey from those dear to me. What was the good of arousing anxiety in a trusting heart, and causing children's tears to flow?

As for anyone outside my family, I was too well aware of my friend's risk to allow myself to enlighten them.

The plan proposed of not only submerging the boat, but of travelling under water from Tunis to Bizerte on the *Dragonfly,* was one that pleased me immensely, since it was quite a voyage.

By sea the distance from Tunis to Bizerte is 56 miles.

The Tunisian torpedo boats belonging to the Defense Flying Squadron, with their speed of 22 knots, cover this distance in two hours and a half. A submarine, with a speed of only 12 knots under water and 15 on the surface, would take five or six hours, even more, if the commanding officer were willing to deviate a little from the usual itinerary.

The excursion was worth the trouble.

I should certainly have preferred a day trip. But the choice was not offered me; and no doubt Jacques had pitched upon this hour so that my arrival at Bizerte might not be noticed.

I put on my waterproof leather costume, and a cap resembling that of the naval officer, yet without daring to add any band. I put some provisions in my pocket—chocolate, wafers, dates—to defy sea-sickness, which is, however, unknown in submarines, and, an hour before the time appointed, I was eagerly pacing up and down the Customs Wharf, somewhat excited, I confess, by the prospect of what I was about to experience.

Now and again I stopped to gaze at the broad watery avenue of over five miles cut by the Tunis canal through the Lake, and I was wondering why I saw nothing, when, in the very harbor, not more than 50 yards away, a sort of land-surveyor's staff appeared, gliding slowly along the calm water. Then, a little nearer, a small mast hove in sight, increasing gradually in size as the wharf was approached.

Suddenly, the surveyor's staff sank from view, and, two or three seconds later, a metal shell of slight convexity seemed to float on the yellowish water at the very spot where the staff had vanished.

At first, the shell looked like a tortoise; but the aspect changed almost immediately, for a big, grey-painted cylinder now emerged, and below it a turret, about two yards in diameter, thinning off on one side pretty much like an ironclad's spur.

Simultaneously, oblique stays, starting from the turret's summit, shot down to the surface; then, at about 20 yards from the wharf, all forward movement ceased.

A moment afterwards the shell-cap was slowly raised, and a head showed beneath it, covered with a naval officer's triple-braided headgear.

I could not refrain from calling out:

"Jacques!"

He saw me, smiled, gave an order, and his body half issued from the narrow aperture.

Straightway, a species of squaloid creature exhibited its back on the water; two long metallic grooves, with narrow plates between them, formed, so to speak, its backbone; another turret smaller than the central one emerged in front at the same time as a small mast behind. At the top of this mast hung a tiny tricolor French flag, and, although so meager and reduced to the state of a bit of wet rag, it appeared to me prouder, more triumphal than the ensign flapping at the masthead of a man-of-war.

The *Dragonfly* was now lying flush with the water throughout its length.

From the smaller of the two turrets, whose lid had just been raised, a sailor bobbed up like a Jack-in-the-box, and flung on to the wharf one end of a metallic cable. A few moments later the submarine was alongside.

"So you have come through the canal under water," I remarked, when we had exchanged our first greetings.

"Yes; it was part of my program for today; but neither the most interesting nor the most difficult."

"Then I am to be a witness of this latter."

"I suppose so, since you are set on the thing. Anyway, it is less risky here than elsewhere, because on this shore of the Mediterranean there are no bores and no tattlers."

"Happy land!"

"And as it is quite understood that you will tell nobody, and that the escapade shall be kept to ourselves!"

Poor Jacques! Could he suspect that this escapade, as he then called it, would be his voyage into eternity; that the whole world, seized with ardent curiosity, would seek to know the particulars of our journey under the sea; and that I myself should break my word by giving a full account of the event in these lines?

But no anxiety at present disturbed his high confidence, for he went on:

"This is what I propose: first, dinner, in a jiffy; then, voyage through the canal at the surface, so as to be in the Gulf before dark; then, a descent right to the bottom."

"What depth?"

"About 30, or perhaps 40 yards on the line we shall follow. However, I haven't yet definitely settled our exact route."

"Could you go lower still with the *Dragonfly*?"

"Yes; the hull is a very strong one, and can withstand a pressure up to 90 or even 120 pounds per square inch, which allows a depth of between 30 and 40 fathoms."[17]

"But the hull is double, isn't it?"

"No. The double hull is peculiar to submarines built by Laubeuf, and of the *Narval* type; the *Dragonfly* was designed by the engineer Romazotti, and comes from Normand's yards at Le Havre. That's a good builder."

"I thought Normand's yards turned out only torpedo boats?"

"They make everything there; and we are fortunate to have them, and the yards at La Seyne, Penhouet, and Saint Nazaire, too; for, with the insubordination prevailing in the arsenals, and the six hours and a half work-day, we shall soon find it impossible to obtain anything good from the State's shipbuilding yards."

He pulled out his watch and called:

"Jeanson!"

A beardless face, with rosy cheeks, above which showed the cap of a naval second lieutenant, appeared inside the turret.

"Be ready, Jeanson, by 6:30 p.m.!"

It was the end of August; the day had been warm, and it was the hour when the sea breeze was about to restore life to the old Muslim city. At the end of the day, on Marine Avenue,

---

[17] The British fathom is a thousandth of an imperial nautical mile or 6.08 feet, or 6 feet in the common practice. (Ed.)

a motley crowd of loiterers could be seen, belonging to every nationality.

A band, that of the 4th Zouaves, was playing in front of the French Resident-General's Palace; women in light dresses, and with partly colored sunshades, walked with undulating gait amidst thick-set Maltese, burnoose-clad Arabs, and baggy-trousered Zouaves.

We passed through the crowd, with the joy of life in our hearts. D'Elbée shook hands with one or two officers, and, at last, we sat down to table in the Grand Hotel.

"If you had told me we were going to dine before starting," I said, "it would have saved me getting a supply of provisions." And I exhibited the pocket of my leather coat, in which bulged my morning's purchases.

"Why, you'll find all you want on board," he replied. "Didn't I tell you my *Dragonfly,* replacing an old-fashioned and much smaller submarine of the same name, was a craft of considerable tonnage; so that we have much more room than on the 35-yard torpedo boats that you used to visit?"

"What is the length of your submarine?"

"180 feet from end to end."

"Why, she is a regular little steamer!"

"Of course. Didn't I mention I had crossed from Brest to Bizerte without help, putting in only at Ferrol, Gibraltar, and Mahon?"

"Convoyed?"

"Yes, during the first portion of the way. Advantage was taken of the dispatch of the *Justice* to the Mediterranean Squadron of ironclads to give me her as an escort. But I left her at Mahon and arrived at Bizerte alone."

"Wasn't it rather imprudent?"

"Not a bit. You are safer even in a big submarine, hermetically closed, like mine, than on a large torpedo boat. If bad weather overtakes you, the submarine descends, and, at a depth of ten yards below the surface, the water is quite calm."

"So the problem of submarines acting over a wide radius is at last solved."

"Very nearly, at any rate; and today, it is certain that an autonomous submarine like mine can start from Brest, enter English roads without being seen, carry out some well-organized plan there, and return without needing to get fresh provisions on board."

"And Germany? She is no longer an adversary to be disdained at sea."

"Germany? If we have to do with her, she will restrict the war to *terra firma*. Placing her fleet in safety within the roads of Kiel and Wilhelmshafen, she will defend the entrance so as to render it impracticable for our submarines, or English ones, using for this purpose stockades, chains, and wire nets; and, while preserving an absolute defense on sea, she will act around the Moselle and Meuse with all the offensive skill acquired under William II during the last 20 years."

I had no reply to make, and we were about to rise from table when a knock was heard at the door of the small room where we had been dining *tête-à-tête*.

"Come in," cried Jacques.

A quartermaster, standing straight as an arrow, appeared on the threshold. He made a military salute, and took off his cap.

"Commander, the boat is ready. Departure at 6:30 p.m."

"Thanks, Yvonnec. Will you have a glass of wine?"

"I can't refuse, Commander."

"You would perhaps prefer a bowl of good Pont-Aven cider, but here they don't keep it."

"Their wine isn't bad in this place, Commander."

"Your health, my good fellow."

I touched glasses with Jacques and glanced at Yvonnec.

His eyes were as honest as a child's—blue eyes that looked out from his hairy face; for the Breton grew a rough, blond beard, whose bristliness contrasted with the mildness of his features. Tall, strong, and stalwart, he was a fine specimen of the Armorican race, and the double wool stripe he wore on his sleeves testified to his excellent conduct.

He twirled his cap, and said:

"The engineer asked me to buy him a handsaw file as big as I could get. He wants it for the journey. I don't know Tunis, Commander. Perhaps you could tell me where to go?"

"We have still the time to smoke a cigar," observed Jacques, taking out his watch; "we will go up as far as the Place de France. Don't trouble about the file, Yvonnec; I will bring one back with me."

"But the engineer gave me the money."

"Keep it, and we can settle up on board."

The quartermaster put on his cap again, saluted, wheeled round in correct style, and went out.

"That's a fine type of seaman," I remarked, waving my hand to him in friendly fashion as he closed the door.

"You never spoke a truer word. He is a real Breton: sober, in spite of the reputation for drinking attributed to his race; obedient, even to self-sacrifice; as devoted as a dog to us; and quite smart enough to get an early promotion as a petty officer."

We were now out in the street.

"Ah!" he continued, "what a splendid recruiting-ground for sailors we have in that province so wonderfully sung by my friend Botrel [18]—Brittany, the home of the corsairs of old. It is not because I belong to them that I praise our Breton lads. But what couldn't one do with them, if only they were understood and loved!"

He clenched his fists and ceased speaking. We had reached an ironmonger's in the Rue de la Casba, situated beyond the small Place de France, which allows entrance into the Arab town.

"Here," he said to me, handing over the file, after choosing it; "the pocket of your leather coat is more convenient than

---

[18] Jean-Baptiste Théodore Botrel (1868-1925) was a French songwriter best known for his popular songs about his native Brittany, including the famous *La Paimpolaise*. During World War I, he became France's official "Bard of the Armies." (Ed.)

mine. You are rigged out as if you were going on a long voyage."

He laughed heartily. I hear him still. He little suspected of what importance would subsequently be to me this file, which he ought to have kept himself, and which I forgot to give back to him.

At 6:25 p.m., we were back on the wharf, by the side of the little trolley that plies along the Avenue de France et de la Marine.

The second lieutenant was there; the Commander of the *Dragonfly* introduced us to each other.

"Monsieur Jeanson, the second lieutenant."

There was another second lieutenant. He was down in the engine-room. I did not see him... I never saw him.

"Get in. We are going to start. Nobody happens to be about."

A small movable gangway afforded access to the top of the hood. I stepped on to it, and just as I was about to pop into the aperture, I turned round.

"Must I enter?"

"Unless you prefer to wet your feet during our passing through the canal."

"How do you intend to make the passage?"

"On a level with the surface."

"Can I stay up?"

"If you like."

"Then I will. I should like to enter only when you are going to descend under the water. But you will give me due notice at least?"

A laugh was his sole reply at first. Then he said:

"I see your enthusiasm has cooled. But, anyway, we shan't go under without warning you. And I will leave Yvonnec with you; he can tell you what way we shall take."

Jacques now disappeared in his conning-chamber. A young, beardless sailor—I remember him well—barefoot, and wearing a blue-and-white striped jersey, cast off the mooring-rope that fastened us to the wharf, and I heard the order spoken inside:

"Go ahead, slowly."

A seething of the water arose to the stern of the boat. Gently the *Dragonfly* pivoted round, turned her invisible prow towards the canal entrance; then another order caught my ear:

"150 revolutions."

The speed increased; the banks grew narrower, and the row of palms and eucalyptuses, which, as far as the Goulette, formed the Tunisians' favorite promenade, stretched along in front of us until it vanished on the horizon.

Nine kilometers further, the canal opened into the Gulf of Tunis; and, 16 kilometers beyond that, would come the plunge.

CHAPTER II
THE DESCENT INTO THE SEA

Standing near the turret, on the narrow gangway that ran from end to end, I was scarcely half a yard above the level of the water, and the *Dragonfly* showed no more than her two turrets clear of the surface.

It was as though I were sliding along the smooth liquid, and I wondered how the master of this craft was able to maintain its horizontal position so constantly.

A dip of a few centimeters, and I should be having a foot-bath.

Through the fore-window, I dimly perceived two eyes, those of Jacques or else of the helmsman, guiding the silent boat, in a line as straight as that of the canal itself. We were hugging the right bank, and, behind us, spurned by the screw, the swirling water dashed up the sloping sides.

Near the middle of the canal, we met a tug towing three *mahonnes*.[19] The tall funnel of the tugboat was belching forth volumes of black smoke, and its engine throbbed, rousing veritable waves. For a moment, I was afraid we should foul; but notice had been given from La Goulette to Tunis of the submarine's passage, and a wide berth was allowed us. But a backwater swell followed our encounter with the tug, and crept over our steel shell.

"Look out!" Yvonnec called to me.

And I saw him pull himself up with his hands on to the slanting buttress of the turret, at the same time quickly raising his legs.

I tried to imitate his example, but was too late. I had already taken my foot-bath; and through the Breton's bristly beard and white teeth a gleeful laugh rang out.

"Ah! Captain, I told you to be on your guard!"

---

[19] A type of barges. (Ed.)

I joined in the laugh, though annoyed. The water had gone through my shoes; and I should be obliged to perform the rest of the voyage with damp feet.

If I jot down this disagreeable impression, it is because everything that preceded our immersion, even the most trivial incidents, I have engraved on my mind; and, moreover, it contrasts so oddly with the seriousness of what was about to happen.

Passing by the Zouaves' barracks at La Goulette, I made a friendly signal to the trumpeters who were practicing on the canal side. They were far from supposing that I, in my seaman's costume, was a former officer in their regiment. They answered me with a *fan, fan, l'Arbi* [20] in double-quick time, and the drummer corporal, a big fellow with a flowing beard, added a merry cock-a-doodle-do.

As we came to the end of the canal, the boat's speed was relaxed, and Jacques' head appeared outside.

"You must come in," he observed; "if you don't, the swell in the Gulf will soak you up to your waist."

"Oh! A little more or a little less—what will it matter?"

"Come, we will leave the hood open for a few minutes longer, and you can have a glance at Carthage, its hills and ruins."

"Hum! As to its ruins, there's nothing left: *etiam periere ruinæ!*" [21]

"Gad! You are in a poetical vein! Hurry up, so that we may put on speed. I want to be at Bizerte by 2 a.m."

I clambered over the iron ladder running along the side of the turret, and when I was close to him he said:

"I have only a few moments to do you the honors of my boat. Just now, I will put Jeanson in charge, and we will go over the two stories together, so that you may see the machinery and the torpedo compartment."

---

[20] The Zouaves' March. (Note from the Author.)
[21] Lucan (39-65 AD). (Ed.)

"I am at your disposal, whenever you wish," was my reply.

"Profit by the sunset to admire the landscape. Later, we shall plunge into submarine darkness."

The Sun was at present low down on the horizon; it was about to set behind the citadel of Byrsa, which we were skirting at the same distance as when I passed the evening before on the steamer travelling in the opposite direction.

I saw again the Kram and Kheredine with their palm trees and villas, then the Bey's palace, near the promontory where Scipio Africanus had begun the famous mole that blocked the ports of Carthage seawards; and I remember that I made out abreast of these, in the sandy dunes, a slight depression which had been described to me before. It was at this spot the besieged Carthaginians had cut through the rock, re-established their communications with the sea, and opened a way out for their last fleet.

I remember, too, that I once more said to myself: it would be possible with the *Dragonfly* to go under the water at the place where we were, to discover by means of our searchlights the debris of the lost triremes that had not yet been devoured by the sea, to pick up certain antique remains, and even to find ruins, for some learned archaeologists assert that the original Carthage had a portion of her quays invaded by the sea.

As a matter of fact, the *Dragonfly* was constructed so as to permit of egress under water.

She was one of the first French submarines to which had been adapted the *sluice* characteristic of the engineer Lake's American boat, and I was eager to get a glimpse of this novel and interesting invention.

What a relief, indeed, for a crew to feel they can escape at will from this sealed hull! What courage had previously been necessary for men shut in a floating tomb to navigate it in a case of accident! Even with the risks attaching to egress under water, the present prospect was infinitely more agreeable.

And, absorbed by these reflections, I looked, without seeing them, at the russet hills on which stood the monastery of Saint Louis, the small chapel marking the spot where the Holy King died of the plague in the midst of his army,[22] the museum of Père Delattre, the convent of Carmel, and, beyond it, the ancient cisterns fed in the Punic epoch and still fed to-day by the pure waters of the Zaghouan.

Suddenly, my attention was drawn to the new-built little villa standing on the edge of the Byrsa plateau, which I had remarked as we went by the evening before. There it was, again all white, and its garden, studded with trees, sloped downwards with its surrounding wall topped by railings.

On its terrace, a woman's slender figure could be seen upright, and the red, setting Sun, as it glowed behind her, cast an aureole about her head and limbs.

And I thought of *Salammbô*, at Tanit, whose silver crescent, at certain periods of the year, hung over the summit of Bou-Khornine, the famous mountain of the Warm Waters still visible in the twilight on the other side of the Gulf.

The girl—for evidently, she was young—who thus showed her fair silhouette amidst the landscape of a bygone age, was looking towards the sea, and, suddenly, she caught sight of our turret skimming along the water; she raised her arm and waved a handkerchief.

No other boat was in view, and this *adieu* so natural, this almost instinctive signal made to those who were starting across the blue ocean could only be meant for us.

Immediately, I climbed the rungs of the inside ladder. Despite Jacques' remonstrance, I got down on to the outside gangway, recklessly wetting my feet again, and, in turn, I fluttered my own white handkerchief.

She must have seen it; indeed, I know now she did see it; and the movement of her hand seemed to increase.

---

[22] Louis IX (1214-1270), a.k.a. Saint Louis, King of France from 1226, died in Tunis during his second crusade, from either the bubonic plague or dysentery. (Ed.)

The life of two men was influenced by this gracious vi-sion!

And blessed be the exquisite child named Marie-Thérèse, and the white villa bearing the same two words on its portal.

Are there any real presentiments? I shall often want to repeat this question during my story.

Why did I linger replying longer than was needed to the unexpected signal, linger even when the girl's arm had ceased to move?

Jacques called me out of my reverie. He had been watching me for several instants.

"How silly you are!" he exclaimed. "One might imagine you were bound for South America!"

"These greetings between strangers are pleasant," I answered.

"Well! Here is the twilight; we will reach the opposite side before dark, by going under water for half an hour."

"So we shall cross the gulf breadthwise and come up over yonder, in front of the Two-Horn Mountain."

"Not exactly. We are steering towards the point you can see there more north. Abreast of Hammam Lif, there is not water enough."

Hammam Lif was the Tunisians' favorite seaside place; it was just visible, a small white line on the water's extreme edge.

"We are 15 miles from that point, Cape Ras-al-Fortas," continued d'Elbée. "I should like to reach the spot I have fixed on without coming to the surface on the way, and calculating the distance solely by my speed and the depth-chart, which latter has been most carefully drawn out for this coast."

"Shan't you use your instrument which from the conning-tower allows you to see all the vessels passing near you?"

"The periscope, you mean? No; I shan't use that. My experiment consists in regulating the speed and direction under water in such a manner as to emerge at a given spot. If I had to solve the problem at a great depth, I couldn't use my peris-

41

cope, since the sight-tube measures only five yards, and yet I should have to reach my destination somehow."

"Is it very deep here?"

"In the middle of the gulf the depth is about 25 fathoms; but here, three miles from the coast, it is 12-1/2 fathoms at most."

"What is the height of the *Dragonfly?*"

"22 feet."

"Then, if you were to touch the bottom, we should have about nine fathoms of water above us?"

"We shall have them shortly, and more. But don't let us lose any more time. I am going to send the boat under. When we are at the depth I want, I will hand over the steering to Jeanson, and we can have a look round."

"Then, you are going to shut the hood?"

"You will see it shut automatically."

"How?"

"In proportion as I introduce water into the water-ballasts, and the water-level rises round the turret, the lid will gradually close. I could shut it straightway with this key-handle, but I prefer to verify the working of the self-acting apparatus."

"I understand; it was the *Farfadet's* accident which caused this arrangement to be adopted."

"Yes. As you can imagine, one gets so accustomed to risks in the Navy that certain commandants might always imprudently wait till the last minute before closing the hood. And if, just then, a big wave should sweep over the aperture, they would be swamped, and drowned."

"But I have heard that one could never be sure of an automatic apparatus acting in time."

"That is so; but this one seems all right. Look."

We were alone in the semicircular conning-tower. On a mahogany table-top, with a cast-iron central support, were several nickel switch-handles; and about each of them there were metallic arrows bearing the brass letters: *open, shut.*

Knobs, dials, and other instruments stood in rows on the table, and on the raised edge that ran along one of its sides.

"This is the *immersion manometer,* with its needle, and, beside it, there is the *immersion register,* which traces for me on a sheet of paper the curve of depths reached; so I have a double check. Those fly-wheels are the governing apparatus of the three rudders."

"Three rudders?"

"Yes! Submarines have, in addition to the vertical rudder of every craft, horizontal rudders ensuring their *isobatia.*"

"Isobatia? what a funny word!"

"It's a new one, peculiar to submarine navigation, and refers to the boat's continuance, when under water, in the same horizontal plane. But you are not going to have me give you a lesson in navigation?"

"No, I am content to know your boat is *isobatic.*"

"Very good. May it remain so! Or else our progress is a groping along. Now, here is the *axiometer,* which, at each moment, indicates the position of the rudders; and here the fly-wheel that sets the boat in motion; then you see the control of the pumps that bring the water from back to front; the switches that release the safety-leads; and there are other things that would take me too long to explain. Let me show you something better, the effect produced by the chief parts of the mechanism, those that regulate the descent. Look."

At the top of the switch-board I read, in large letters, the words, *Water-Ballast;* and, below, *Fore, Centre, Aft.*

The lieutenant gave about the sixth of a revolution to each of the handles, and in an instant the hood described an arc and slammed down. A wheel, like that of a motor-car's steering-apparatus, now projected above the handles regulating the entrance of the water. Two strong hands had just given it a twist. I perceived then that one of the seamen had climbed into the conning-tower to effect this operation.

"It's simple, and safe, as you see," remarked Jacques. "As soon as the water-level reaches the windows, it not only causes, by electric contact, the closing of the hood, but it rings up whoever is in the watch-tower, which is just under the turret. At this signal, the look-out man must ascend and assure himself that the hood is quite shut, and must screw it tight."

"Then the water continues to rise?"

"No, we go down."

"How can you tell?"

"You have only to use your eyes."

I hadn't a word to reply. Along the four thick-glazed windows, with their massive brass frames, the sea was rising. A moment more and my gaze was parallel with the water's surface, on which danced myriads of tiny waves.

Soon the emerald color covered all the glass, the tint grew darker, and the turret became obscure.

I felt a choking sensation in my throat. We were sinking.

It was the descent I had yearned for; and yet if, at that instant, a fairy had offered to place me, with a motion of her wand, on the Tunis Wharf, I believe my first impulse would have been to accept…

I felt also an uncomfortable coldness in the stomach like what is experienced in a rapidly descending lift; and, more than all, a real anguish created by reminiscences of disasters and of newspaper articles.

But athwart the increasing gloom three electric lights suddenly shone, and I beheld my friend's calm face bent over a manometer, whose needle was turning slowly on a graduated dial.

"See," he exclaimed, "we are at +0.15; that means the water-level is still 15 centimeters below the turret. Now we reach 0; the top of the turret is on a level with the water; we show nothing now but the periscopes, and, even while I speak, they have disappeared. Meanwhile the water is still entering the reservoirs, slowly, because there is no hurry, and I allow it only small opportunity. We might have sunk much more quickly; but I should have had to take certain precautions so as to avoid a descending impetus that involves risks. Now we are 0.60m, 0.80m, 1 meter below the level of the Mediterranean. I will accelerate the rate a little."

He turned one of the handles below the word *Fore,* and, a few seconds later, the floor on which we were standing seemed to tilt. The tilt was real enough, and I was obliged to hold on to a brass rail that ran round the conning-tower.

"Why, we are slanting," I ventured to observe.

"That's so, and for this reason. We are going forward as well as down, but at a very slack speed. As long as I let only a small quantity of water enter the three reservoirs, fore, centre, and aft, we sank vertically, without the slightest tilt. Now, I have just opened the front reservoir entirely; and the fore part tilts in proportion. We are advancing obliquely."

"We are sinking still more quickly," I remarked in a whisper.

And my eye followed the needle indicating: 6, 8, 10, 12, 13 meters...

"Don't you think we are deep enough?" I asked, in a scarcely audible tone.

"We are going down to a depth of eight fathoms, to be surer."

"Surer of what?"

"One can never know. Suppose a big English ironclad of the Malta Squadron, a Dreadnought, for instance, should happen to come this way. As we can't see, we might strike across her path. The draught of such a vessel is as much as five fathoms and more. It is better not to get near her keel."

"And if the keel caught us?"

"It would make a hole in us."

"And the water would swamp us?"

"Yes, since we haven't a double hull."

"And then?"

"Well, then, unless the cellulose acts, and I haven't much confidence in the supply I had to accept, under protest..."

And Jacques finished his sentence by pointing downwards.

"If I am not mistaken," I said, "your cellulose is a cotton-like substance which swells when in contact with water, and of itself stops up holes made by projectiles. It used to be put, I think, in certain water-tight compartments of ironclads."

"This practice has been abandoned. Today it is replaced by coal, for which there is never too much room."

"So the cellulose you have on board doesn't satisfy you?"

"Not at all. The contracts made by the Rue Royale department are no good. I am convinced that our cellulose would let the water enter during the first few minutes, which would be the same as letting it come in altogether. What is the use of stopping a hole when you already have tons of water in the boat?"

"But you have numerous water-tight compartments in the *Dragonfly?*"

"Numerous, no; yet more than on any other submarine in the service. I am experimenting with some doors of automatic compartments. The Naval Engineering Department has had them placed, as it happens, in the compartments containing the cellulose in front."

These last remarks had made me somewhat uneasy. It was evident that the Commander, who was responsible for his boat, whatever might befall, and liable to be court-martialed if an accident occurred, regarded certain portions of his material as defective. And discipline forbade him to speak. I now understood better how such a vessel as the *Vienne* had been lost with all on board, since the captain must have been compelled to sail, not daring to complain, with his boilers in bad repair.

However, I tried to regain confidence, and resumed:

"But when you ascend again, there will be a critical moment during which you will see nothing; and you will have to run the risk of striking against an ironclad."

"We shall be near enough to the coast to have nothing to fear from big ships, since we shall be out of their track. Still, you are right; until one can hoist the periscope on emerging, one is sure of nothing, and there is a possibility of colliding with another craft."

"And then?"

46

"Oh! Then, it's chance-work; just as with an anarchist's bomb."

The needle marked 15 meters. Jacques touched an ivory key below the handle regulating the inlet of the front reservoir, and, watching the water-level at the bottom of the switch-board, he waited.

"By pressing here," he explained, "I introduce compressed air into the reservoir, which had too much water in it. I expel the surplus, and now we are again in a condition of normal equilibrium. The entire talent of a submarine commandant consists in empirically maintaining his balance, alternately using the water's weight and the inrush of compressed air."

Gradually, as I noticed, the boat's horizontality was re-established. The way in which she answered to the steering was marvelous.

I found no more questions to ask. Instead, I reflected.

I reflected that over our heads were eight fathoms of water, a pressure of 22 pounds per square inch weighing us down, and that we were at the mercy of an open valve, an imperfect joint, a clogged apparatus.

"Ask the second lieutenant to come up," Jacques called out.

And when his subordinate arrived he said:

"I leave you in charge. Keep the speed at 255 revolutions, and the depth at eight fathoms for about 20 minutes. By the end of that time, I shall be back."

"In what direction?"

"Steer north, 85° east."

"Right."

"You don't guide your submarine with a mariner's compass?" I ventured to remark.

"A mariner's compass! What a landlubber you are! The compass is a difficult thing to use in this narrow space surrounded by iron on all sides, and traversed by electric currents. We have to employ the gyroscope."

"Foucault's instrument?"[23]

"Yes. The steadiness of its rotation gives us a basis to go on in steering, yet a basis not altogether reliable."

"I have come to the conclusion that there is a good deal of haphazard in your profession."

"Yes, there is luck and ill-luck…But don't let us waste any time! Go down this ladder, and mind your head; our rooms haven't very lofty ceilings."

Beneath the conning-tower we descended a vertical ladder leading into the watch-cabin, which also served as an instrument-room. Sitting at a table was a seaman examining the indications of several instruments that I recognized, having seen them in the conning-chamber. On this table lay a hydrographic map, covered with figures, and showing every depth within a radius of 100 kilometers round Bizerte.

"Here, on the right," said Jacques, "is my cabin; then those of the sub-lieutenant and the midshipman, to which access is obtained by the lateral turret. Corresponding to them, on the left, are the mate's room and the crew's quarters. You can have a peep at them later, with Yvonnec, if you like. The most interesting part to see is lower down."

He opened his cabin door for me to have a glance inside; and, when he had switched on the electric light above his berth, a white ball rolled off the bed and, frolicking round my friend's legs, began to bark joyfully. It was a handsome black and white poodle, with its hair carefully trimmed to look like a lion's mane.

"Hallo!" exclaimed d'Elbée, frowning, "that confounded Vincent has let Phanor embark again…Come here, Phanor! Lie down there!"

But Phanor, glad of his freedom, had made off through a trap-door which a sailor had just opened.

---

[23] The gyroscope was invented in 1852 by the French physicist Leon Foucault (1819-1868) as part of a two-pronged investigation of the rotation of the Earth. (Ed.)

"The rascal!" grumbled Jacques. "He takes advantage of his size to dodge in and out everywhere, and has learned to climb up and down our vertical ladders just as if he were a cat. I am sure he is off to the engine-room, where Renaut stuffs him with tidbits."

"Is it forbidden to embark dogs on a submarine?"

"No; but I don't like them on a boat where there are so many delicate pieces of machinery. They may get into the gearings, jump on to the periscopes, damage an apparatus, or slip on a switch. Consequently, I ordered my man to see that Phanor did not sneak on board before we started. Anyway, the dog is here, so we must put up with him…"

A moment later, still using the vertical ladders, we came into a workroom where some men were engaged with a torpedo. Set on two wooden supports and stripped of its fore part, the terrible weapon seemed enormous.

"Why, it's not an ordinary Whitehead?" I cried.

"On our submarines we have recently adopted the new 450 torpedo invented by Whitehead. The Japanese navy adopted it almost at the same time as us."

"It is as big as a man?"

"Bigger. I am sure a man could easily get inside the tube."

"It would be a novel way of quitting a submarine," I laughed.

Already my uneasiness had vanished, and I was all eagerness once more in presence of these redoubtable engines of war contrived by man's genius.

Why did I think of escaping so frequently? Was it a fresh presentiment? No, for I laughed as I expressed my thought. But, manifestly, to any one confined in a boat under water, the question of escape became a sort of obsession.

"I was under the impression that the torpedoes discharged by submarines were placed outside, and that they were merely shot from the interior," I observed.

"This was so in submarines of small tonnage which could not find room for weapons so cumbersome; but, in this one, we are able to carry five, three in front and two at the back; and we discharge them, as on board an ironclad, by means of submarine tubes. It is the first time a tube has been placed behind; and the experiment will probably not be renewed."

"With the strong pressure you have in descending to depths of 25 and 30 meters, aren't you exposed to an irruption of water through the launching-tubes and their compartment?" I queried.

"No. The stronger the pressure, the tighter the compartment closes."

And my admiration was boundless when, after passing through the engine-room without stopping, we reached the chamber behind, where the huge launching-tube was situated.

It was a sort of cannon, without limber, resting on the floor to which it was fixed by broad steel bars. The arrangement for closing the breech, with which I was unfamiliar, appeared very simple; but when I tried to seize the bronze knob that controlled it Jacques checked me.

"If you are particularly interested in it," he said, "you can come back with Yvonnec, whose task it is to look after the torpedoes, since he is the torpedo quartermaster. And then you can see how Jaubert's oxylith apparatuses act. I have had one installed here. There it is on the left."

By the light of the single electric lamp radiating in this shuttle-pointed chamber, I was able to distinguish a sort of double cylinder with tubes of varying caliber branching off from it. Already my friend had raised the panel situated in the hind part, and he called me.

"See, here is the peculiar excellence of my craft. It is the *sluice*—the sluice allowing a diver to go out and walk at the bottom of the water. We had a good deal of difficulty in obtaining it... Now, that's a real improvement."

He switched on another light, which rendered the whole of the cavity visible. It was a rectangular pit, two yards deep, into which two men could scarcely descend at the same time.

I had begun to put my foot on the topmost rung of the ladder, fixed, like those beneath it, into the vertical wall of metal, when again Jacques checked me.

"We have no time," he said. "To equilibrate the pressures between this compartment and the sluice properly so called, to open the pit and show you the water held back by the compressed air, would take a quarter of an hour and more. Yvonnec can do that for you."

Yvonnec; it was always Yvonnec. He was the Jack-of-all-trades. Returning with my guide, I came once more into the engine-room.

Here my amazement increased, for the machinery was a marvel of clockwork; and the chief engineer who superintended its action must have paid it the minutest attention, since it was a mass of glittering copper, brilliant nickel, and blue-tinted steel.

At once I recognized the explosion motor. But what a motor! And what power!

Cylinders with a probable diameter of 14 to 16 inches, pistons with a stroke of 12 inches at least, there were six of them on each side; and the whole set were strongly held in a base of massive steel that formed part of the boat's frame. A huge, solid fly-wheel revolved on the machine's flank with such swiftness that it could easily be fancied motionless; and in front a powerful dynamo was waiting to be connected with the motor, in order to recharge the accumulators that supplied the light.

All this machinery made so little noise that I scarcely heard it until the trap-door was opened which led into the instrument-room. But if the motor was remarkably silent, the throbbing it communicated to the long steel spindle-shaped craft was felt in every part of her, and made her seem alive.

The engineer was there. He wore a gold stripe on his sleeve; and, on the commander's entrance, he smiled and looked under one of the supporting beams of the engine.

I followed the direction of his eyes, and immediately understood. A short tail tipped with a black and white tuft was wagging between the two stanchions.

This spot was Phanor's usual lodging when he could slip on board.

"It's your fault, Renaut," said Jacques, smiling also, for he understood as well. "It's your fault this animal insists on accompanying us. You stuff him with sugar."

I tried to divert the scolding, for I took a liking to the engineer straightway.

"How do the gases escape that you produce by combustion?" I asked.

He smiled again and pointed upwards, then added: "They go out of the boat, sir; but, when we descend to a depth of ten fathoms, we have to utilize part of the engine's power to drive them."

"Call him captain," interrupted Jacques. "I don't want you to think that we have a civilian on board, Renaut."

"I thought the gentleman, I mean the captain, was the engineer who had installed the oxygen-producing apparatus on board."

"He is not the inventor, but it is owing to him and his relations with the inventor that we are able to experiment with the apparatus."

"Then, captain, let me thank you," said the engineer, with an earnestness that surprised me. "To tell you the truth, it was the first problem that should have been solved for these sealed-up hulls, and it's a shame we've waited so long. It's easy enough to fish up a shipwrecked submarine; but only when the air is exhausted, and the crew are all corpses. And what a death it must be to die by slow asphyxia!"

"Come, come, Renaut," answered the commander, "you don't want me to imagine…"

Suddenly Jacques stopped.

"I was forgetting," he said.

And going nearer to the engineer he added in a lower tone:

"You are going to get married at what date?"

"At the end of the month, commander, if you will sign my furlough for the 22nd."

"Certainly. I am expecting your substitute by the 20th, and you will have time to tell him how to manage…. And where are you going for your honeymoon?"

"Oh, as for that, in the mountains, sir, Switzerland or the Tyrol, in a country where there is air, space, snow, glaciers, and where one can breathe and enjoy the Sun…"

He spoke eagerly, and I remarked him more closely.

He was a fine, handsome fellow of 30, with keen eyes, intelligent head, elegant moustache, and a stalwart build, denoting strength and agility.

"And your artificer?"

"Niclaus? Oh, as full as ever of his theories. When he thinks I am not listening, he hums the *Internationale*. I shouldn't care to start on a campaign with a fellow of his sort; he is capable of damaging or tampering with the engine, in order to hinder us from going. It wants so little, a bit of sand in a clip, a nut loosened near the fly-wheel, or on the driving-shaft…"

"Do you really believe Niclaus would do that?"

"He was one of the ringleaders among the malcontents of the Rochefort arsenal; I am sure of it."

"You are quite right to mention the matter to me, Renaut," replied d'Elbée, in a graver tone. "As soon as we get back, I will ask Admiral Boehme to remove him. It's the last voyage he will make with us."

The last! If only a sibyl had come and told my friend it was his last voyage too…

This conversation recurs to me now as if it came from beyond the grave. At the moment the words were spoken, however, I had lost all the uneasiness experienced on my embarkation, and was taken up with the novelty of the surroundings and Jacques' explanations. The engineer's reference to Niclaus re-awoke some of my previous sensations, and I was reflecting on the contingencies it suggested when Niclaus himself appeared in the trap-door, and slowly and nonchalantly descended the steps in the corner of the engine-room, opposite to the compartment behind the torpedo-launching tube.

At the sight of his superior officer, he took off his cap, with an awkward, listless gesture, glanced slyly at me, and, to keep himself in countenance, carefully closed the panel of the trap.

"Leave the panel open," cried the engineer sharply. "You can see that the commander is just going up."

He executed the order without hurrying himself, his eyes the while avoiding ours. The man was a southerner, short, thick-set, with black glossy hair, a sallow complexion, and greasy skin. His small eyes were shifty-looking; but, if once they caught your own, it was easy to discern their expression of sullenness.

How different he was from Yvonnec so straightforward and frank, with his ruddy complexion redolent of health and good-humor, and with his deferential, cheerful demeanor towards his superior!

Suddenly a short, quick ring was heard, and a call followed.

"The 20 minutes are up, sir."

I tried to find out where the voice came from, which I recognized to be that of the lieutenant who had been left in the conning-tower, two stories above us. The voice was so loud that it seemed to have spoken, at most, three yards away only.

My friend guessed my astonishment, and pointed to the wide bell of a speaking-trumpet projecting from a frame in the metal ceiling.

"It is the loud-speaking telephone," he said.

And, without raising his voice, or needing to put any apparatus to his mouth, he spoke back as if to someone close at hand:

"All right, I am coming up."

As we climbed the iron ladder he said to me again:

"I am going to show you another provision for our safety which will help to tranquillize you. At the top of the conning-chamber there is a metal cable which can be unrolled by simply pressing a knob, and which is then carried to the surface by a buoy."

"I remarked the buoy; it bears the name of the boat."

"Exactly; and it is painted with white varnish, which causes it to be visible at a great distance. Anyone then coming to the buoy can speak to us by means of the loud telephone you have just heard, if only they connect an apparatus to the buoy."

"Where is the knob that releases the cable?"

"In my conning-tower. In case of accident, or untoward event, I have merely to put my finger on it, and, whatever the depth, I am directly in communication with the surface. The thing is so simple that one cannot forget how to use it. And now," he continued, "remember, please, that you came on board to see for yourself the action of your friend Jaubert's apparatus. Yvonnec will show it to you as soon as you like."

He exchanged a few words with the midshipman; and I gathered that the engine had just been stopped, because, at the end of the 20 minutes, the officer feared they might be too near the coast. What seemed to justify his hesitation was that the notice accompanying the sea-chart drew attention to the existence of a current of three knots athwart the Ras Durdas.

"Then," asked d'Elbée, "do you think we have drifted a little towards the south-east?"

"Yes, sir, I do."

There was a moment's silence, while both bent over the chart. The midshipman indicated the measures with a compass.

"To make sure, we must emerge," concluded Jacques.

I was just putting my foot on the ladder to go down again; but on hearing my friend's decision I turned back quickly.

I had only been shut up for half an hour, and already I longed for a mouthful of fresh sea air, for a glimpse of sky and tossing wave. I heard Jacques' order:

"Hoist the periscope!"

Then the electric lamps were extinguished in the conning-tower; and gradually a dim twilight replaced the inky black that the extinction of the lamps had plunged us in.

"Night has nearly fallen," exclaimed Jacques.

I strained my eyes to catch the fading day through the glazed apertures.

"Aren't you intending to open the hood for a few minutes?" I asked.

"So soon?" he laughed. "So it weighs on you, this water above your head. You'll get used to it before long."

"Perhaps; but I should be glad to inhale a little of something else than my friend Jaubert's oxygen."

"And yet that's why you came here. Why, you haven't even taken a look at his apparatus, nor spoken to me of it either."

"I've time enough. We have still several hours' traveling to do; and, since you have placed Yvonnec at my service, I will go with him and examine the oxylith installation."

"Pay particular attention to our new machine. To have solved the problem of replacing the air required for explosion engines by oxygen mixed with the gases produced by combustion is, in my opinion, the great and essential innovation in submarine navigation."

While speaking, the commander of the *Dragonfly* had his gaze fixed on a plate of crizzled glass, on which were projected the exterior images reflected by one of the periscopes.

Today there are two periscopes in a submarine: one for observing by day, the other for observing by night; the latter has a wider field.

The plate appeared like a broad opaline leaf; but the light outside was so dim that I could distinguish nothing.

"Look," he continued, pointing with his finger, "do you see that?"

"I see nothing at all."

"That small bright spot on the plate, I mean."

"What is it?"

"That's the lighthouse of Bou-Said, perched 140 yards high, at the extremity of Cape Carthage. It has an eclipse-light of 20 seconds' duration, visible 25 miles away.

And that other, much paler, on the left, is the beacon, at the entrance to the canal, near which we passed an hour ago. By calculating the angle between the two points, I shall know exactly where we are. And I want this knowledge, on account of the sea-bottom, which varies from 18 to 30 fathoms in depth."

"To obtain the angle, you are going to emerge?"

"Yes. In fact, we are approaching the surface." He was right. A moment later the dome of the boat was out of the water; and, as soon as the hood was raised, I rushed out with all speed, while Jacques, laughing heartily at my hurry, ensconced himself on the edge of the conning-chamber, with his angle-measuring instrument in his hand.

Ah ! How I enjoyed being outside! It was the hour when the set Sun spreads round the horizon below which he has disappeared that melancholy tint, flitting through all the shades of mauve, heliotrope, and lilac, which subsequently blends with the dark blue of the slumbering east.

The lights that studded the shore I did not even perceive. Those towards which I turned were the stars which, in the direction of the Ras-al-Fortas, twinkled above the lofty cliffs of the granite coast.

Ah! What dear radiance, what splendid reflections of the infinite, I saw in those innumerable rays, beholding them with imagination as well as with sense. And, as often happens when healthy emotion causes the heart to throb, some lines of the poet Anatole Le Braz [24] occurred to my mind, and bathed my reverie in sweetness:

> *Stars, O stars in the skies!*
> *Gaze of the dead that we love,*

---

[24] Anatole le Braz (1859-1926) was a famous Breton folklore collector, translator anf poet. (Ed.)

If God should put out your eyes,
Our spirits would lose the above,
Stars, O stars in the skies !

But long meditations are not very apropos on board a submarine, at any rate not when one is outside, facing the sea. They are best kept for when one is sojourning in ocean depths, where other visions arise, awaking other poesies. And Jacques' voice called me:

"The soundings give here 23 fathoms and a half, with a sandy bottom. Come, we will go down in earnest and touch the bottom."

"Is it in your program?"

"My program is what I choose it to be."

"But for experiments of the kind, isn't it better to be convoyed?"

"If I were not sure of the boat's being stanch, I should not venture. But she has been tested at 33 fathoms."

"You went down as deep as that?"

"I was not on board on the occasion; but I have been down myself to a depth of 23 fathoms. It was just before I started. Everything was all right. So you may make yourself easy."

"With you I feel quite safe. But what shall we do next?"

"Come up again to 11 fathoms, and forge ahead at a maximum speed of 13 to 14 knots, steering towards Bizerte."

Listening to him, I climbed in. Before the hood was closed, I cast a final glance in the direction of the Carthage coast; and it seemed to me that the little villa I had remarked on the promontory of Byrsa was brilliantly illuminated. Then, I gave a last look also at the firmament which had called up my poetic fancy. And the hood blotted out the whole.

Once more I watched the preparations for descending; and already the needle marked 4.50m of water above the conning-tower, when the commander suddenly checked the handles regulating the inrush of the sea into the compartments.

"After all," he remarked to his second, "I think we will choose another day and another hour for the 20-fathom dive... This evening I will confine our experiment to testing our rate of descent. If I am not mistaken, we can exceed an average of 14 knots; but I should like to start from the Ras-al-Fortas, and we shall gain a few miles more in the east. Near the coast there are depths of 17 fathoms. We will steer from there straight for Plane Island. The distance measured accurately is 22 miles. In this way we can verify our speed to a fraction."

The midshipman bowed his assent.

I was tempted to ask Jacques if my observation as to the imprudence of a night experiment in such deep water had influenced him and made him change his plans. But I forbore.

I forbore; and today, I say to myself that if I had not spoken so and, perhaps, caused him to doubt, he would have followed out his plan, and would probably have carried it through, whereas, half an hour later...

"We will meet again here, when you have had enough of below," cried Jacques, as I proceeded to go down again into the instrument-room.

"Agreed. I shall rummage about with your Breton. Don't trouble about me."

"All right. Make yourself at home."

In the engine-room, for a short time, I amused myself with examining the valves, the revolutions of the fly-wheel, the indications of the speed-register; and then, finding the door open that led into the compartment of the torpedo-launching tube, I entered. Yvonnec was there, as I expected; and apparently he was waiting for me, for he grinned, and began at once to talk.

"This is the principal part of a submarine, captain. The rest, y'see, is secondary. What we do here is to contrive so that this pretty little plaything may be shot off just at the proper minute and exactly the way it has to go. Here, it's my domain. I was sure you would want to see my tube."

This big fellow pleased me infinitely. His manner of speaking was above that of the common sailor. He had received some education, and his integrity was as visible as the blue sky in clear water.

My first question referred, not to the oxylith apparatuses, which I knew to be everything that could be desired, but to the way of launching the new torpedoes. I was amazed at the sight of this enormous tube bearing inside it an engine capable of sinking an ironclad that had cost 50 millions of francs. I had already seen tubes for the same purpose on board torpedo boats, but they were in the open air, and launched the torpedo into the sea without difficulty. And the torpedo, once in the water, went under, and traveled by means of its own mechanism.

In the submarine, since the tube was itself in the water, there was a vital question to be dealt with both before and after the launching of the weapon, to wit, the boat's protection against an inrush of the sea. At my request Yvonnec showed me how the lever worked that opened and shut the sluice.

"Do you always drive the torpedo out with a cake of powder?" I asked.

"Yes, captain; but we shall soon be able to use compressed air, which is more convenient; the installation will be made next time the *Dragonfly* is docked."

"Is there much compressed air on board?"

"Pretty nearly everywhere, but not in my department, so I don't know much about it. I've seen tubes in the magazine which are charged up to 1800 pounds; it's the same pressure as that of our torpedo engines."

My attention was now drawn to the torpedo itself; suspended on a small car whose wheels ran along the inside of two rails fixed in the floor, it seemed, with its huge, glittering bulk, its tapering end, its many-bladed screw, like a sleeping monster that one would hesitate even to touch with one's fingers.

"Four men at least would be needed to get it off the cradle and slip it into the tube," I remarked.

These words had just left my lips, and Yvonnec, with his arm raised to show me something else, was about to answer me, when a shock occurred that felt as though the submarine were being wrenched asunder. The floor yielded beneath my feet, and I was thrown heavily on to my back. In his turn, the quartermaster was flung on the top of me, while the torpedo-launching tube, which, an instant before, was lying horizontally, assumed an almost vertical position.

"What is the matter?" I cried.

And a nervous trembling shook me from head to toe.

We had both of us rolled against the partition separating us from the engine-room.

Suddenly, Yvonnec, jumping up again, sprang to the iron door in the partition, which was opening, and, having slammed it to, began to screw the bolts that kept it fastened.

Behind the door thus shut, a bellowing noise filled the engine-room. I heard angry cries and howls, and distinguished Renaut's voice giving an order. Then hoarse, gasping sounds prevailed.

It seemed to me also as though, farther away, someone was knocking at the iron walls, but soon the tappings ceased.

After my first exclamation, I had remained for some seconds with staring eyes, incapable of movement. At last, however, I found strength to repeat my question to the quartermaster. He did not answer me, but continued to screw his bolts, leaning over the door, which had quitted its vertical position and was slanting back.

A prey to terrible anguish, I groped for a bar or rail that I might hold on to. While I was feeling about, the floor sank again to the horizontal with a slight tilt sideways, and then all motion stopped.

The engine itself was no longer working. And a tomb-like silence fell upon us.

CHAPTER III
FRENZY

When I carry my mind back to that terrible moment, my heart stands still.

And today, as, sitting quietly in front of my desk, I try to bring order into the medley of sensations and shocks that then rioted within me, I find the task a difficult one.

At first, I could not believe that what had occurred was a disaster. Among the various submarine commanders, Jacques had a high reputation. For 18 months, he had been in charge of the *Alose.* And subsequently, he had been transferred to the *Dragonfly,* our largest submarine, because he was the one in whom most confidence was felt. Unless he had had a like confidence in himself, he would not have resolved to make a trial experiment of the boat's speed in descending without the presence of a convoy-ship, and by night instead of by day. His acceptance of special conditions proved how sure he felt of his craft, of his crew, and of himself.

Yes; but this shock!

This shock had been caused by something: by what?

It did not come into my mind at the time that the *Dragonfly* might have collided with an ironclad, since I was unaware that, on account of the great depth of water close to Cape Bon, vessels from Malta hug the coast in this spot.

My first thought was: we had struck on a rock rising up from the sea-bottom, and had damaged our prow in consequence.

The damage must be serious, for we had dipped down with a suddenness indicating the instantaneous invasion of one or several compartments.

My second thought was: Jacques would get us out of the dilemma.

I knew by my conversation with him that, in this new submarine, there were water-tight compartments well separated from each other, and that, in the front part, there was one especially adapted for resisting collisions, and arranged so as to render an inrush of water harmless.

I knew also that several compartments were filled with cellulose, and provided with automatically closing doors.

I knew that, from inside his conning-chamber, Jacques could cast off the safety-leads, either individually or collectively.

Last of all, I knew that, when freed from the weight of the eight or ten tons these leads added, the *Dragonfly* must rise to the surface like a cork, even with one or two water-logged compartments.

And I waited for the ascent. I waited, holding on to the brass rail running round the place where we were, and my pulse beating more rapidly at each second.

No movement happened.

I put my ear to the partition that cut us off from the engine-room. What was taking place on the other side?

"Yvonnec," I cried in a choked voice, "do you hear? What is it?"

A fresh gasping rattle was again audible in the engine-room, and a queer gurgling like that of a person trying in vain to speak.

"You must open," I exclaimed. "Open quickly!"

And I seized one of the knobs on the nuts which the quartermaster had just finished screwing in.

But Yvonnec's hand was on mine directly. "No," he said. "You mustn't."

"Why not? If there is anything the matter, it's only through there we can escape."

"When anything is the matter," he replied, "our orders are to shut the doors… all the doors!"

At this tragic moment, this man thought only of his orders; and, without pausing to ask himself whether it would be fatal or not to him, he had, first and foremost, executed them. There was grandeur in the manifestation of discipline which I had before me; but, to my shame, I confess I did not see the thing in the same light. Since we were at the further extremity of the boat, the way for us towards deliverance, so it seemed to me, was through the room containing the engine; and to close the door giving access to it, I looked upon as madness.

I renewed my attempt. But Yvonnec checked me again; and, without speaking, pointed to a thin stream of water trickling from beneath the screwed-up door. Then, I perceived, what my distraction had prevented me so far from noticing, that my feet were ankle deep in the stream.

The machinery was flooded, and we should have been ourselves submerged if my companion had not acted so promptly.

There was a moment of intense anguish. We looked at each other, Yvonnec and I, without daring to open our lips.

No noise now came from the other side except an occasional whining, which must be that of Phanor. I held my breath, trying to catch an echo of Jacques' voice. I said to myself that a sailor would soon come from him to reassure me.

I had forgotten the water which continued to trickle from under the door, and now filtered along the gutta-percha paddings, until at length the pool crept up to the torpedo tube. Its greater depth against the door showed that the submarine still remained in a somewhat slanting position, the back part where we were standing being less invaded than the fore part. Was our room going to be flooded too?

Once more Yvonnec set himself to twisting the nut handles, and ultimately the water ceased entering. When he had finished, he turned to me and said:

"Captain, we are at the bottom… and shall have to stay here for some time."

This sentence, so dreadful in its quiet brevity, aroused me from the torpor into which I had sunk.

At the bottom, like the *Farfadet,* like the *Lutin.* Was it possible?

If so, it meant death, hideous death, with physical and mental torture, lasting several days, such as I had never thought of without shuddering.

I had formerly read a full account of each of these catas-
trophes, which had both occurred near to Bizerte, one in the
lake, the other not far from the jetty; and I had cursed the lack
of foresight responsible for the absence of cranes sufficiently
powerful to raise the submarine before its crew were asphyxiated. I remembered that the *Farfadet* had been brought to the
surface four days after its accident, and that the imprisoned
men had been heard knocking for assistance at the moment
when the boat slipped back to the bottom.

If the means requisite for raising the *Farfadet* had been
wanting in the Lake of Bizerte, in calm water only four or five
fathoms deep, it was not likely they would be forthcoming in
the Gulf of Tunis. It was not even likely we should be found.

Who had witnessed the catastrophe? No one, since it had
happened at night. On the morrow, when it was perceived that
the submarine did not return to Bizerte, the authorities would
be anxious, would institute a search... which would be fruitless. We should not be found, because no one had caught sight
of us since the moment of our going under water abreast of the
antique citadel of Byrsa.

The girl who had waved her handkerchief from the villa,
and to whom I had waved mine in return, was the last human
creature that had seen us on the surface of the sea; and, after
disappearing from her eyes, we had navigated for 25 minutes
under water in a direction unknown to any one save ourselves,
but which would be rather supposed to lead to Bizerte, whereas we had steered for several miles in an opposite direction,
in order to have a freer field towards the east.

Consequently, however prompt such search might be, it
would not be in our vicinity. We were lost.

These reflections, rapidly traversing my mind, drove me
nearly mad. I called out to Yvonnec, beseeching him to get us
out of this prison. I asked him to do all sorts of impossible
things. Then I began to stride about the narrow place in which
we were confined, incapable of mastering the wild beast's
restlessness which a man always feels when pent up. Silence
reigned... a silence such as I could never have imagined. It

enwrapped us like a thick shroud. Since the engine—the boat's pulse—had ceased to throb, all noise had died away; and no one can realize the despair and frightfulness of absolute immobility who has not experienced it at the bottom of the sea.

Exhausted at length, I stopped once more in front of Yvonnec, who was still standing against the door; and the tranquility in his look restored me somewhat to myself.

It must be the hope of escaping from our dreadful situation which caused this man of inferior social condition and limited education to exhibit such calmness of mind.

"Is all hope gone?" I asked with choking voice.

"Gad, Captain, I don't know any more than you do... We can only wait till somebody comes."

"But who will come?"

"That's more than I'm able to say."

"The commander?"

"Oh! The Commander! It's not likely any but ourselves are alive now in the boat."

"You really think the other compartments are full of water?"

"Since the water is in the engine-room, it must have filled the conning-tower, the forward compartments, perhaps those of the crew and the officers' cabins... if they didn't shut them in time."

"Then are we the only ones left?"

"You see the slant, the fore part is at the bottom, that's sure, and we, who are aft, still float, because there is air here, and perhaps, too, in the compartments below the engine, because they are always shut..."

"What compartments are those?"

"The magazines and the compressed air reservoirs."

There was a fresh silence, until my anguish broke out into a sob.

"My God! my God!" I cried.

"You are right, captain," exclaimed the Breton, with a grave voice, "only the Good Lord can deliver us from this!"

My companion's tone was so impressive that it momentarily diverted my despair. His clear blue eyes gazed at me, and, with his hand on one of the nut fastenings, he seemed like a sentinel placed in front of the fateful gate.

His tranquility at such a time confounded me. I could understand that contact with permanent danger had engendered a habit of resignation, but that in such a desperate pass he should count solely on a problematic intervention appeared to me hardly human. I felt angry with him for staying there so apathetically, and especially for belittling me with his serenity.

A new fit of excitement attacking me, I began to pace backwards and forwards again. It seemed to me I should soon go mad.

Today I cannot well analyze, in the quiet of my recovered life, the tumult of sentiments that agitated me during that revolt against destiny. And what would be the use of evoking the utterances of that miserable piece of humanity I had become? I am ashamed enough to have to expose my weakness, ashamed to have found myself so cowardly, after embracing a career in which death has to be faced.

Death, yes; but not a death like that!

Death in broad daylight, as I had often dreamed of it, in a day of battle, leaving behind me the remembrance of a great warrior-effort, of a supreme assault! Yes, my mind was familiar with that. I had no fear of it.

But the agony of this burial alive! When I think of it even now, it causes me to break out into a cold sweat.

Exhausted again by my emotions, I sank into a state of complete prostration.

How long it lasted; by what hallucinations it was traversed; what noises I thought I heard, calls produced only by the bubbling of my own brain, visions of safety rising amid the chaos of my hurtling ideas—I have no clear recollection now.

When I came back to the consciousness of our situation, I looked round for Yvonnec. He was no longer beside me. By the light of the Edison lamp shining above the torpedo-tube I perceived him leaning over the fore part of the tube, with his head hidden in his hands.

I spoke to him in a low tone; but he did not answer.

Alarmed, I rose. Was he sleeping, or had he fainted? Had he felt the first effects of asphyxia? It could not be that, for I myself still breathed freely.

I went up to him and touched him.

"Yvonnec, are you asleep? Answer me," I said.

The Breton lifted his head slowly, and I saw round his clasped hands a chaplet of big boxwood beads, terminating in a small crucifix.

He was praying.

I was neither a skeptic nor a church-goer. It was long since I had prayed. During the years that had followed my Confirmation, I had listened to my mother as, kneeling at my bedside, she repeated the prayers with which she had cradled me; and, on reaching manhood, I had joined her in saying them whenever I went to see her, but with none of her sincerity, fervor, and faith.

At the moment of performing any important act, it would never have occurred to me to ask help from God, in whom, however, I believed. My mind being impregnated with fatalism after a dozen years spent in Africa amongst Arabs, I had lost all conception of a Providence interfering in small human interests, and capable of succoring the atom of humanity buried in the infinity of worlds. Even at this hour of doom, I had not thought of such aid.

Yet, I believed in another life, with its rewards and punishments. I had a settled conviction that the souls of men after quitting the body would receive what was their due; it was strange, therefore, that, on seeing Yvonnec kneeling and praying, I did not imitate him, though a voice within me said: "That man is stronger than you."

"Come, Yvonnec, we must do something; we can't stay here doing nothing," I said.

"At your service, captain; but I have been doing the first thing that was to be done. I have prayed to our Saint Anne of Auray."

"You've done right, since you believe she can help to get us out of this. But now we must act…and act quickly, because, if the light should fail…"

I did not finish my sentence; the consequences it suggested were the most terrible of all… our being in an obscurity rendering all action impossible, an obscurity peopled only with nightmare phantoms! Something must be attempted, at any rate, before such a thing could happen. Yvonnec kissed the cross on his chaplet, put it in his pocket and replied:

"I am at your orders, captain ! "

This simple sentence, with its recognition of my rank, strengthened my will. In our desperate position, which might have been supposed to destroy social distinctions in favor of the animal instinct of self-preservation, this sailor attributed superiority to me, and showed that he relied on me.

In order to justify his confidence in the officer, I summoned up all my energy. Twenty years passed in the army had given me a fund of coolness. It was time I proved to this sailor, who was 15 years my junior, that I was able to master my weakness.

Getting up, I glanced round the compartment. In the corner near the door, my friend Jaubert's oxylith apparatus was working silently, and automatically diffusing throughout the narrow space in which we were confined the gas we needed to breathe; at the same time, it absorbed the carbonic acid our lungs exhaled into the air.

Its two big cylinders went up to the ceiling. I knew they had been charged at our departure, and could therefore supply us with oxygen for a week; so it was not asphyxia that was our immediate danger.

A week! The apparatus might even last longer; for it was intended also to feed the engine; and the big copper tube communicating with the engine-room passed through the steel partition an inch or two above the door.

Since the machinery was swamped, all the excess oxygen would be utilizable for ourselves. There was no reason to fear that our gas-producing apparatus might be invaded by the water, since the inside pressure of cylinders and tubes sufficed to keep it out.

I was making these reflections to myself when Yvonnec, stroking the torpedo that hung from the ceiling, said:

"If only we could get out like the torpedo, captain!"

I turned round, and for a few instants I stared at the monster, hypnotized by its glittering form. The thought just expressed by the Breton had passed through my own mind before the accident, and I had mentioned it to d'Elbée; and indeed the torpedoes used on board the *Dragonfly* were of a diameter equal about to the body of an ordinary-sized man.

Since the launching-tube communicated with the sea, one might take one's place in it, like a torpedo, and be shot out. Then, once out...

"Yvonnec," I cried, "quick, open the shutter."

My companion at once seized the knob, somewhat similar to that of an old cannon of 80, turned it a sixth part round, and the shutter opened, allowing us to see inside.

I stooped down and put my arm in. If a torpedo had already been introduced in readiness, the plan was not feasible. But no, the tube was empty.

"Now, Yvonnec," I said, "can't we escape through there?"

"At first, it seemed to me we could, captain; but after a bit of reflection, I fancy it's impossible."

"Why?"

"Because we are not torpedoes."

"You told me they were driven out by powder."

"Yes, in that tube; in the other, compressed air is used."

This was unfortunate, for compressed air was preferable to powder with a man in front. However, the powder could not be really dangerous, having only just the expanding and driving force to project the torpedo out into the water, where its own screws came into action as propellers.

"Try if you can get in, Yvonnec."

"It's not necessary, captain; I did try some time ago with one of my comrades, just for fun. There isn't much elbow room, but one can get in."

"Do you think I could?"

"Surely. You're no bigger than me."

The hope of employing the tube as a means of escape began to shape itself. I weighed the objections; but they presented no insurmountable difficulties, although, the evening before, I should have said they did. Feverishly I questioned my companion.

"How is the tube closed at the other end?"

"By a thick cap garnished with leather rubbers."

"And how is the cap held tight?"

"By the water."

The question even was useless; for evidently the pressure of water on the outside held it the tighter in proportion as the depth increased.

The next question was more doubtful.

"At what depth are we?"

A column of water measuring ten meters corresponds to a pressure equal to that of the air at the Earth's surface, and is balanced in the barometer by a column of mercury of 30 inches. If, therefore, we were 20 or 30 fathoms under the surface, we had a pressure above us of between 60 and 80 pounds per square inch, and the same pressure, of course, on the cap of the tube. It was enormous.

I tried to collect my ideas and to remember. A little before the accident, I had seen the boat's hydrographic chart. It was dotted all over with quotations of depth. Even in the Gulf of Tunis they varied from five to 15 and 20 fathoms. And a trifle further northwards, it seemed to me I had noticed figures showing depths of between 30 and 40. If the accident had occurred in these parts, we could not possibly get out. Nor could any human aid reach us at such a depth.

No professional divers would risk themselves at this depth. At between 15 and 20 fathoms it would appear that they are attacked by giddiness, which forces them to return to the surface at once. I had read somewhere, at the time of the disaster to the *Lutin,* which lay 17-1/2 fathoms deep, that a trained diver could never go deeper than 25 fathoms.

Where were we?

The sweat broke out on my forehead as I asked this question aloud.

When the commander of the *Dragonfly* gave up his project of descending to 20 fathoms, his last words to the second lieutenant were an order to steer towards Ras-al-Fortas.

This was the cape opposite Cape Carthage, on the other side of the gulf. Since the eastern side of the gulf was rocky and ran sheer down into the sea, there must be considerable depths there, for I recalled the dotted curves indicating the submarine differences of depth for each ten meters of distance; and, if I was not mistaken, the first three of these curves passed close to the shore, very near together.

If, therefore, our boat had reached anywhere near that shore, we must be in a depth of 16 fathoms. But if, on the other hand, we had already veered in the direction of Plane Island, towards Bizerte, we might have sunk in a depth of 35 or 40 fathoms. And then we had no hope.

I cannot say that I argued the matter out exactly in this orderly manner at the moment. My brain was too confused. Amidst the rush of thoughts, my one fixed idea was to get out through the tube, if possible.

Still, I was forced to reckon with the shock that would be felt from the explosion of the powder; with the mephitic gases created by the explosion; with the distance to be covered in reaching the surface. To lessen the force with which my head would be driven against the cap of the outlet, I would protect my head with a pad made of my clothes; and, since it would be the pressure of the powder-generated gases which would open the cap, not the impact of my head, I should stand a decent chance of getting through without a fractured skull.

The powder-generated gases were mephitic; but, as I should be affected by them only for a moment or so, I concluded they could not be fatal to me.

What would be the most difficult was the having to rise through 15 or 20 fathoms of water, in order to reach the surface; yet, even here, I argued I was bound to come to the top, though perhaps unable to hold my breath long enough to avoid swallowing water, for I would surround my neck, arms, and waist with pieces of cork. There was no lack of this article in our prison. It hung on the walls in the form of chaplets and flat sections; and I had remarked similar supplies in each other compartment, a reminder of the ever-threatening danger.

As if one could escape from a submarine!

Once in the upper air I should be saved; the coast could not be far away. I was a good swimmer; I should be held up by the cork; and the joy of being free of this tomb would increase my strength tenfold.

Throughout these interweavings of plans and hopes, I had not once thought of Yvonnec, who stood motionless and silent beside the open tube. Or, rather, I had just once thought of him, but solely because he would close the shutter behind me, and fire the powder necessary for my being thrust forth.

But I had built up my plan without asking if he were willing to play the role of staying and dying alone. But now the question arose: Why should he stay, and not I? By what right could I save my life in sacrificing his? If there were the least chance of escape, it ought to be utilized for both; and, if a choice were to be made between us two, it ought to be made by casting lots. Yvonnec must have read my thoughts at present, for, on raising my head to look at him, he said:

"Captain, if you feel yourself a good enough swimmer to reach the coast, I will send you off as soon as you like!"

CHAPTER IV
THE TORPEDO-TUBE

So he consented to stay, not even waiting for my request, which, I am sure, would have become a supplication; for hope had just revived in me, mad hope, which leaped all obstacles, the hope which sustains criminals condemned to death, and which has been declared immortal.

It is indeed strange how quickly, in the worst extremities, man passes, sometimes without reason, from the most profound discouragement to the wildest confidence.

Dying people are ready at any moment to imagine they are recovering; with the least improvement, they believe themselves out of danger, and, after accustoming themselves to the notion of death, they come back to that of resurrection.

My imagination had worked a miracle in a few minutes. I saw myself swimming with savage energy towards the near coast, gaining it in a last effort, scaling the rocks with bleeding hands and feet, but with gleefully beating heart.

I saw myself running to the Cape Ras-al-Fortas signaling-station, telephoning to Tunis... *In fine*, I saw myself delivered by the heroic consent of this sailor, to whom no one could render the same service.... *and who was aware of this.*

I looked at him as one looks at a man in whom previously nothing extraordinary has been noticed, and who has just been discovered to be a hero. His face wore still its impassible expression. Without apparent revolt or hesitation he had decided to remain alone and to confront the dreadful fate that hung over our heads.

Again he spoke:

"Do you know how to swim, captain?"

"Oh, yes, well!"

"And to dive? Can you hold your breath?"

I answered in the affirmative, although at bottom, I was vaguely conscious of possessing but little proficiency in this latter art. What I was sure of was that I would do anything and everything to get out of this hell.

"And you, Yvonnec," I asked in turn, "can you hold your breath?"

"Oh, yes; when I was a child, I used to play with the fishes."

I could have wished he had said he did not know how to dive. In spite of the evidence I had had to the contrary, I feared he might create difficulties at the last moment.

From the wall I took down the pieces of cork, and put them round my neck, and then upon my chest, this latter precaution being essential, not only so that I might use them to keep me above the surface when I got there, but so that I might, on entering the tube, be able to shift them and gird them round my waist, if more convenient.

And now I was ready for the experiment.

"You must push me behind, Yvonnec," I said to him. "Alone, I can't get right in."

I was kneeling down in front of the opening when I spoke. Bent over a low box which was fixed in the floor at the other end of the compartment, my companion did not reply. I heard him, however, murmur something to himself; and, rising, I went to him.

"Captain," he said at length, "we shall have to give up the attempt… There is no powder."

"No powder?" I repeated in a terrified tone.

"Generally, there are two charges in a canvas bag that remain in the box."

"They are not in?"

"No, they must have been taken away and locked up in the magazine."

"And there is no way of managing without them?"

"None."

I sank rather than sat down on the tube. The door of deliverance, which had seemed to be half-opened, was shut upon me again.

I was overwhelmed.

Today, I wonder how I could ever have believed in the possibility of escaping in such a manner.

I had fancied that the outside cap was opened by the expansion of the gas, and now I know that it could only be removed from the tube opening by sliding down, an operation effected from inside the boat, which allowed the outside water to enter the tube before the torpedo was launched.

The inrush, at the depth we were, would have been tremendous; and this shock and pressure I should have been obliged to support, while waiting for the powder to explode. Moreover, the powder employed in torpedo-launching was adapted only to depths of from four to eight fathoms. Down where we were, it would have been powerless to force the hood open; and I should have been driven against the cap, with the result that my spine would have been broken, or my head been smashed in, notwithstanding the padding afforded by my clothes.

My folly was as great in supposing that I could have passed successfully through the last phase of the experiment. Even if not killed outright, while in the tube, and even if I could have got into the water, I should have drunk in such a quantity of the liquid as would have completed my asphyxia. Stunned by what I had gone through, I should have risen to the surface as an inert mass, and have been drowned without the least chance of coming to the shore.

It was, therefore, in reality a piece of good luck that the means for carrying out this foolish project were lacking. But my disappointment at the instant was so bitter that nothing in the world would have convinced me I had been mistaken.

Afresh I began to wander about the cabin, uttering senseless cries...

Huddled up at the further end of the compartment, Yvonnec did not budge, and his almost weird immobility exasperated me. I wanted him, like myself, to rave against fate. No doubt he was saying his beads again, for his lips opened and closed from time to time, while his drooping eyelids hid his gaze from me. I must, in this fit of frenzy, have hurled both reproaches and insults at him; but he probably did not hear them, his mind being manifestly elsewhere.

My rage soon spent itself. A nervous trembling seized on me; and at last I slipped down to the floor, beside my companion; and looking for some moments as if hypnotized at the water lying at the opposite side of the cabin, on which the Edison lamp cast its pale radiance, I fell finally into a heavy sleep.

A horrible nightmare harassed those first hours of slumber. I shall never forget it; and I don't know which was the worst during that night—the dreadful reality that had overtaken me, the more dreadful dream that followed, or the return to the same reality that had become a veritable instrument of torture...

I was on a field of battle. Bullets were hurtling through the thinning ranks; melinite shells were bursting amidst clouds of black smoke streaked with red lightning. The air was impregnated with their acrid fumes. I could hardly breathe.

Where I was fighting or why, I did not know!

Was it the war of revenge so long dreamed of?[25] Was it a civil strife? What was this wood-crowned ravine towards which my fevered eyes were bent?

Near me infantry men were firing unceasingly in the trenches... Behind them were subaltern officers. I recognized friends' faces, and tried to call them... Gay?... Vothelin Destainville?... Henriet?...

Then, the scene vanished, and another took its place. There were zouaves now, soldiers I was partial to. The others were "*Bluebottles*"—these were the "*Corncockles*" of the battlefield.

An order was shouted: "Forward!" And to the accompaniment of a rousing tune, with bits of the *Marseillaise* and the *Sidi-Brahim* intermingled, the entire column swept on.

---

[25] Revenge against the Germans for the French defeat of the Franco-Prussian War. (Ed.)

I raised my arm, brandishing a saber that seemed to me as unwieldy as an axe or a mace. I tried to echo the forward shout; but, suddenly, a sharp pain shot through me. I clearly perceived a nearer hiss amidst the intense humming of projectiles that swarmed through the air, and I sank to the Earth, pointing to the hill with my arm, which an intolerable weight dragged downwards.

A bullet had entered my side, with a thud of crushed flesh and bone; then another struck me in the middle of my forehead, and I thought my brain had split like a ripe pomegranate.

An icy hand laid me at full length in a trench, among the *Corncockles* and the *Bluebottles.*

There was a silence; the cannonade slackened; the firing died away: gloom spread in the firmament.

All at once, a general movement was effected in the midst of the corpses surrounding me, amongst which the Moon's rays shone with russet gleams.

Gradually, the bodies drew nearer each other, and assumed the appearance of rows. I felt myself seized by my head and feet, and placed together with the others.

I was close to a beardless soldier, on whose blue hood I could see a number one—that of a battalion I was especially fond of.

His eyes were shut; he seemed asleep; but, like me, he had a hole in his forehead.

The battle was finished. I was considered to be dead; and this charnel-house, in which I was being put, was the common resting-place for the slain.

Upon the heap of corpses, other rows were deposited by invisible grave-diggers. I felt stifled, I tried to free myself; I made efforts to shout, but the words refused to leave my throat…

It was horrible! I was being buried alive!

No more hurtling, no more shells bursting, no more bullets hissing; but, above me, the noise of shovelfuls of earth falling, falling, thickening my shroud!

I lacked air; I could not breathe… I tried to turn round… My nails penetrated into some cold, rigid flesh, that of the infantry man whom Death had laid beside me. The weight on my chest was too heavy… I felt the dreadful anguish of those that suffocate. At last, I succeeded in crying out, and my cry finished in a hoarse gasp!

Suddenly a quiet voice replied to me:

"Captain, wake up; it will be better for you."

I opened my eyes and sat up. Yvonnec was holding my hand; and such was the rebound from the horror of my dream that, on realizing I was awake, I threw myself into his arms.

With the refound liberty to breathe, I was, at first, like a man born again; but the illusion did not last long. Memory told me that I was, none the less, in a tomb. Again I asked Yvonnec:

"Is there no way of escape?"

All at once, I sprang to my feet, with dilated eyes. On the other side of the door, I heard something—a stifled, inarticulate cry—it must be a cry! And I fixed my ear against the metal partition.

The quartermaster shook his head. He had heard nothing; and the cry was only an echo of the fever that racked my brain.

However, there was something else. Beneath the door the water was oozing more quickly. Yvonnec tried to stop up the crevices with bits of his woolen belt. To strengthen the stopping, he tore up his cap, and then his flannel shirt, showing his muscular body and his white Celtic skin.

And now, in our prison, we began to suffer from the heat and damp, which caused my forehead to drip with perspiration. I took off the leather coat, in which I was uncomfortably warm, and was just going to throw it on the floor when I perceived that in the fore part of our cabin, there was hardly any water left.

I couldn't believe my eyes. Just before my nightmare, the electric light had been reflected in it as in a mirror. Had I slept so long?

But that indeed was not the question. At present, another more important one suggested itself. Where had the water gone? It could not have evaporated; and certainly, not long previously, it was really there. It must, therefore, have found an issue. What was this issue?

I had not long to seek, since I came to the cast-iron slab which Jacques himself had raised, when he was taking me round. Underneath was the hole communicating with the sluice. Through the interstices of the slab the water had filtered away. So there must be under us compartments empty like our own. The sluice was empty, no doubt; and, through there, it would be possible to get into the sea, as it was possible to get from the sea into the submarine.

Now, again, insinuating, tenacious hope appeared to me in another form. I did not know how the sluice worked; but Yvonnec would know, since Jacques had asked him to explain it to me subsequently.

I wondered why my companion had not yet thought of this way out. Coming back to him, at the end of the torpedo-tube, I seized his arm, for he seemed to be again praying. If he did nothing but this, it would not be possible for me to utilize his services.

I was mistaken. He was asleep.

And my shaking his arm produced no other effect than to make him raise his head, which had sunk on his arm. Like myself a while before, he had fallen into a deep slumber.

I did not disturb him further. It was better indeed he should have his turn. If we both slept at the same time, there might be some signal important for our deliverance which we should not hear; and it would be concluded there were no survivors in the *Dragonfly*.

Other questions occurred to my mind, one that I had asked myself ever and anon since the accident. Were we being sought for? Was it daylight? Instinctively I took out my watch.

By its tick-tack I knew it was still going. The hands pointed to 3:20. But was it afternoon or morning? Having dozed off twice, I had lost consciousness of the hour. The accident must have happened about nine in the evening. Had we been no more than six hours and a half in our present condition, or was it not rather 18 hours? If the latter, then everyone in Bizerte and Tunis must be in great anxiety, because we were due at the Bizerte Wharf about two in the morning, and ought, in any case, to have arrived before daylight.

So we must be the object of some one's search at this moment. Would anyone think of coming in the direction of Cape Ras-al-Fortas? Had Jacques spoken either to a comrade or to the head of the Flying Defense Squadron, on whom the fleet of submarines depended, of his idea of making for this spot, in order to proceed thence in a straight line as far as Plane Island ?

I was reflecting whether it was likely a lucky sounding would reveal our position, when a thought flashed through my head. The buoy attached to the telephonic wire must have been released at the time of the accident.

"It is the first movement to be made," had explained Jacques himself. He could not have forgotten to carry it out.

So the buoy was probably floating now above our prison, and we could be spoken to, if an apparatus were adapted to the wire. For right against the partition wall was the receiver with its broad trumpet magnifying sounds. Indeed, this cabin was the place, above all others, where the receiver was necessary, since in it took place during a battle the launching of the torpedo. The boat being in obscurity and its commandant directing it by means of the periscope, it was only in this way he could communicate to the two men shut up in the compartment the order to shoot off the missile.

However, it was still doubtful whether the buoy at the surface could be put into direct communication with our own cabin; one could only surmise that they who installed this safety-apparatus would think of the possibility of such a case as ours occurring, and provide for the call being heard in every compartment of the boat.

And my eyes wandered at each instant to the trumpet whence I kept hoping some signal might reach me. After I had repeated this act more times than I could count, I was suddenly recalled to the consciousness that I had eaten nothing for a long while. I was hungry. My stomach felt empty. Until now I had overlooked this contingency.

Drowning and asphyxia were the only forms of death I had anticipated. I had come on board after a good dinner with Jacques, and, engrossed by my first plans of escape, I had forgotten what we might have to suffer from hunger and its accompanying thirst after a few days' confinement.

The pangs in my stomach served to answer the question I had asked myself a few moments before. It was not six hours, but 18, and rather 24 hours that had elapsed since the accident. We were at least at the end of the first day of our submarine imprisonment.

I was hungry, hungry! And mechanically I put my hand in one of my leather pockets. I drew out an orange, a packet of dates, then some waffles and chocolate. They were my provisions of the evening before.

"One would think you were embarking for South America!" Jacques had said to me, joking at my precaution.

What a good thing I did not get rid of them, when I arrived on board, by sending them down to the galley.

There was another parcel, somewhat heavier. I opened the paper. It was the file we had bought at the ironmonger's in the Rue de la Casbah.

I should have preferred another tablet of chocolate.

I put the tool down at the bottom of the shutter. It was a handsaw file of the largest size, without handle.

Being famished, I greedily ate two waffles; I nibbled a few squares of cream-chocolate, and was about to start on the orange, but stopped.

What I was doing was wrong. These were our only eatables. With them we might hold out longer, waiting till the telephone should speak.

I ought to husband them. I ought especially to share them with Yvonnec.

Yet the selfish impulse which, a few hours before, had prevented me from troubling about the lot of my companion if left alone face to face with death, seized upon me again.

What a poor creature man is when he is under the influence of his instincts, and is urged by want. How quickly he once more becomes the self-seeking animal of the struggle for life.

If I were to keep these provisions for myself! If I were to hide them in the torpedo-tube! Yvonnec did not know I had them. I should eat them only during his sleep. He would know nothing, and I should sustain myself longer.

But a revolt of my inner being almost immediately vanquished this odious temptation. The brave fellow's life was well worth mine. We would live or die together.

To tell the truth, there was egotism even in my veering round. Supposing there were some means of escape that was possible, and that we had not yet tried, I could do nothing without him, and had nothing to hope for without his help. He was acquainted with the boat, at least with the compartment where we were, since his duties required his frequent presence in it; and, besides, I remembered Jacques' saying: "Yvonnec will show you, Yvonnec will explain to you!"

It was necessary, therefore, he should preserve his strength and brain as long as I did. I put aside for him a portion equal to that which I had just consumed, and I examined how much remained.

There was a bag of dates I had not touched; it contained about 30. Then there were a dozen waffles and about half a pound of chocolate. As for the orange, we should want it to quench our thirst; and it would have to be used parsimoniously, for we hadn't a drop of drinkable water in the cabin; and, although we were surrounded with water on all sides, we were as certain to die of thirst, if not delivered, as the traveler lost in the Sahara, 100 leagues from every fountain or well. We were even worse off than he, for he might seek and walk, scratch the sand with his nails, drink the blood of his camel or his horse. My blood was already feverish. I was thirsty.

Yvonnec had just stirred. He stretched himself, looked round, as if stupefied, and when his blue eyes met mine, I saw them fill with tears. It was my turn to cheer him.

"Courage, my poor Yvonnec."

"Ah! Captain, I have been dreaming of my native place."

"Of Larmor?"

"Yes, and especially of my lass, poor Annaïc."

"Then you are betrothed, like that unfortunate engineer."

"Yes; but his marriage was for next month. Mine was not so near, since her parents wanted me to have my stripes. But we loved each other all the same."

The tears ran freely down his rosy cheeks slightly tanned by the weather, and wetted his bristly, blond beard.

"Then there are the old folks…"

"Your parents? Have you got them both?"

"Yes."

His chest heaved under the sobs that broke forth. The thoughts of his village, his parents, the Breton fisher-girl, had conquered his sailor's impassibility and religious serenity.

And his grief was contagious. Absorbed in the efforts of the first moments, and assailed by nightmare, whilst this simple fellow dreamt of his home, I had not yet begun to trouble about those I had left in France, in a small and far-off provincial town, where they were waiting to return to Paris with me.

A fair silhouette passed before my eyes; little curly heads enframed it. My wife knew nothing. I had told her nothing before leaving. No one having seen me embark on the *Dragonfly,* she could learn nothing from the newspapers, and only in six or eight days would she begin to be anxious and to worry. Would she ever know the truth? How should she?

And it was an extra grief to think that now when all the other members of the crew, whose names would have been given by the papers, were being mourned, no one was troubling about me.

And what would my disappearance mean to my old mother who was living alone in the Aisne department, where she had been since my father died, and whom I had left in a poor state of health? It would be her death.

I seized Yvonnec's hand, and I wept with him. It was no longer the mad despair of the first moments that afflicted me now. Our two griefs dwelling on the same sort of reminiscences and regrets had brought us to a common condition. We were two prisoners condemned to a like fate.

I offered Yvonnec his share of the provisions. He thanked me through his tears, ate, and, as if struck by an idea, went and fetched his sailor's jacket, which he had thrown into a corner. From one of the pockets he pulled out a big lump of coarse bread, from the other a pipe, some tobacco, and matches.

"I hadn't eaten much before starting," he said. "I meant to nibble my bread during our journey. It's lucky."

I quite agreed with him. By economizing we might make our eatables last three days.

"I really believe, Captain," he added, "it must be a sign from Providence."

"Perhaps you are right."

And I listened to the Breton with an attention I had not paid him a few hours before. Faith is contagious, just like grief.

"He has evidently spared us, and afforded us means that may lead to our escaping," Yvonnec continued.

"It is true," I replied, "our both having food in our pockets is extraordinary, as also the fact that we are in the only part of the boat which is not flooded."

"Now I come to think of it, Captain, the sluice perhaps is not flooded, either."

"You are right; the sluice can't be flooded, since the water that was on the floor here has run away through the lid joints."

"That's so, I declare! Let's have a look."

"Do you know how the sluice works?"

"Not very well. I have only seen the pressure taps used twice: when the second lieutenant explained them to us, and once before when a diver came to La Pallice [26] to go down into the sea through the well."

"Is there a diving apparatus in the sluice?" I asked quickly.

The quartermaster reflected an instant.

"I don't fancy so. The man who went down took off his dress when he came out of the well; but he carried it away with him after. He belonged to the Rochefort arsenal."

"But there must have been a diver in the crew."

"Yes; it was Simon; but his apparatus is bound to be in the magazine, or perhaps among the machinery."

While talking, Yvonnec had raised the circular slab and put his foot on the topmost rung of the vertical ladder used in descending. He went down and disappeared in the darkness, for the lamp in our cabin lighted only the upper portion. I tried to find the switch that Jacques had turned inside the well, but could not.

"There is water at the bottom," announced Yvonnec.

"It's the water that has run from the floor here. And the sluice door?"

"I am afraid to open it… if there should be water on the other side…"

I should have liked to go down to where Yvonnec was, but should have interfered with his movements. The well was about the size of a sentry-box, and I did not know how the door was fixed, and whether it opened from the outside or from the inside. I heard my companion try the bolt-nuts which could be screwed and unscrewed by hand, like those fastening

___

[26] The industrial harbor of the city of La Rochelle. Ed.

the machine-room door. He paused, listened, and uttered a cry of joy.

"There is no water," he called; and his voice sounded farther away as he added: "Now the door is open."

I scrambled down the ladder in a jiffy, and was met at the bottom by a partition of thick sheet-iron. At last I managed to perceive or rather to discover the low opening through which the Breton had disappeared.

"There must, however, be a lamp somewhere," Yvonnec said, speaking to himself; "a lamp with a thick glass to it."

Suddenly a light illuminated the place where the door was. I passed through the aperture with beating heart. We were now in the sluice properly so called, and in a position to communicate directly with the sea. The only separation between us and the water was a steel stopper.

My hopes began to rise sharply.

CHAPTER V
IN THE SLUICE

The antechamber of the sea—the name given by an American engineer to the sluice—was a semicircular compartment following in its shape that of the boat's stern. It allowed just room enough for a man to stand upright, was not more than 8 feet 3 inches in length, and was about half as broad as it was long. Its capacity, therefore, was hardly 210 cubic feet.

The sluice was situated exactly under the two propellers whose driving-shafts passed symmetrically to the right and left of its ceiling, revealing their passage in two semicircular bulges.

During the boat's motion, the screw propellers revolved close to the sluice walls, and produced a peculiar noise very audible to those in the compartment. Divers, whose task it is to explore the sea-bottom in the vicinity of submarines, or to examine the boat's hull, cannot leave the well when the screws are revolving. The seething water would upset their equilibrium, in spite of their leaden-soled shoes, and would cause them to spin round.

The well affording an outlet from the sluice was at the extreme end of the boat. It was formed by a bronze tube only 1 foot 6 inches deep; but its 2 feet 6 inches diameter allowed a diver wearing his dress to enter and leave it easily.

A heavy steel stopper turning on a horizontal hinge, and provided with a thick crown of gutta-perchaed leather, closed the orifice hermetically; a chain was employed to raise it when the diver had come back into the boat, and the pressure of the water was sufficient to hold it in its position against the inner rim of the exit-tube, as soon as the pressure of air was relaxed in the sluice. For greater security, a second stopper was adapted to an inside rim of the same tube, and opened inwards, by means of four hand-screws. The well, therefore, was something like a kettledrum, or rather, considering its size, a large drum, projecting somewhat beneath the stern of the boat.

The walls of the sluice, unlike those of the other compartments, were not made of steel plates riveted together, but, since it was necessary for the chamber to support great pressure, they were constructed out of a single sheet of steel seven-eighths of an inch thick, and the door was still thicker.

Yvonnec, through fear the water might enter, unfastened the screws of the topmost covering very carefully; and, when this lid was raised, the inside of the drum was seen to be quite empty, while the yellow surface of the slightly bulging valve at the bottom announced to us that the sea was there, but was held back by its interposition. The important question for us to solve was what density of water we should have to overcome, by the aid of compressed air, in order to remove the stopper.

"Captain," said Yvonnec, rising, after he had unhooked the chain that permitted of the heavy valve being put back in its place, the lamp is burning away up there... We must economize our light."

"You are right, Yvonnec. I will extinguish it."

The brave fellow thought of everything. Just now it was essential we should have the use of the lamps at any moment; if the light were to fail us, all our efforts would be vain. How long, I asked myself again, while switching off the electricity up above, would the accumulators last us? According to Jacques' statement, they had been recharged at Bizerte the day before the boat started. Probably, if we burnt only one lamp at once, we might keep the light for several days.

We had, however, to face the possibility that, in the other compartments, though flooded, the lights might have continued burning. As in all submarines, the glass protecting them, being thick and comparatively little heated, might have resisted the water. And, if this were so, our supply was rapidly diminishing. When this hypothesis flashed through my mind, I felt a fresh agitation attack me.

"Quick, Yvonnec," I cried. "Don't let us lose any time. How are you getting on?"

"I have found the compressed air tap, Captain. See, here is the manometer. We can reach 75 pounds with it."

"I dare say 75 are more than you have ever tried."

"The second lieutenant did try 60 pounds one day, just to test if we could support so much; but he didn't go beyond."

"And you were able to bear the test?"

"Yes."

"Then be quick and open the tap."

The quartermaster hesitated a moment.

"We must close the door hermetically first. But have you reflected, Captain? Do you think you had better stay with me?"

"Why not?"

"Because if we go this time to 75 pounds, there is the possibility of your not being able to support it. For instance, any one whose heart is affected would be unwise…"

"Oh! My heart is all right. Besides, if I stay in the well, while you are in the sluice, I shan't know what you are doing."

"Yes, you will. There's a thick pane of glass in the door. You haven't noticed it. Look! Through that you can see all that goes on in the sluice."

He showed me a small round window about two inches in diameter strongly fixed in the steel. "Of what use would it be to see, if I could not get in to help you, in case you should be overcome?"

"That has been provided for. Outside, there is a special tap for lowering the pressure in the sluice. The officer who has to watch the divers can always turn it in case of need. I'll teach you how to manage it. If you see me fall, you'll only have to give the handle a twist."

In my turn I hesitated. If I remained, I might possibly interfere with Yvonnec's movements by fainting. And then the stopper would not be removed, and this second chance of escape would vanish like the first. Still, to separate seemed to me impracticable. I felt I could do nothing if I were left without the quartermaster even for a moment. Having been in daily contact with the complex machinery of the submarine, he knew all about the parts which we now had to deal with, and I was completely ignorant of them. At this moment he appeared to me like the commander on board; and, indeed, by the regulations, he was, since he was the sole survivor of the crew. As for me, I was merely a passenger, unacquainted with everything, and more especially with the means of escape that might be within our reach.

"It's only a first experiment," added Yvonnec, in presence of my reluctance. "We'll see if the compressed air manometers act properly, and the conduits too. Then, when I've had a look at the well when open, I'll close it again, and we can begin again together, and get out."

What he said was sense and reason. But I couldn't face the prospect of our being cut off from each other, even for so short a time. The vague fear I had of some unforeseen accident, due to the great depth at which we were, which might stop the action of certain valves and shut Yvonnec up in the hole from which I couldn't liberate him, this and the need I felt of his remaining close by me, prevented me from approving of his argument. Wouldn't it be better, also, to try in this preliminary experiment, whether my lungs and arteries were able to support the tremendous pressure?

"My heart and chest are strong enough, Yvonnec," I again asserted. "I will stay with you."

"Very well, Captain. I will shut the door."

He had just begun to turn one of the screws, when I stopped him. There was something else we had to face.

"Tell me, Yvonnec, will it be impossible to open the door again as long as the high pressure subsists?"

"Of course."

"Then we risk being shut up here for good, and not being able to get up into the cabin again?"

"Anyway, we shall be kept here until the compressed air is got rid of."

"Are you sure of getting rid of it?"

"Oh, yes. Here is the tap."

He showed me another manometer by the side of which was a small brass wheel. On the wall painted light grey, red arrows with the words *Open* and *Shut* over them indicated in which directions they were to be manipulated.

"I understand. But where does the compressed air go?"

"Ah! That's more than I can tell you, Captain."

Yet the question was an all-important one for us to answer. If the air, issuing from the sluice, were driven out of the boat, the exit valves would evidently be blocked by the water, on account of the enormous pressure it exercised; and the compressed air, once in the sluice, could not get out again. This consideration must have caused the submarine-constructors to provide for the evacuation of the air into the contiguous compartments, especially the larger ones, in order that the pressure might be raised only by degrees, and so as not to incommode the crew.

But if these compartments were themselves filled with water?

This was what had to be feared; for then the valves would not act, and the compressed air, remaining in the sluice, would make it impossible for us to get out. We should merely have changed one prison for another, with this aggravation of our condition that, being confined in a high-pressure atmosphere, the air of which could not be renewed, we should not live long in it. Must we, on account of the risk, abandon the only chance remaining to us of quitting the boat? No, a thousand times no; and such was the opinion of the quartermaster, to whom I explained my anxieties.

"Only," I added, "I will go and fetch our provisions from up yonder."

What a clinging to life there is in the heart of man! There was I seeking to prolong our miserable existence even in the case in which we should be hemmed up in a place that divers would not dare to loiter in. A minute or two later I was back with my leather waistcoat pockets stuffed full of the food we possessed. It crossed my mind that perhaps we should need to devour the leather of the waistcoat also. Leather had helped

Massena's soldiers before Genoa and Kleber's soldiers in Mayence to prolong their resistance.

I made a second journey in order to gather together in the sluice all the pieces of cork that were hanging on the walls of the cabin above.

"According to the second lieutenant's recommendation," observed Yvonnec, as he turned the pressure tap slightly, "it is best to open the valve gradually. It is easier to support the air."

A gentle hiss was heard. At the summit of the steel ceiling a plug had just dropped a little in the centre of a copper disc. The compressed air was entering our new prison. Slowly it penetrated into us, filling all our organs; and, at first, it seemed likely to affect us but slightly, since the inside and outside pressures thus supported would counterbalance each other.

The quartermaster again ascertained that the clamps securing the door were screwed tight; then he returned to the manometer, the needle of which was gradually moving from zero towards the right.

"15 pounds," he said at the end of a few minutes.

"And now," he added, closing the pressure tap, "let's see if our exhaust apparatus works all right."

He turned the brass wheel in the direction of the "*Open*" arrow, and I saw the needle of the pressure gauge come back towards zero, thus showing that the air introduced into the sluice was passing into a compartment prepared to receive it. There was, however, one little thing we ought to have noticed, and did not: the arrow did not come quite back to the point it had occupied at the beginning. It oscillated for a second or two a little beyond zero, and finally came to rest at three-tenths. Consequently, there remained in the sluice about a quarter of the pressure that had been admitted into it.

"It works well," he exclaimed. "We need not fear not being able to get out. Now I will begin again."

And he once more opened the pressure cock. I went and sat down on the edge of the well, with my feet dangling in the space below. I wanted to be the first to see the heavy stopper fall, and the water show itself held in check by the compressed air. Through this channel we could both escape at once, without its being necessary for either one to be sacrificed.

As for the diver's dress we had hoped to find in the sluice, I reflected that it could not have served us. For even supposing the apparatus had been capable of supplying air and rendering the diver independent in his movements, and admitting that one of us could have reached the bottom of the sea in it and walked there, how would he have been able to guide his steps, having no compass or other means of finding the way? Plunged in darkness, he would risk going out seawards rather than in towards the shore; or, if walking shorewards, he would probably be stopped by a wall of rocks impossible to climb.

"30 pounds," pronounced Yvonnec.

I felt no oppressive weight, but a slight heaviness in the temples only, and, so to speak, a sagging sensation in my backbone. My brain was not affected, and I continued my reflections. Perhaps the best mode of accustoming one's self to this new physiological condition was not to think about it.

Since escape in a diving-suit would not have been practicable, it remained for us to get through the well one after the other, and, once in the sea outside, to gain the surface as rapidly as we could, aided by the cork on us. The only danger that seemed to threaten us was meeting with a blade of the screw-propellers, which were in the vicinity; but, having no clothes on us that could catch, they could only check us for a moment, and, at the worst, bruise us a little.

"45 pounds," again announced my companion's voice.

It sounded rather muffled to me, and I tried to twist my head round to look; for, seated as I was, my back was towards him. The effort was a painful one. My neck was quite stiff, and my brain began to weigh like lead in my skull. Then a buzzing noise that I had not so far noticed became very perceptible. It was the noise in the ears which assails divers when they descend to great depths, the noise from which those who passed the hawsers under the *Lutin's* hull in five fathoms of water had suffered much.

The pressure we had introduced into the sluice corresponded already to a similar depth. But now it was greater; and, in another minute, I experienced sensations that were unbearable. My throat became too narrow for the air which continued to enter.

"Slacken the ingress of the air a little, Yvonnec. It's coming in too quick," I said.

And I left my post to approach him. But my legs were like masses of iron, and I reached him only by crawling.

"It does begin to weigh a bit," he replied, and his voice sounded still more muffled.

"There," he added, an instant later, "now it's a bit slower. But if you want to go up into the tube-room, say so, and I'll stop the air coming in."

On my knees I kept looking at the needle of the gauge, but a mist that grew thicker and thicker—though existing only in my brain—shut out the divisions of the dial.

"Whereabouts have you got to, Yvonnec?" I asked.

"Nearly 60 pounds, Captain."

"And the well?"

I was incapable of taking a step towards it. Yvonnec went instead, and he staggered. I vaguely saw him sit down on the edge and kick the stopper.

"It sticks still," he murmured; "it sticks fast, still!"

When he came back, I saw on his bare back and chest the veins swell and stand out... It was the same with the veins of my hands.

"60 pounds!"

These two words reached me as if they had been spoken in wadding. They were, in fact, the last I heard. The buzzing in my ears had become a roar, and my heart beat at irregular intervals, threatening complete cessation. A few more instants passed, while the circle of iron I felt round my temples grew tighter still and tighter. The Edison lamp flickered on the ceiling, and appeared to be multiplied into a dozen. At the same time, it changed its color, and my eyes saw nothing but violet glimmerings.

I was incapable of further resistance... Iin my head there seemed to be a liquid as heavy and as unstable as mercury... I could not even open my lips to beg the Breton to close the tap.. My hands beat the air as if I were drowning... My heart ceased beating; then there was a blank in my mind and a dull pain in my forehead. I had fallen at full length on the iron floor.

When I recovered my senses, Yvonnec, who was leaning over me, had his hand on my heart, trying to find out if it were throbbing still. He uttered a cry of joy on seeing me open my eyes.

"You frightened me, Captain!" he exclaimed.

It was some time before I realized the situation. My breathing was comparatively easy, but I ached all over... My thoughts were confused, and I felt as though I could never get up again. As for moving my tongue, it was quite impossible. In my mouth I seemed to have only a swollen, inert mass.

Yvonnec squeezed a little orange juice between my teeth, after prizing them open sufficiently with the blade of his knife. I thanked him with a look, being unable to utter a single word.

The experiment had been made; I could not support such pressure, and, even if I were to succeed in accustoming myself to it, like Yvonnec, I should be, nevertheless, incapable of the effort required to escape through the well, for the Breton owned to me that the strain on him had deprived him of all his energy. And there was something still graver. The stopper of the well had not been removed. As soon as I was able to speak, my first question was:

"How far did you go?"

"To 70 pounds," replied my companion. "It was just at this moment that you fainted; and, as I felt myself giving way too, I closed the pressure cock quickly and opened the other one. One minute more, and I should not have had the strength to do it."

So we were more than seven and a half fathoms down. This fact was incontestable. What human help could ever reach us there? On realizing our situation as it then was, I abandoned myself to apathy. There was no use in struggling further. I regretted not having succumbed to my swoon. Why had Yvonnec had the presence of mind to shut off the air's ingress just when it would have been fatal to us, and to bring us back to an existence heavier to bear at this moment than the worst physical pressure? We should have done with our troubles, whereas at present we had to face fresh ones before entering eternity.

This terrible word, which I had learned to dread when listening to my mother's warnings as a child, and afterwards at school, when studying Descartes and the great spiritualists, to fill with the idea of God, had become void of meaning to me during my life of indifference and fatalism which I had led as a man. Now that I was on the brink of the unknown, this same word arose in my mind with terrifying significance. Unconsciously I repeated it aloud.

Beside me I heard Yvonnec's voice repeat it gravely; then he added:

"You are right, Captain. It's time we thought about it; for we can do nothing more."

I saw him get up, go to the door, push it with all his might, then return and sit down beside me again.

"What is the matter?" I asked.

"There is at least 15 pounds pressure here over and above what there was," he replied. "I can't open the door."

This announcement gave me a shock, and I scrambled up on to my knees by dint of a tremendous effort.

"What! The door won't open? Are the clamps unscrewed?"

"Quite."

"And you can't open...?"

"See for yourself."

He went to the door and renewed his attempt, with a purchase on the partition to help him. It was useless. The door did not budge. The extra pressure sufficed to keep it closed. The experiment of the Magdeburg hemispheres at once recurred to my memory. Monsieur Bouty, our professor of physics at the Rheims Lycée, used to perform it for us regularly each year.[27] I recalled it now in all its details. It used to amuse the class exceedingly. When the pneumatic machine had exhausted the air from between the two hemispheres adhering to each other along their leather-lined edges, two pupils used to harness themselves to cords threaded through rings in the hemispheres and pull in opposite directions. Their strivings were in vain. The atmospheric pressure, acting on the two convex surfaces, with a vacuum between them, was powerful enough to weld the two halves into a single piece. The experiment gave me a most convincing proof of the atmosphere's weight and force.

One day, however, either because the air had been insufficiently exhausted, or because the sly professor had previously slipped a bit of paper between the leather edges, thus withdrawing the air, the two hemispheres had suddenly come asunder, and the two athletes who were pulling had tumbled backwards to the floor. I was one of them, and the joke—for so it was—crossed my mind now in singular contrast to the distress of our situation. Its effect was to restore to me a little of my self-possession.

While waiting for my physical strength to return, I tried to understand what had happened, and the explanation was not hard to find. The compressed air, after leaving the room in which we were at present confined, was forced into an empty compartment, probably either the water-ballast one or else the crew's mess room, which latter, with the engine-room, was the most spacious chamber of the submarine. But on entering, the pressure of the air there was increased, and ultimately an equality of pressure was established between the air in each compartment. That this would inevitably happen, had been shown by Yvonnec's first attempt to increase the density of our atmosphere. Only we had not noticed the indication.

---

[27] This experiment was designed by German scientist and mayor of Magdeburg, Otto von Guericke, in 1650 to demonstrate the concept of atmospheric pressure. Ed.

I did not carry my reasoning further. Yvonnec was again at the door pulling desperately and, as before, in vain. There was no sign of its yielding. A horse's muscles would be required at least to unfasten it, unless, indeed, a something introduced between the two leathern surfaces could produce the same effect as the professor's bit of paper. A metal blade, perhaps...

"Have you got your knife, Yvonnec?" I said.

"Yes, Captain."

He took from his pocket a strong knife attached to a steel chain, which must have been bequeathed him by an ancestor, for the horn handle was polished by rubbing as if it had been ivory. I opened it, and did my best to insert the blade between the door and its framework. I failed. The adherence was so perfect that I should have broken the knife, if I had continued.

Again, the tenacious Breton tackled the clamps. This time I aided him as well as I could, for I felt somewhat recovered. We alternately used continuous pulls, and, following on these, sharp tugs. The result was the same. We were hopelessly trapped in this tiny den, where the oxygen could not be renewed. Before long we should be asphyxiated.

If I had been now as I was a while previously, I should have begun to rage once more. But, in the course of our imprisonment, my mind had undergone a change. My apathy was growing, due no doubt to my physical exhaustion and the weakening of my brain. There was some analogy between my state and that of the sick man about to die, who looks with a sort of indifference on the fatal moment.

Worn out, we both slept side by side. On awaking, I rubbed my eyes dolorously. Absolute darkness surrounded me. I sat up and groped about, wondering if I were really awake, and if my eyes were really open. Yes, I was not dreaming. The light had gone out. And I uttered a cry of anguish which aroused my companion. I heard him get up and go towards the door. I called him with a hoarse voice.

And all at once the lamp shone out. The blessed light returned. The Edison lamp was our sun—a sun whose rays

Yvonnec was economizing, for he it was who, feeling sleepy, had switched off the light.

But, almost immediately, another cry of distress escaped me. I wanted to see what time it was and found my watch had stopped. How could I have forgotten to wind it up? It marked half-past three when I looked at it before we had begun our sluice experiment. In my excitement I had lost all count of the hours that had elapsed since. In circumstances like ours this inability to estimate duration of time has been frequently noticed. The miners imprisoned at Courrières for 15 days thought that they had not been shut up more than three. On me, the effect was to lengthen the hours. It seemed we had been confined for a week.

"Have you got a watch, Yvonnec?" I asked.

"No, Captain."

What I missed most was the little familiar tick-tack; in the dreadful silence around us, it was a sort of companion. I wound my watch up again, observing that the fingers indicated ten minutes past seven. Whatever happened, I would not forget to repeat the operation as long as I had strength for it.

Near me, Yvonnec murmured:

"I am thirsty."

We shared the half of the orange he had cut to recover me from my swoon. Then we took from our provisions six dates and two waffle-cakes for each. We should still be able to have three similar meals.

"Let us try once more," said my companion. "It is stifling here."

We united our efforts, but the door remained immovable.

The sluice, which was an invention I had so much praised when the engineer Laubeuf introduced it into our French submarines, the sluice—the one means of escape from the submerged vessel into the sea—was now a dungeon excluding us from exit either seawards or towards the interior of the boat.

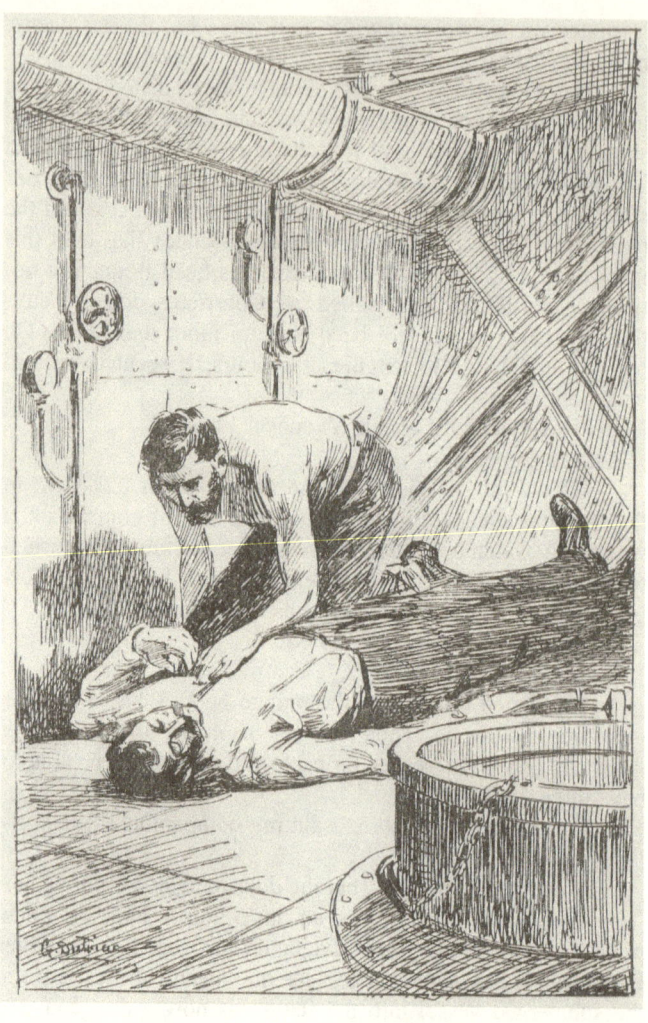

CHAPTER VI
TOWARDS SUICIDE

Several hours passed, during which we wasted our strength in useless attempts to open the door. After each vain trial we sank to the floor, panting and weary; and again we recommenced in sheer desperation. At last we fancied that, with the help of a cord fixed to one of the clamps, we should exercise more force or at least should pull more together. We made one out of my shirt, and the result was the same.

But this last strain finished us. The expense of muscular force had covered us with perspiration and dried our throats. To quench the intolerable thirst that assailed us, we halved our last piece of orange, and I flung myself down by the door. This time I felt there was nothing else that could possibly be done.

My companion was apparently of the same opinion, for he knelt down in a corner. I would have liked to do the same; and envied him the faith that seemed to reveal to him beyond death a world free from horrors and suffering. What I experienced was not resignation, but anger against the destiny which thus, in cowardly action, was killing two beings full of health. If this destiny were really the infinitely good Creator, why did He not listen to the cry of two men dying beneath His eyes? If He were really Providence, why were there in the world so many unanswered prayers, so many undeserved pains, so much unjust despair? What wrong had I committed to be subjected to this dreadful torture? Why this difference made between me and other beings happy and free at this moment under the open sky?

After all, why not end the torture myself? Why not anticipate the fatal moment? But how?

I glanced around me. My companion would not allow me to re-open the pressure tap. Suddenly I thought of the knife he had lent me not long before.

A simple cut in my wrist, a vein opened, and my life's blood would ebb away. It was thus the Ancients rid themselves of existence, when its burden became too heavy. They, however, proceeded to carry out their intention at the end of a banquet, amidst flowers, and under the eyes of their slaves and friends. Whereas, I should have to hide myself, and to lie with my arms hanging down into the well, in order to hide from Yvonnec the blood flowing from my hands.

Unfortunately I had given him his knife back. As indifferently as I could, I asked him to lend it me again.

"You will only break the blade, Captain," he replied. "Perhaps it may come in handy later. Don't try now."

Later! Did he think other attempts were still possible?

"It's not to open the door I want the knife," I said.

Something in my tone and my embarrassed look struck him, for, after a few moments' silence he approached me, and gazing steadfastly at me, he answered in a low tone:

"I don't like to guess why you want it."

And as I remained silent, he continued:

"Tell me the truth... Am I not right in my supposition?"

I turned away my head. He came nearer.

"Listen," he said. "Do you wish to leave me alone? It would not be kind of you. Together, we can endure longer, and contrive more. Perhaps there is yet something we have not thought of."

"You know better."

"Even if there's nothing, you ought not to hasten your death voluntarily, since you know I can't imitate your example. I should be left alone with you lying there. Why should we not die together, when the time comes?"

Taking my hand, he went on in a supplicating tone:

"I am only a poor man, and am far from having your education, your knowledge; but we sailors have got something in larger measure than you, and I'll tell what it is."

He took my other hand, and with his eyes fixed on mine, he said:

"Death terrifies you, doesn't it?"

"Yes, death in this form," I murmured. "I want to dash my head against these iron walls. I am going mad with being shut up here, stifling and suffering this agony of thirst."

"I understand," he answered gently. "With us sailors, it's different. We are obliged to think of death often. When we embark, we never know whether we shall get back to land."

He paused and his gaze was lost in space.

"Have you ever seen our cemetery?" he continued. "Against the wall are written the names of the Larmor sailors... There are many of them; and beside each are these three words: *LOST AT SEA*. Often there is no date; only the year, because the day of the shipwreck is not known. When you are only a cabin-boy, and go there, quite a little chap, to pray with the old salts, you get used to the idea... You know that all those whose names are there are not lying in their own native ground, but are buried in the waves somewhere near Iceland or Newfoundland... It's the natural death of the sailor and you think it will be yours someday... So you are better prepared than other folks when an accident happens, with death in its train."

"That's true, Yvonnec. But those who die at once, overwhelmed by the waves, like your fellow-seamen in the *Dragonfly*, go off, without knowing it hardly, whilst we... It's horrible!"

"Well! I prefer our situation to theirs," replied the Breton quickly. "Those who were overtaken suddenly hadn't the time to repent of their sins. We two, on the contrary, can..."

"You are fortunate, Yvonnec, to have such resignation. I haven't it. I prefer making an end of the thing and not waiting."

"No!" he exclaimed, shaking his head; "no, you mustn't do that. It's forbidden. We say it is cowardly. And then, you won't leave me alone."

"Look here," he went on, feeling that I was affected; "am I not a bit your friend, since now we are making a good fight together? Well! Among us, a friend is never forsaken—never. At Port Louis, opposite our house, there was the old Kemeneur, who was at least 62. Last year, he was at Newfoundland, where his boat was cut in two by a passing vessel. His comrade couldn't swim; so Kemeneur, who was a good swimmer, tried to keep him afloat until they could be picked up. Unfortunately, the sea was running strong, and before help could reach them they both sank. Kemeneur could have saved himself, but he preferred to sink rather than desert his friend."

Brave fellow! His story was related to make me give up my project, by an appeal to my self-respect, which my companion believed to be stronger than religious motives. I was conquered.

"No, Yvonnec," I cried, holding out my hands to him; "I won't leave you alone either. It's quite enough, having already meditated doing so."

"What do you mean?"

"Oh ! You know; when I thought of escaping through the tube…"

"That was different, Captain!"

"Don't call me Captain anymore. Let there be no distinction between us. Will you be my friend?"

He made a gesture of surprise, and on his face appeared the first smile seen in our prison since the disaster.

"D'ye see, Yvonnec, it's I who ask your friendship, to get from you the strength and resignation that are lacking to me."

"It won't last long…"

"But it will be all the closer!"

"Then I am willing… my friend."

The word affected me strangely, as I heard it pronounced. What subtle bonds are created between people threatened with the same death! They are like those existing sometimes between comrades in the same regiment.

I lay down on the floor, with my leather coat rolled up under my head; but almost immediately I rose again. I had just felt beneath the back of my neck a long, hard object whose presence in my pocket had been quite forgotten. It was the file which I had taken from the floor and put back.

Ah! After all we possessed a tool capable of attacking part of the steel shroud that enveloped us, and I had never thought of it! There was no need to make a hole large enough to pass through. Such a work was more than our strength could accomplish. All we had to do was to bore a small hole. We were in an air-tight compartment. What was necessary was to create a leakage. When once a communication had been established with the exterior air in the part of the vessel on the other side of the door, the door would easily open.

"Yvonnec," I cried, "here is the file. I ought to have remembered it."

"The file!"

"Yes; we can escape by its means. Let's go to work quickly."

And I explained to him my idea.

"That's true," he agreed. "But where can we make the hole?"

We walked round the sluice. Everywhere, except in the door, the metal was too hard to be attacked. We decided to try the door on one of its projecting edges. It was about an inch thick. By taking our turns, we might dig a groove deep enough to reach the opposite partition. My companion straightway set to work with a backward and forward movement of the file; and after a few minutes I replaced him.

For more than two hours, we toiled on feverishly, under the most inconvenient conditions, for, there being no handle to the file, the difficulty of working with it increased as the groove grew deeper.

"We shall never manage like that," said Yvonnec, finding that the effect each rub produced was diminishing.

The groove had not penetrated to half the door's thickness. I sat down discouraged, and with a more intense thirst than before.

Suddenly, the Breton uttered a cry:

"Look there, Captain."

And he pointed to the glass bull's-eye at the top of the door, through which, from the inside, the divers could be watched at work.

"It can't be thick enough to resist a good jab," he continued.

And gripping the file, he struck it pointways against the surface. The point of the file broke. As for the glass, it did not even crack. Intended, like the metal, to support a pressure of 75 pounds, it must be of exceptional thickness and toughness.

"We want a hammer, or something as heavy..."

Yvonnec glanced around, then leaning over the interior lid of the well, which he had closed, he opened it again, and tried, but in vain, to take off the nuts.

"The pin!" he exclaimed. "If only we could use the pin as a hammer."

And, with savage energy, he began to file one of the ends of the steel cylinder serving as a hinge to the huge lid. The task took us several hours, for the metal was exceedingly hard, and I was quite limp when we had finished. And, besides, my eyes began to be dim, and my breathing labored. Evidently, the air was getting mephitic, through lack of oxygen, whence the effort of my lungs to extract all that was left of it. Yvonnec was just forcing the pin out of the hinge, when he dropped his instrument and, putting his hands to his throat, gasped out:

"I am choking."

Were we going to be asphyxiated just at the moment when we had a chance of a respite? I picked up the file to go on with his job, but I turned giddy and nearly fell into the well, over which I was bending.

"Air, I must have air!" murmured the quartermaster, his face assuming a purplish tinge.

I rushed to the pressure tap. Anyway, there was air to be had through it, though compressed; and our lungs needed its oxygen, however contained. Having opened the admission cock wide, I turned the exhaust too, so that there might be less danger of the pressure becoming too strong for us to bear. In this way, I reflected, a sort of air-current would be created in our narrow den: the carbonic acid gas would be partly carried away, and, even though the pressure should become troublesome, some time would elapse first.

It never once occurred to me that what I had just done would effect a mechanical change in another part of the boat from which our deliverance would ultimately result.

A few moments after the taps had been opened, Yvonnec ceased gasping and got up.

"It was time," he said.

And, without another word, he went to work again. Nearly an hour more was spent in freeing the pin from its sockets. When, at length, we had the piece of steel in our hands, I experienced a veritable emotion on seeing my companion take the file and begin to attack the bull's-eye once more, using now the heavy pin as a hammer. It was, in fact, our last chance of safety, or rather of gaining a little longer time.

"Try not to break the file any further, Yvonnec," I said to him, "since we have nothing that could replace it."

At the end of about ten minutes, the glass yielded, broken on one of its sides. I looked at the needle of the gauge. The air in our prison, which was at 30 pounds odd, spread into the entrance well like a jet of steam. The needle sank to 15 pounds, oscillated a little, then stopped. For a few instants longer we waited, and again tried the door. It opened on being pulled slightly.

Free to quit our horrible dungeon, we rushed up the ladder, and reached the compartment where we had been before. Lighting the Edison directly, we rejoiced to be able to look on the torpedo tube, and especially on the oxylith apparatus, thanks to which we could prevent ourselves from being asphyxiated. There too was the loud-speaking telephone. Had it spoken during our absence, and, if so, would it call us again?

The water no longer oozed through the engine-room door, so this latter must be hermetically closed. And in this cabin, we should not experience the stifling sensation, it was four or five times as spacious. In it, also, every object seemed familiar to us; we felt ourselves less isolated. Yet here, I had raved and stormed with despair. What philosopher will ever explain man's complex nature under the stress of pain and threatening death?

In our first sensation of relief we had forgotten our thirst. Soon, however, we were conscious of it again. Our skin had grown dry and hot, our tongues clammy, our throats contracted. The arduous labor we had gone through had quickened our perspiration; we longed for something to drink.

While still in the well, I had thought of the possibility of obtaining a few drops of water out of the apparatus for producing a fresh supply of oxygen. The operation consisted in the reaction of water on the stony composition called oxylith, and was similar to that employed in producing acetylene by the action of water on carburet of calcium. I even remembered the figures indicated by Jaubert; one pound of oxylith yielded 160 cubic feet of pure oxygen. But in the apparatus before us there was water, not the marvelous stone of the inventor. How were we to collect it?

I explained what I knew to Yvonnec, but was not sure of the way in which we ought to proceed. We had before us two cylinders of about the same capacity. In the lower parts they were connected by a brass tube bulging in the centre, where a gauge was fixed. The needle of this instrument pointed to 67. What did the graduation mean? It could not refer to atmospheres. From the upper portion of the larger cylinder, which ended in a convex cap, a tube issued which extended to the pipe joining the two vessels; and in the tube I remarked another bulging part ending in a square pin somewhat resembling the old-fashioned watch-key. It must be a valve.

To make use of it, a special key, no doubt, was required, the constructor wishing to prevent any careless handling.

At the top of the smaller cylinder a second gauge pointed to one and a half ; and at the back of this there was a copper spout, like that of a watering-can, very flat and pierced with tiny holes. It was evidently through these that the oxygen was diffused about the compartment. Last of all, near this orifice, another bent tube issued from the smaller cylinder and passed through the bulkhead separating us from the machinery.

As I have already mentioned, our apparatus renewed at the same time the air to be breathed in both compartments. I tapped on each of the two cylinders, and discovered from the sound that the larger one was much thicker than the smaller. I searched for an opening into which to introduce the water, and for another into which to introduce the oxylith. I found neither. I was obliged to confess that the apparatus here before me was quite different from that which I had seen act in the chemist's laboratory.

My embarrassment was great. I turned to Yvonnec who was watching me, with his hands behind his back. I questioned him.

"Do you know how the thing works? Did you see it put in?"

"No, my friend, it was here when I came back from my holiday."

"And nobody explained it to you."

"No. It was not in my department."

"Who had charge of the new apparatus when it was put in?"

"Kerren, the first mate, and the cook."

"The cook?"

"Yes. The supply of oxylith is in his galley."

I turned on the two taps on the small cylinder, taking care to turn them back as they had been. One of them, situated in the lower portion, must establish and cut off the connection between the two vessels. Then, looking behind the apparatus, I saw hung up on the partition, a key which was probably the one fitting into the square pin I had noticed a minute previously.

I seized it, inserted it, turned it once, twice, thrice… Suddenly, a jet of white smoke gushed out with extraordinary force at the base of the pin, striking the partition with so much violence that the steel resounded as if under the impact of drops of metal. Immediately, I reversed the action of the key, and the jet stopped.

This escape of oxygen gas was a revelation to me, by the very fact of its violence. I now recollected that Jaubert had had two different apparatuses installed on board the *Dragonfly*. The one produced breathable gas, using water and oxylith, in proportion as it was needed. If I remembered rightly, this apparatus had to be refilled every two days. The other did not produce oxygen, but contained it under high pressure—1800 pounds, if I were not mistaken—and liberated it automatically at any required pressure. This was the one placed in our compartment.

Now I understood the part played by each of the two vessels. In the larger one, the gas, originally stored at a pressure of 1800 pounds, still remained at 1005 pounds per square inch, after several days' drawing on its supply. When it passed into the smaller cylinder it was reduced to 22 pounds. The curious thing about the invention was the action of the automatic valves regulating the transformation of pressures.

Now, also, I felt sure, for my ideas were becoming precise on the subject, there was not a single drop of water in the apparatus before me. However, instead of having to be refilled every two days, like the other one, it could supply us with breathable air for six days to come. Ought we to regret this?

We must be at the end of our third day's captivity. Yvonnec and I had calculated that out, when I had wound up my watch. If the apparatus in our cabin had been one of the kind containing water and oxylith, its contents would have been exhausted by now, since no one had been there to refill it, and all we should have found at the bottom of it would have probably been a little muddy water quite unfit to drink. With this one, we had, at least, food for our lungs—yet no water.

All that remained of our provisions was a little chocolate and a few dates—four each. Our waffle-cakes were gone, and, even if we had had some left, our mouths were too parched to masticate them. Alone, the dates gave us the sensation of freshness, and we now proceeded to eat them. Alas! They did not quench our thirst.

The hours passed, while we discussed the most unlikely projects; then the dryness of our mouths rendered conversation too painful. I closed my eyes and strove to go to sleep again. I wanted to sleep and never to wake. But the fever of my thirst made slumber impossible, so I rose and began pacing up and down our cabin like a wild beast. Yvonnec remained sitting on the tube, and, from time to time, repeated his refrain:

"Oh! I am so thirsty."

I paused opposite the Jaubert apparatus, asking myself whether there might not be in it something capable of replacing the water we required—or of lessening our sufferings. Back to my mind there came some words used by the chemist when explaining his invention to me.

"This new apparatus," he said, "might be named the Life and Death machine. The gas it contains, if dosed out economically, is a sustainer of life; if distributed in greater quantities, it kills. Mixed in a proportion of 23% with the nitrogen of the atmosphere, it renders the air breathable; inhaled under a pressure of 60 pounds only, it burns the lungs, and, curiously enough, brings about an end as agreeable as it is rapid."

"Agreeable!" I cried as I listened.

The inventor went on to explain to me that oxygen breathed under strong pressures produced throughout the organism a feeling of more intense vitality, and permeated it with a strange comfort. I objected that such knowledge was impossible, since whoever tried the experiment would have to succumb in order to prove the matter. Jaubert replied that a Monsieur Mouline had gone through the experiment involuntarily, that he had been withdrawn in time from the oxygenated atmosphere, and that he had regretted being taken from the Paradisaic visions and voluptuous sensations in which he was plunged.

At present all this recurred to me with great distinctness. I remembered I had spoken to Jaubert of Tiberius, who used to invite to his table patricians he wished to get rid of and to kill them beneath a shower of roses. Of my promise made in the sluice I refused to take account. One thing only I could think of. Here was the means of converting into an agreeable death tortures that were becoming intolerable.

The prospect thus offered restored to me a little of my self-possession. I pocketed the key that served to free the oxygen, sat down on the torpedo-tube and ate my last date but one. When the last one was finished I would open the tap.

While waiting for the moment to arrive, I oddly enough fished out my pocket-book and pencil, and began to busy myself with calculations. I hardly knew why; perhaps to kill time before myself being killed. I wanted to find out the capacity of the reservoir. It was a sort of sum I worked out. Here it is:

Given a gas at a pressure of 1005 pounds, contained in a cylindrical vessel of $\pi \rho^2 h$, what will have become of this pressure in a semi-conical compartment of $\dfrac{\frac{1}{3} \pi R^2 H}{2}$ when the cylindrical vessel has been opened wide?

The calculation was an absurd one under the circumstances, yet, for a while, I was fascinated by it. Having approximately obtained the dimensions of the cylindrical reservoir by a sort of hand measurement, I succeeded easily in determining in cubic meters the gas it contained under the atmospheric pressure of 760 millimeters.

It was 53.6^{mc}.

Diffused in our compartment, would these 53 cubic meters make the pressure increase to 60 pounds? That was the question.

Yvonnec watched me with astonishment, and approached:

"What are you doing there, my friend?" he said.

"I will tell you, Yvonnec; we have something within our reach which will diminish our sufferings... You are thirsty, are you not?"

"Yes... And if it lasts much longer..."

"Well, wait a minute; I will tell you my idea."

There still remained to be calculated the dimensions of our compartment. Its form was not semi-conical, but semi-ovoid. The lack of exact outlines interfered with my ciphering. I walked to and fro, took measurements, covered my pocket-book with figures. My heated brain grew tired out with the task, and, being weary, I abandoned it. I thought there could be no doubt, *a priori,* that 53 cubic meters of oxygen diffused throughout the space in which we were would yield the pressure that would spare us a repetition of the sufferings we had already undergone in the sluice, and would set us both free. I returned to my companion, who was patiently waiting for these calculations to be finished which he could not see the use of.

"Listen, Yvonnec," I began, "we are sure to die, are we not? Nobody will come to let us out of here?"

"My opinion is like yours, friend."

The tone in which he pronounced the word "friend" expressed both affection and deference. I felt the brave fellow was grateful to me for breaking down all social distinctions, as if the approach of death had not contributed to this more than my will.

"Well, Yvonnec, I will tell you what is the effect of pure oxygen on the human body, if it is absorbed in large doses such as the apparatus there can give us."

And I went on to explain all I knew, adding as I finished:

"You understand, Yvonnec, we have there the means of avoiding the worst pangs at the last..."

I shall never forget the expression in his face when he grasped my intention. His kind blue eyes that had been fixed on mine began to quiver. He drew his hand several times across his forehead, glanced for a second at the figures in my notebook, then reared himself up.

"But, my friend, it is once more suicide you are proposing to me; and this time for both of us!"

His voice was full of deep reproach.

"I am not going to forsake you, Yvonnec; I shan't leave you alone, as you said I was going to do in the sluice. By the way I suggest, we can both go together."

"But it's none the less suicide, friend," he repeated, in a low tone, as if the word were a horrible one. "And you know it's forbidden."

He pronounced the last word very deliberately.

The day before I should have made light of his eternal objection. Now I dared not. I parleyed.

"It's not suicide in the manner which is forbidden," I answered; "our time has come; all that I do is to suppress the agony."

"You haven't the right."

"God cannot be angry with us for avoiding such agony."

"If God has thought fit to impose it on us, friend, you have no right to go against His will."

"But who tells you such is His will? And, if I assert on the contrary, that He has designedly placed this anesthetic at our disposal, this gas which drives off the agony, we can surely utilize it."

This argument seemed to produce some effect on my companion; for, sitting down again on the torpedo-tube, he buried his face in his hands and did not reply. But, after a moment's silence, he raised his head once more and said:

"No, friend, I am sure man has no right to advance his last hour; the priest has often told me so."

"But since I assert to you…"

"No, no, my friend," he repeated; "there is a commandment against it, as you know."

I tried to be calm; but this obstinacy exasperated me; moreover, I was in pain, and to speak only increased it.

"Look here, Yvonnec," I said, "have you ever seen people in the last stage of hydrophobia?"

"Why do you ask me that?"

"Because such unhappy people are exactly in the same case as ourselves. They are doomed, and nothing can save them. They cry, howl, bite the bed-clothes, struggle and suffer dreadfully. Well, it often happens that they are stifled under a mattress in order to abridge their agony."

"Say rather because they are a danger to others," the Breton replied. "And yet I say nobody has the right to kill them."

I was struck with the retort, and did not know what to say. "What if I were to turn on the gas during your sleep?" I asked after a pause.

The quartermaster's eyes flashed.

"You would commit two crimes," he answered. "First, a suicide, then a murder, for I don't want to die; you hear me, I don't want to die."

There was terrible energy in his last words. Still exasperated, I raised my hands and clenched them.

"And I will not go on suffering as I am," was my reply.

We were both on our legs, opposite each other, as if we were two enemies challenging each other. Suddenly, Yvonnec took my hand and broke into sobs.

"Oh, friend, my friend!" he said.

My heart gave way; we fell into each other's arms.

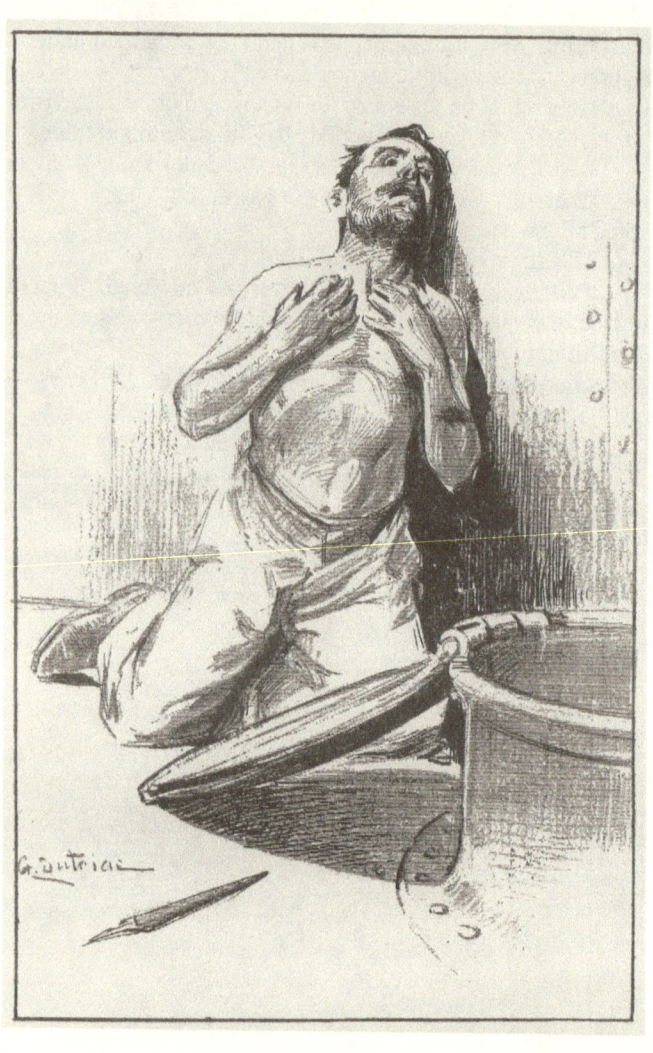

CHAPTER VII
THIRST

A long fit of dejection followed this explosion. We panted; from our chest issued hoarse breathings. The torments of our thirst increased every minute. I thought no more about the oxygen, or rather, I tried to think no more about it. I was ashamed of my conduct.

Suddenly, we both started up, and, both of us thrilled by an unspeakable emotion, we stared at each other.

"Did you hear that?" exclaimed Yvonnec, in a hollow tone.

"Yes, I heard."

"There were two knocks, weren't there?"

"Yes! I thought perhaps… but, if you heard too, it can't be a noise in my ears."

"Listen!"

Two other knocks, somewhat fainter, yet sufficiently audible, reached our ears. Only a human being could have knocked thus on the iron plates of the submarine; and a hope, an immense hope, rose in our hearts. Near us, within earshot, there was a living creature. Where was he?

Before being able to answer this question, we must reply to the signal made us… or to the appeal addressed to us. And seizing the heavy steel pin which had not long before served us as a hammer, Yvonnec struck two blows with all his might on the door of the engine-room.

The noise resulting from the blows was quite different from what I expected, on the hypothesis that the room was filled with water. The resonance of the blow should have been duller. On the contrary, the metal vibrated strangely. However, I drew no particular conclusion from this fact, being preoccupied with the idea that for us to be heard at the other end of the *Dragonfly*, whence the noise seemed to come, our own blows should be struck on the hull of the boat. So, at my suggestion, the quartermaster struck the steel roof above us several times as hard as he could. We waited, holding our breath.

Again the noise reached our ears, making us quiver from head to foot; and, as if to show us that our response had been noticed, the mysterious being who thus revealed himself now struck several blows, as we had, almost at the same intervals. Whence came the call, from the outside or the inside? Was it from a diver or from a survivor of the crew? If a diver, he must have perceived we were at the opposite end of the boat and would undoubtedly approach us, and we should hear blows struck nearer to us. I expressed my opinion, while still listening, but Yvonnec shook his head.

"If it is a diver who is walking along the bottom of the sea, he won't be able to get near us," he said.

"Why?"

"Because the boat only touches with its fore part, while we are at least four or five fathoms above the bottom."

"That's true; but can't he hoist himself on to the deck and get to us with the help of the handrails and gunwale that runs from one end of the craft to the other?"

"Perhaps, if he has an electric lamp on his helmet. If he hasn't one, at the depth we are, it's almost black night even at midday."

"Listen… There the knocks are again…They are just as far away as they were."

We hushed our conversation, after replying. But the signal was not repeated.

"The noise doesn't come from the outside," said Yvonnec. "Blows struck outside in the water have no force; we should only hear them if they were above our heads."

"Then it's one of the crew… shut up like ourselves."

"Yes, he must be in one of the compartments or small water-tight magazines on the other side of the crew's room. There are two or three storerooms there."

"It looks as though he is alone. But how is it he has begun only to knock today?"

"Perhaps it's we who hear him for the first time today."

And we neither of us happened to think there was perhaps something changed in our environment, and that a modification of the contents of one of the compartments near us might have rendered a sound audible now which was not in the hours immediately following the accident. Nor did we remark that the floor of our cabin sloped more than when we had quitted it to try to escape through the sluice. If we had been struck by these things, we might have been spared some long hours of torture yet to come.

For a long time we remained listening with staring eyes and clenched fingers, for, though this revelation of someone else's being alive did not alter our lot, it impressed us. Maybe, there was a selfish feeling in our emotion, a sort of consolation in realizing that we were not so thoroughly alone.

During the moments of expectation we had forgotten our thirst, but it returned as soon as the cessation of the signals seemed final. Our difficulty in speaking increased, yet we endeavored to exchange our thoughts further on what had occurred.

"If it had been a diver," I said, "they would have called us through the telephone," and I glanced up at the ceiling.

Yvonnec nodded his assent. Even if Jacques had no time to unhook the buoy allowing communication, the diver's first care would have been to seek the buoy and to fix the telephone wires to it. Moreover, it was folly on our part to have imagined a diver could descend to the depth of more than 22 fathoms, at which the pressure-gauge showed us to be fixed. The noise we had heard could only be one made by someone inside the *Dragonfly*; and, this being so, our gleam of hope, which had for a moment made us thrill, died gradually away.

Was the man inside the boat Jacques?

I uttered my thought aloud, wondering whether he might be shut up in his conning-tower. Yvonnec hearing me, shook his head.

"If the Captain had been alive, he'd have spoken to us," he said, pointing to the telephone. "And, besides, he would have cast off the safety leads."

I acknowledged the truth of the remark. These leads in submarines of recent model are distributed fore and aft and in the centre, and are so arranged as to be either cast off altogether or by lots. The latter method is employed to restore equilibrium, the former to raise the boat rapidly to the surface of the sea. If Jacques had remained alive after the accident, he would have cast off all the leads at once, and our craft would not have pitched down to the bottom.

While thinking about these leads, I remembered that they were held in position by cables, wire ones, no doubt, which must pass through the boat in order to communicate with the conning-tower. Since every weight was distributed as equally as possible about the submarine, I argued that one of the cables might be somewhere near to our cabin, perhaps within it; and, if I could discover it and file it through, the weights it held might thus be released. My brain was once more off on a new track, and I began wandering round the cabin again, while Yvonnec sat on the tube watching me.

I know today that the safety leads are unhooked by means of electricity, like so many other things done at sea now through this agent. My cable theory, therefore, was false, but just then it assumed the form of a hallucination. I seemed to see a cable running along one of the corners of our prison; there it was encased in lead, and, taking the file, I attacked the place with a frenzy which was exhausted almost as quickly as it arose. A film covered my eyes, and I fell at the foot of the oxylith apparatus.

Closing my eyes, I tried to doze off, as Yvonnec was now doing, but sleep would not come to me. Travelers who have suffered from thirst have well declared that its claims are more imperious than those of hunger and sleep. My suffering allowed me no repose; it reached a state of paroxysm, and I spent some hours of the worst kind I ever remember in my life.

Here I must place an interruption in my reminiscences, for after all I sank into a semi-comatose condition which must have lasted more than 12 hours, since my watch stopped again. I must also have been delirious at times, for I subsequently found I had taken off my woolen vest, which I wore under my shirt, and had torn it into shreds. I must too have prayed, for, on recovering my normal consciousness, I was on my knees, with clasped hands, against one of the reservoirs of the oxygen apparatus.

At this moment my hand happened to touch the square tap allowing the gas to escape; and the thought recurred to me what relief I might obtain from turning the key in it. I longed for some of the oxygen as if it had been a spring of fresh water, and, this time without any intention of suicide, I twisted the key three times round.

The oxygen gushed forth violently. For the moment Yvonnec did not wake, even with the noise, and indeed there were chances he would never wake, since I was risking his life as well as mine. However, I gave no heed to this, but, dropping the key, I lay down and inhaled what I believed to be a balm for my lungs.

I was mistaken. In my state, the gas was not the food or drink I needed. It seemed as though I were breathing the burning air that escaped from a furnace, and, soon, as though I were drinking fire. Yet, strangely enough, my prostration yielded to a physical excitement which caused me to leap to my feet, and I began to stride about once more, knocking myself against everything, Yvonnec as well. At last he roused himself a little, with haggard eyes and lolling tongue, panting like a bellows. The oxygen continued to gush out with all the force of its 1005 pounds, inflaming the innermost vesicles of our lungs.

"Water! Water!" gasped Yvonnec.

Yes, it was water we wanted to calm the burning which was devouring us and threatening to reduce us to mummies.

All at once I rushed to the door of the engine-room. Behind it there was water, the water of the sea, it was true, which would increase, not quench our thirst. But it was water— something liquid, which would moisten our clammy tongues and parched palates. With the door open it would enter, would bathe us and cover us with a humid shroud. I had no thought of suicide. It was simply that I had lost my power to reflect on consequences.

Before Yvonnec could stop me—though indeed he was incapable of trying—I successively unscrewed the three nuts that held the door fast. They had been made tight some days before by the quartermaster's strong wrists, but at this instant I had muscles of steel. The oxygen had accelerated all my vital functions and given to my organism an exceptional vigor just as it was consuming me.

The last nut being off, the force of the water would wrench the door open! Yet, no, it was I who dragged it open! Now, the sea might enter and deliver us!

The sea did not enter; it was no longer there. The engine-room was disclosed to my eyes. Not a drop of sea-water was in it. But, if I were to live 100 years, I should never forget the sight I looked upon. Two lamps were still burning in the square, low, convex-ceilinged room; one lighted the engine, the other, the wall opposite the heavy flywheel. They caused the brass and steel to glitter, and shone on the twelve big cylinders in couples, and on the cast-iron framework buried in the floor, and on the dials of all sorts arranged along the partition. And above all, they revealed a tragedy of a dreadful kind.

As I have already said, access was obtained from the engine-room to the instrument-room above by means of a ladder, and through an oval trap-door just large enough to allow the passage of a man's body. This trap-door in the ceiling was just in front of the door I had opened. It was the only aperture allowing the engineers to escape in case of danger. To try flight by our door was, of course, to get into a pudding-bag. On the ladder, leading up to the trap, two corpses were clasped in attitudes that indicated only too clearly the struggle that had taken place between them.

I recognized Renaut, the engineer, with whom Jacques had talked for a moment in my presence, and who had spoken so enthusiastically of his approaching visit to the country. I seemed to hear him still saying: "Air, space, snow, glaciers, a landscape where one breathes freely in the Sun." Poor fellow! He longed for space.

The other was Niclaus, the assistant, the woolly-bearded sailor with the hard, deceitful eyes.

Both were stiff and cold. And their attitude! Alas !

The lid of the trap worked in a groove by means of two brass handles. Four nuts, like those I had just unscrewed, served, when the lid had been closed, to fasten the inner leather covering against the rubber frame, so as to shut the aperture hermetically. I could see that the lid was not entirely closed, prevented by the forearm of Niclaus, which was thrust between it and the side. The assistant's other hand clutched Renaut's face with brutal force, and his teeth were fixed in the engineer's left arm, which, as also the right one, was engaged in a fruitless endeavor to slide the lid home. In this position death had surprised them both, Niclaus half hanging, and Renaut straining to accomplish the task which his assistant thwarted.

In the engine-room, as elsewhere, the orders were: Shut all the doors. And the engineer had thought only of obeying them.

Renaut's face bore traces of the assistant's long nails; one of the scratches had furrowed his neck, which must have bled freely, for, unlike that of Niclaus, his face was bloodless. Not a sign of the bleeding, however, subsisted; the sea had carried it all away.

But could the sea have withdrawn, and how could this compartment, after filling with water which oozed through into the tube-room, have become empty and almost dry? The problem presented was a strange one, and my troubled faculties, my fevered head did not help me much to elucidate it at the moment. Even the deductions I had just made only came to me later. The horror of the spectacle constituting this battle of corpses, so to speak, held me spellbound on the threshold.

Soon a single idea assailed me, summing up my disappointment: No water!

My amazement was such that I did not remark Yvonnec creeping between my legs and disappearing under the lower case of the engine. But I can never forget his voice, crying out to me, as he paused in his drinking:

"Water, my friend... water... quick!"

Lying on his back amidst the heavy uprights in which the motor was fixed, he was holding his mouth under the discharge tap of the cistern that contained the water for cooling the cylinders. And this water could not be salt; it was, it must be fresh. Yvonnec was gulping it down.

"Quick, my friend... your turn!" he said, pointing to the clear, thin stream as he rolled aside. I rushed towards the best, life-giving liquid.

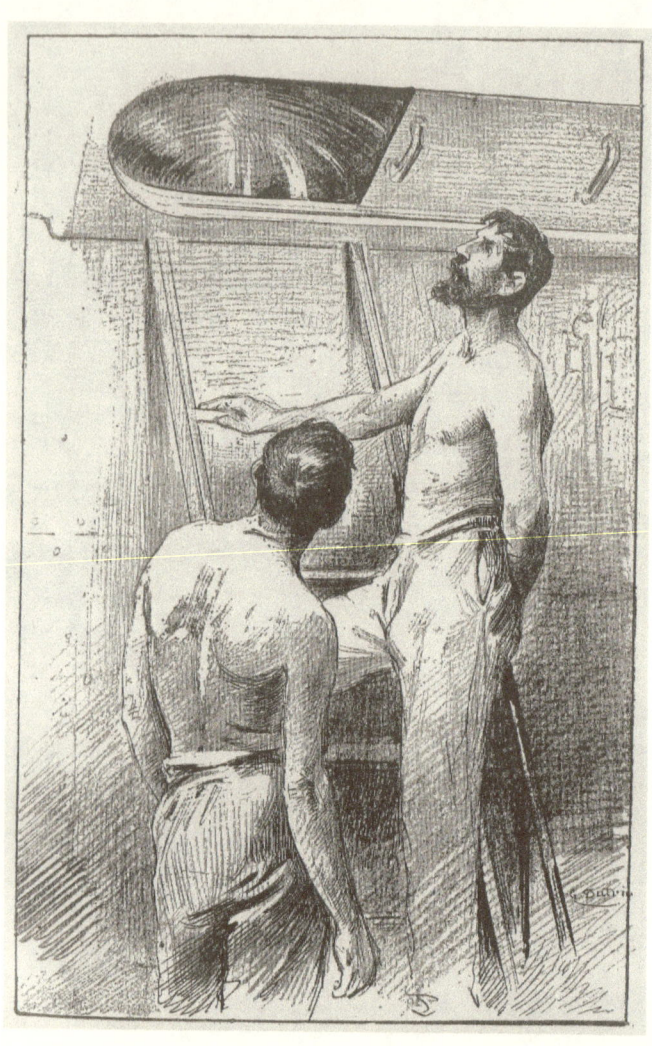

CHAPTER VIII
IN THE ENGINE-ROOM

I no longer thought of the horror of our situation. I drank, drank greedily, holding the tap with one hand, as if I feared someone would take it quickly away. An infinite sense of well-being distilled itself throughout my body, like oil entering into the joints of a machine, and, with a feeling of delight, I regained possession of myself. My blood ceased coagulating and commenced again to circulate freely, and my paralyzed tongue was restored to its flexibility, while my brain assumed its control over my various functions.

Ah! I no longer dreamed of suicide. For the moment I forgot to anticipate the future. I lived only in the present, and enjoyed only as one can enjoy who has suffered torture.

When at last I rose, I found Yvonnec standing pensively in front of the two corpses, and the dismal sight brought me back to reality. I went up to him and placed my hand on his shoulder.

"It's dreadful!" I said. "We can't leave them there like that."

"What I am afraid of," he answered, as he pointed upwards, "is the return of the salt water here. Look! There it is above our heads."

He was right; and, indeed, it was strange. Through the narrow opening the water could be seen as if separated from us by a transparent sheet of ice. How came it that the water did not fall?

If our minds had been at the time scientifically preoccupied, we should certainly have found this effect of compressed air extraordinary, notwithstanding what we knew of it already. After thrusting back the water from the engine-room, it held the liquid volume suspended above the opening, while we, plunged in this same air and at present sufficiently accustomed to it to breathe it without embarrassment, were able to contemplate our enemy, at once powerless yet threatening, through the hole by which its egress had been made.

What now concerned us most was that it should not return. We had to shut the trap-door immediately. The quartermaster, mounting on the lower steps of the ladder, tried to pull Niclaus' arm out of the aperture. His first effort did not succeed. The dead man was literally hanging by the wrist, which had been half crushed by the lid when the engineer had pushed it to. In order to release the hand we should have to pull the lid open a little.

My fear was that in doing so we might cause the water to invade this compartment which we had, so to speak, conquered; and, after escaping from the effects of the oxygen and our thirst, it was not worth while being drowned like rats. My reflection reminded me that the oxygen was still gushing forth in our other room, and I hastened to turn the key and remove the risk of our being consumed by its vapors. But at the door I was met with a fresh obstacle. It was closed, and refused to open. Yvonnec came, and together we tried to overcome its resistance, but our united strength was in vain. We were shut up in the engine-room.

Like a vigilant jailer the pressure of the gas we had set at liberty closed one compartment to us as soon as it had opened another. We had again changed prisons. But this time the change was advantageous, since here we had at least a temporary cessation of our thirst torment. After several more fruitless attempts, we resigned ourselves to our new situation. What had happened was that, in entering the engine-room, one of us must have unconsciously closed the door behind him. And, as the oxygen continued to pour out, the pressure of air in the torpedo-tube room had soon become greater than that in the engine-room, so that at present the door remained fast without there being need of screws to hold it.

Now that my memory, aided by the discoveries made in the course of the Government Inquiry, enables me to reconstitute more fully the several stages of our adventure, I am

tempted to give a short summary here of the series of pheno-
mena that contributed to our deliverance. With the forces that
we somewhat blindly set in action, we might have succumbed
ten times over. And yet, it so happened that each of our efforts
and each of the effects produced did really tend to the object
we had in view.

We had gone down into the sluice and had shut ourselves
in there in order to produce the pressure needed to open the
well leading out into the sea. We obtained 67 pounds per
square inch, which, though formidable, had not sufficed. I
know today that, being at a depth of 30 fathoms, we required
15 pounds more per square inch.

Unable to support the 67 pounds, we had driven it out.
And where had it gone without our knowing ? Into the engine-
room, whence it had chased the water. This water was forced
back by way of the instrument-room, which could only have
been half-filled, and into the wardroom which the sea had not
entered. Without suspecting it, we assisted this liberating operation by again opening the compressed air tap of the sluice,
in order to get the oxygen that we were lacking. Yet how
could we imagine the repulse of water would occur with the
sea weighing on us to the extent of its 75 pounds per square
inch?

*The answer to this problem shall be given in its proper
place.*

From the circulation of compressed air in and out of the
sluice had resulted the increase of pressure in the torpedo-
room, where we succeeded, after breaking the bull's-eye, in
re-establishing communication between this compartment and
the sluice. But this pressure would not have been enough to
bring about the opening of the engine-room, where a pressure
of 37 pounds prevented the water from re-entering. Then it
was I had unwittingly made the thing practicable by opening
the oxygen reservoir, and for a brief space of time there was
an almost equal pressure in the two compartments, so that we
were able to pass from one into the other. If we had let the
favorable moment go by, we should inevitably have perished

under the consuming action of the oxygen. Next, the oxygen continuing to escape had shut the door behind and fastened it, thus ceasing to invade our lungs. In the engine-room, it is true, we had to put up with 37 pounds of air pressure, but the latter was of normal composition; our lungs grew accustomed to it. We could live in it, and we wanted to live.

But we could not go on living in presence of these two corpses, and I regretted that the passage towards the sluice was cut off, for we might have thrown them into the well. Here, in an air strongly impregnated with oxygen, their decomposition would be hastened.

Yvonnec climbed on to the ladder and pushed back the trap-door a little, the task being all the more difficult as Renaut's fingers were stiffly clenched round the brass handles. When finally the lid was a trifle more open, Niclaus' arm slipped out of the aperture, and the two corpses tumbled on to the floor together, for the sailor's teeth were still in the engineer's forearm. The thud they made in falling caused me to shiver in spite of all I had gone through during the past few days.

The quartermaster was nearly carried off his balance by the suddenness of what occurred, and had to clutch the rail of the ladder. For a moment or two he stood motionless. I called to him; and there was a quiver in my voice, which increased when I noticed him trying to pull the lid gradually more and more open instead of shutting it. Before he answered me it was quite half open, and in the space that it had occupied there was what seemed to be a slightly concave sheet of glass. This indeed was water, suspended in air, so apparently contrary to nature's laws that I rushed on to the ladder with the intention of closing the trap-door myself. And I cried to Yvonnec at the same time:

"What are you thinking of? We shall be swamped."

"No," he replied, "we shan't. I want to see."

"See what?"

"If the lid can be pushed back entirely!"

"Why?"

"Because," answered my companion in a low tone, "we can thrust the two comrades through the hole; it's time we had them out of the way."

Perhaps his plan was feasible. I watched the water closely, and, as it didn't budge, I nodded my head approvingly. I had already remarked the odor characteristic of decomposition. What would it soon be if we did not remove the bodies?

Yvonnec's experiment was carried out successfully in its first part. The trap-door was now wide open, and not a drop of water fell.

"We must get them through quick," said the Breton, descending to the bottom of the ladder.

Bending down, he took his knife and with it prized Niclaus' teeth asunder so as to free one body from the other. I turned sick at the sight. The assistant's bloodshot eyes were open, and their ghastly stare was turned towards me.

"If they had anything to eat in their pockets, it wouldn't be amiss," observed Yvonnec phlegmatically.

His words served to restore to me my coolness, and I helped him to search the dead men's pockets. But neither on the one nor on the other did we find the least bit of food.

From the chief engineer's pocket I took out a pocketbook, and did not put it back. My action was not dictated by curiosity. At such a moment the contents of the pocket-book were of such little interest to me that I did not even trouble to look inside. I was influenced in what I did by the same unconscious or subconscious motive power which had acted in me previously. The pocket-book I placed in a drawer filled with tools, which was situated under the small, carpenter's bench where Renaut effected his petty repairs.

Vaguely I must have thought that I might have an opportunity of giving this souvenir to those who would care for it—to the girl he was to have married and who, at present informed of the disaster, was weeping bitter tears. Are we to believe in presentiments, I ask again? Personally I do not believe in them; and yet, under circumstances like those of Yvonnec and myself, one's mentality changes.

In the engineer's pockets were also a packet of tobacco, a briar pipe, some cigarette papers reduced to pulp by the sea-water, a very fine knife bearing a name on it—Germaine, no doubt that of the betrothed. His watch had stopped at 11:16, proving that it had continued for two hours to go though surrounded by water; and, hanging to his steel chain, I remarked a fairly large mariner's compass with two movable, vertical glass faces, like those used in rapid surveying.

While I was engaged in this lugubrious inventory, Yvonnec raised Niclaus in his arms and painfully bore him to the top of the ladder. Fortunately the body was perfectly rigid, and therefore lent itself easily to the experiment. I now seized the legs of the corpse to help my companion, yet anxiously wondering what would occur. Niclaus' head at length touched the liquid vault and passed into it, though with some difficulty. We pushed, and it seemed as though we were thrusting the body into a thick viscous liquid. Gradually the trunk and legs disappeared also, but we, at the same time, were deluged with water.

At once we paused, tempted to loose our burden. What if the operation should result in the re-flooding of the engine-room? Yet no, the compressed air was there, opposing itself, better than any metal stopper, to the return of the water. This latter, however, being incompressible, the solid volume we were introducing into it could only find room by displacing an equal volume of the liquid, which necessarily fell into our compartment, and on to our heads. The price was not too dear, since it delivered us from the necessity of living with two decaying bodies.

At length we managed to finish our task; after Niclaus, we thrust Renaut through the aperture. The trap was closed again, and the screws were tightened so as to make further danger on this score impossible.

The water which had fallen into the engine-room gathered on the side opposite the door; and I noticed from this circumstance that the inclination of the boat had increased.

"We are rising aft," I said to Yvonnec.

"Then if we are," he replied, "why shouldn't the boat rise up to the surface?"

I had some difficulty in making him understand that, though we had got rid of the water from the engine-room, there must be the same quantity in the boat.

"But why should the boat go up on our side?" he insisted.

"Because there is less where we are; what we have lost has simply been displaced without leaving the boat."

"Then we have perhaps drowned the comrade who was knocking yesterday at the other end. We don't hear him now."

I was dumbfounded by the justness of this hypothesis which had not occurred to my mind. Yvonnec might be right, and the unfortunate fellow was perhaps calling because of the water which he saw invading his compartment.

"We must repeat the same signal," I said.

"It's just what I was going to propose, friend," he replied.

But in vain we struck at regular intervals, for a long time, one, two, three blows on the side plates and bulkhead separating us from the neighboring compartment, which was the repairing shop, Yvonnec told me. In vain we listened with straining ear. There was no reply. It seemed really that we were the sole survivors of the *Dragonfly.*

"If he is alone, he has perhaps gone to sleep," suggested my companion.

And he added, as though speaking to himself:

"It must be terrible to be alone."

I was thinking just then the same thing. In this distress, I esteemed myself fortunate to have such a companion. I looked at him and recalled the day when I had seen him for the first time at Tunis, in the Grand Hotel, while Jacques was offering him a glass of wine. On that occasion he was spruce, fresh, and rosy, with well-combed beard. Today he appeared ten years older, with gaunt features, hollow eyes, and bristly, shaggy beard. What must I look like myself? In a few days more, at the same rate, we should have the aspect of ghosts.

"What are we going to do, friend?" he asked.

I did not know what answer to make. What could we yet attempt or hope for? Yet to give up, after the manifest good fortune we had had so far—due to the protection of Our Lady of Auray, said Yvonnec, with conviction—would be risking a return of frenzy. While we still preserved some physical energy, it would be wise to examine the place we were in, where tools existed in plenty. Here was a drawerful of them: hammers, pincers, chisels, files of all kinds, screws and nails, with numerous spare nuts and bolts. And there were, besides, four strong bits fitting no doubt into a brace. Where was the brace?

Yvonnec discovered it under the bench. By taking turns, we should be able with these bits and the brace to pierce sheets of iron of from a quarter to one-third of an inch thick. And I reflected that if the oxygen ceased coming to us from the pipe communicating with the Jaubert apparatus, we could bore a hole through the separating wall and receive as we wanted it a supply of the vivifying gas in our old compartment.

Then here was a can of lubricating oil.

"That should feed us," said Yvonnec at once,

He was right. In any case, the oil would be more nourishing than water, and as containing a considerable portion of carbon, was a windfall worth having.

"Heavens! How hungry I am!" exclaimed the quartermaster.

And, after casting a questioning glance at me, he took a pull at the can. It contained a thick blackish oil used by automobilists for greasing cylinders. I made a wry face, in spite of myself, when drinking my share, and hastened to wash my mouth out at the emptying tap, whither Yvonnec had already preceded me.

"Heavens! How hungry I am!" repeated my companion as he paused in his operations.

"We must economize our water, Yvonnec."

"Oh, there are nearly 18 gallons in there, friend. We put in a full supply at Bizerte."

"Yes, but the engine drew on it between Bizerte and Tunis; and then there must have been a good deal of evaporation."

"When the reservoir here is empty," he replied, "you have only to open the tap there for water to arrive from the magazine. So we shan't be left without."

"Undeceive yourself, Yvonnec. Though you were to open the tap now, no water would come."

"Why?"

"Because of the pressure. The density we have in this compartment would prevent the water coming."

"Are you sure?"

"Quite. And, moreover, if now you were to turn the tap you have pointed to, all the water in our reservoir might be forced back into the magazine."

"Always the pressure!" murmured the Breton. "Since one has to count with so many things… it would be better…"

But he suddenly stopped what he was going to say, and, dropping on to all fours, disappeared under the frame of the engine.

"Why, what have you got there?"

"Oh-ho! Well, I never!"

"What is it? Tell me."

And, anxious, I stooped down, just as Yvonnec dragged out a sort of shapeless mass that for a moment I hardly recognized.

"Phanor!" cried the quartermaster, raising the mass into the air.

And I saw that it was Jacques' poodle, with its lion's mane, and hair on only half its body, its back quarters carefully shaved, and its tail terminating in a bushy tuft.

"Here is something to eat, friend!" said the finder, rising to his feet, with eager eyes; and he repeated the words "to eat" while I drank again. The expression reminded me only too well that neither water nor oil was sufficient to quench hunger. My stomach was lamentably empty.

"Poor Phanor!" said Yvonnec, drawing out his knife and sitting down on the one stool of the engine-room. "It was his favorite nook between the two uprights. He took refuge there to keep out of the way, knowing his master would have sent him ashore. When ensconced there, he fancied nobody noticed him; but his tail-tuft always betrayed him."

While talking to himself, the Breton was gutting the poor animal. Afterwards he proceeded to skin it with a celerity denoting practice.

"I once took duty for the cook for three months," he explained. "I will try to dress him up and make him eatable."

"But to cook the dog," I replied, "you want fire; and where can you get any?"

"Oh! You shall see... The meat would be unsavory raw; it is rather high already."

Once more I reflected how extremely lucky we were. This dog had embarked against its master's wishes. Here, its body at a critical moment was about to furnish us with a meal. The service rendered us was a great one. For, at this juncture, the degree of starvation at which I had arrived was such that I was ready to devour anything. Not even the already perceptible smell of the poor beast disgusted me; and, as for Yvonnec, he continued his refrain while eviscerating Phanor:

"Heavens! How hungry I am!"

I am sure that, if this windfall had not fallen to us, and if we had been compelled to fast a day or two longer, we should have been tempted to fetch the two seamen's corpses from their resting-place in the water above us and to live on their flesh.

When the dog was skinned and trussed, we found that there was not very much to eat—no more than could be got off a big hare. Still, we might hope to hold out two or three days longer with what there was. And, if at the end of these no call came at the telephone, we should be practically at the end of our tether. While I was making these reflections, my companion had been exploring Renaut's bench, and had brought thence a soldering-lamp.

"See," he said. "We can get a fire... It is filled with spirit."

"Fortunately."

"And, if it had been empty, we could have fetched some out of the engine."

Yvonnec showed me the large brass reservoir fixed on to the two uprights.

"So you know all about the motor, Yvonnec," I remarked.

"No; not about this one, friend. About steam-engines, yes. But these explosion-motors are new to me."

"Yet you have your torpedo-man's certificate."

"Yes. I am entrusted with the putting together and taking to pieces as well as the upkeep of the torpedoes. I also have to do with the dynamo and the network of electric wires. But the engine is not in my department. I only know that this motor works by means of spirits of wine, because the head man used to say that it was a good thing alcohol had replaced the methylated spirit, since the vine-growers of the South would be benefited."

Before Yvonnec had finished speaking, my mind had begun to conceive a plan, first vaguely, and then in clearer detail. For several years I had been accustomed to a motor-car driven by methylated spirit. All explosion-motors resembling each other, this one I had before me could only, if driven by alcohol, differ in its carburetor. I remembered all the essential parts, which I had often handled, being myself the chauffeur.

The twelve big cylinders of the engine here facing each other had all their explosion-chambers and their lighting wicks, and the valves were all commanded. Here were the magnetos and there the wheel. I looked about for the handle setting the engine going. *If only I could start the engine!* Why not? The peculiarity of the explosion motor in a submarine was its being able to act in a closed chamber; and this one could act as regularly at the bottom of the sea, and at any depth, as when under the guidance of the engineer. It could even have gone on working in the compartment filled with

143

water. Its stoppage was not due to a deterioration of the other parts of the engine, since there they all were in front of me. What had caused the standstill was the engineer's will, or rather that of the commander, who up in his conning-tower could stop or set going his motor instantaneously. Jacques had either stopped the engine himself or ordered the engineer to stop it. If I succeeded in starting the engine again, and in making the screw turn, what would happen to the *Dragonfly?*

This was a perplexing question. And, while I was debating it, a flame flashed from the end of the tube belonging to the soldering-lamp. Yvonnec pointed his finger to it triumphantly.

On the metal bench freed from its tools, he arranged in a line the eight pieces of meat supplied by the unfortunate Phanor's carcass and now representing the sum total of our provisions. They had no very inviting color, but, to men as hungry as we were, they seemed more appetizing than the primest pieces of a fat ox.

Holding his lamp at a suitable distance, the quartermaster directed its blue flame on the pieces in turn ; the meat crackled, and the darker portions gradually assumed a tone uniform with the rest of the roast. By this means our supply was preserved from decomposition. Two of the pieces were thoroughly cooked. They were to be our meal for the day.

At last I asked Yvonnec to cease. The lamp's flame alone consumed more of our oxygen than we two together. It was of no use to risk a deficiency before having the time to pierce a hole in the partition.

We ate heartily. Never had a meal tasted better, never had I had a beefsteak cooked to a greater nicety. If we had obeyed our appetite, we should have eaten a second and a third portion; but the nine pounds of meat yielded by Phanor must last us four days at least. It was a pound ration a day, but without bread or vegetables, and also without salt, a lack we felt keenly.

Yet our enjoyment after fasting compensated for everything. Indeed, our strength, hitherto kept up by nervous effort, was at breaking-point, and without food would have been incapable of further manifestation. For the moment even I was overcome by the eating and drinking; and, lying down, I abandoned myself to sleep. I did just remember, before dozing off, to wind up my watch. It indicated a 2:15, but whether morning or evening I could not say. We must be at the commencement of our fifth day.

I faintly saw the quartermaster, with his tall stature, turn off the two lamps. I had a buzzing in my ears; still, I had grown quickly accustomed to the compressed air. Soon I reached the land of dreams, and found myself rushing along in a monster motor-car at the bottom of the sea, leaping over seaweed, madrepores, and coral.

CHAPTER IX
IN DIVER'S DRESS

When I awoke, my head was heavy and my temples were swollen. My ears tingled and buzzed, and I ached all over. My watch indicated 3:05. I had slept more than 12 hours.

Yvonnec had been up some time. He had lighted one of the lamps, and, on opening my eyes, I saw him bent over me with anxious face. The expression of his features drew me at once from the semi-torpor in which I lingered through fear of too quickly having to face reality.

"What's the matter, Yvonnec? Bad news again?"

"No, my friend," he answered; "but I was afraid you weren't going to wake... I was nigh shaking you. Yet it's so nice to sleep, and not to think... You would have been angry."

"Angry, no. I had a nightmare, as on the first day."

"That's funny. My dreams are all pleasant. I wish I could dream all the time. I dreamt about Annaïc again. I saw her at our 'Pardon.' 'Twas there we got to know each other. I danced with her there for the first time."

He stopped, then said in an altered tone:

"That's all finished."

I noticed a big tear run down his weather-beaten cheek and lose itself in his beard.

A Breton "Pardon"! The word called up before me a peaceful vision. More than once in the country of the golden broom I had seen the Armorican women, with coifs like white seagull's wings, and the sturdy Breton lads with their round hats and embroidered vests; the little children with their virgin voices and garlands of cornflowers. Yvonnec's tear recalled their long processions winding through the sunlit countryside, among the hawthorn bushes, and kneeling in the cross-roads before the granite Madonnas.

While these dreams brought to my companion in our tomb the echo of ancestral resignations, I had been during

147

those twelve hours borne in fantastic course by a motor-car whose cylinders, as large as ancient mortars, resounded with explosions like those of a storm, under the action of sparks as long as flashes of lightning.

In front a huge octopus, clinging and twining round the hood of the motor, waved its tentacles amidst the living blooms of a submarine forest, and belched forth a black miasma which darkened afar the crystal waters. This fiery dragon which I had driven through the Mediterranean plains with my hands clutching a wheel as large as that of a ship for steering, drew our *Dragonfly* in its wake.

Turning round scared, I had seen the submarine bound over the wrecks of modern ships and antique triremes, and I had still before my eyes the phosphorescent furrow hollowed out in the sand by its heavy, unwieldy forepart, in which was a gaping rent.

Was it another presentiment? No, but rather association of ideas, for I had gone to sleep thinking: *Could I only set the engine in movement!*

And my imagination running away with me, under the stimulus of my feverishness, had converted the thought into a nightmare, so that it might recur to me on reawaking.

As a matter of fact, my first impulse was to seek the means to turn the handle. The instrument required was evidently not a fixture, as in the motor-car, but must be somewhere hanging within the engineer's reach. Finding it nowhere, I examined the magneto, hoping to discover there a special arrangement answering the same purpose. Whilst engaged in my search, Yvonnec called me:

"Look here, friend," he said; "I have been continuing the inventory. Just see what I have come upon."

Leading me to a corner, he showed me a strongbox that he had opened, and the course of my ideas was at once changed by what I perceived inside—a diver's dress.

"There is the whole apparatus," went on my companion, "and nearly five fathoms of tubing into the bargain."

He was right. The dress was complete, from the helmet that seemed to belong to some warrior of ancient times, to the lead-weighted shoes that served to keep the diver in a vertical position. The brass helmet, of aneroidal form, was scooped out in the lower part so as to fit on to the shoulders and act as a breastplate on the diver's chest; and three apertures, one circular in front for the eyes, and two elliptic at the sides, were provided with thick panes of glass. At the back, another opening projected, with a thread on the outer edge, to which Yvonnec had already screwed the end of the gutta-percha tube supplying air to the diver. What use did he hope we could make of this apparatus?

The remainder of the equipment consisted of a garment all in one piece, of coarse canvas, lined and coated thick with gutta-percha. To strengthen it there was a leather belt provided with a dagger in a brass sheath, which allowed the diver to cut through any obstacle met with in the water, and attached to the belt was a ring with a cord which connected the man below with those on the surface of the water.

Yvonnec had let me examine all these details without a word. At last he said:

"Well, my friend, what are we going to do with it?"

"That's all right," I remarked, dropping the heavy shoes which I had just lifted. "Unfortunately the apparatus is of no use to us here."

"And yet…"

I interrupted him with:

"Since we can't get into the well."

"Yes, but…"

"And even if we could it wouldn't open."

"I know, yet…"

"And even if it would open, we could do nothing with five fathoms of tubing."

"I don't mean that…"

I was certainly in a humor for interrupting, for again I did not let him finish his sentence.

"And even if we had five miles," I said, "we shouldn't be able to find our way about."

Yvonnec gently shook his head, waited an instant, and then crossing his arms, replied:

"You can object as much as you like, friend, but all the same, we might walk about inside."

"Inside?"

"Yes. Why shouldn't we visit the water-logged compartments?"

For a moment I was confounded in presence of this proposal, which, however, was reasonable enough. Yvonnec continued:

"Look here, friend. The comrade who has ceased knocking is perhaps not dead. If we could get to him!"

I reflected, and he added:

"And if we could reach the tubes of compressed air?"

"Well!"

"Well! I heard that there was compressed air in the magazines, air up to 1500 pounds. This force would be sufficient to drive the water out of the boat, even if we were down in a depth of 30 fathoms."

"Yes, but the hull would not be able to stand the attempt, Yvonnec, even granting we had the means to direct the air in the right directions."

"Then how is it the hull is able to resist where we are the pressure of the sea?"

"Because of its convex form. If we were to bring a still greater pressure to bear on the inside, all the plates would be dislocated."

My companion did not reply to this. His mind was at work on something else. On my side, since I did not believe in the possibility of using the compressed air to drive the water out of the boat, I disapproved of the project of trying to get provisions out of the magazine. But the idea of putting on the diving-dress and entering the water-filled compartments led me to think of another thing.

"Perhaps we might succeed, Yvonnec, in finding the safety leads now."

"Ah ! if we could only cast them off," he answered. "But how?"

"By the switch the Commander should have employed."

"Yes, but you want to know the working of it."

"I do."

"You do, friend?"

"Yes. Jacques showed me how to work the switch in his conning-tower. It's very simple."

"Then what has to be done is to get inside the conning-tower. But is it open, do you think?"

"It must be. If the door had been closed, the Commander would have been alive, and would have called us through the telephone. Since no signal has come to us from him, he must have been drowned, and his conning-tower must be open to the instrument-room below, to which we have access."

Yvonnec nodded his head approvingly.

"Anyway, you will have to look for the switch. Are you sure you can put your hand on it?"

"Yes. It is on the left side of the conning-tower, on the small mahogany table that stands in the narrow part. There are several switches round a central one. This last is to cast off all the leads together, the others to cast off some few at a time."

"Then you would have to press on the central knob."

"Of course."

"If only there were a light in the room!"

"Even without a light, I believe I can find the right place by groping."

"It's not so easy. There are all sorts of handles, levers, and switches on the Commander's table."

"That's true; but I remember that the knobs communicating with the safety leads are covered with a vulcanite cap to prevent any one of them being touched by accident."

Yvonnec remained silent for a moment, then, taking my hand, he said to me gravely:

"Until now, friend, I have never thought we should be able to escape by our own efforts."

"Then all we have done up to the present—our experiment in the well?"

"I had no faith in it. I was convinced we were too deep down."

"How did you know that?"

"When the accident happened the boat plunged head foremost. You recollect, the torpedo-tube was as straight up as a chimney. Well, we took at least half a minute to get to the bottom, and in half a minute you can sink a good distance going down vertically. That struck me. I didn't say anything to you in the well, for I didn't want to discourage you; but I was practically sure the lid of the well wouldn't come off."

"And now, you have hope?"

"A good deal… I remember seeing the *Ruby* in the basin, with its safety leads attached. It takes a lot of water to balance such a weight. If only you can cast off ours, we shall go up like a cork."

"All depends on the number of compartments to the fore which are filled with water."

"This time, friend, I have good hope."

"Then, quick ! Help me to put on the dress."

Yvonnec's cheerfulness had taken possession of me, and I was all eagerness. If I reached the conning-tower I should find the switch, I felt convinced. With feverish haste I hurried my companion at his task, and he, bending over the dress, examined all its parts to assure himself that it was water-tight. He showed me the two taps in the back of the helmet, which served for the pumping of air from outside. I should have no need of them, since I should get air through the tube.

"Do you think you can strike the opening of the conning-tower?" he questioned anxiously.

"Yes; it is at the top of the ladder."

"But the ladder?"

"The ladder is almost vertical, isn't it, and stands in one corner of the instrument-room?"

"Yes; in the corner here."

And he showed me the side opposite to the back. Again with an anxious voice he said:

"Look here, friend. It's I that ought to go up there. I know the place best. There's only the switch commanding the safety leads I don't quite locate; but with your explanation…"

"No, no," I answered. "I mean to go myself. I am sure of finding the way. Don't let us lose any more time."

"But you might faint, friend," urged Yvonnec, once again trying to dissuade me, "and I couldn't come to you. Have something to eat before starting. What a pity we haven't a little rum!"

Whilst speaking he had lit his lamp and proceeded, as the evening before, to prepare our substitute for beefsteak. The one he served me with was double the size of his own. I noticed that the flame of the lamp was not so long as on the previous occasion. The oxygen in our compartment had diminished; we should have to be careful. But there was no immediate cause for uneasiness, as we still breathed quite easily. When I came back, it would be time to see to the matter.

The meat was nicely cooked, and I had to exercise a strong self-control not to be greedy and swallow my portion at once. I seemed to feel the *Dragonfly* quivering and ready to quit the depths of the sea for the upper air.

My toilet was long. Yvonnec lingered over it, scrutinizing the joinings of the trousers to the breast-covering, loosening and tightening again each of the screws that ensured the hermetic closure, and seeing that the large gutta-percha bracelets round my wrists and ankles did not let any water through. At last he said:

"When you enter the instrument-room, friend, you must stay for a minute by the aperture, to get your lungs accustomed to the air inside the dress. Then you will move your limbs and make sure that no water is getting inside. If anything goes wrong you'll have only to slip through the trap, and I shall be here to receive you."

He put the signal-cord into the ring on the belt.

"Three tugs at the cord will tell me you are in the conning-tower, and that you are breathing all right?"

"Agreed."

"And if anything should happen that you don't breathe as easily, you must pull several times sharply."

"But what could you do in that case, my poor Yvonnec?"

"I don't know; but I could come to meet you. I can hold my breath a long time, and, with the cord to help me, I could fetch you back."

When all his recommendations had been given, Yvonnec climbed the ladder, unscrewed the nuts of the trap-door, drew the latter open, and... a bucketful of water soused him. He shut the trap quickly, but the water spurted through the crevices. What had happened? Simply this, that, having absorbed oxygen, we had exhaled carbonic acid, and the pressure having decreased in the engine-room, we were informed of the fact by this descent of a certain quantity of water from the compartment above. And now I reflected that our cooking-lamp was the great culprit. It had absorbed a great deal of the oxygen, which had not been replaced. We must borrow some from the neighboring compartment.

We looked for the tube of the oxylith apparatus feeding the engine. It was in the corner on the left side of the door. At my suggestion Yvonnec lighted a match in front of the orifice formed like the rose of a watering-can, flat and pierced with three small holes. The match burned with a small, short, meager flame. If the oxygen had been coming into the room, we should have seen, on the contrary, the combustion grow stronger and the flame brighter. Consequently, the apparatus did not act. Later I discovered the reason. The second reservoir was regulated so as to supply oxygen under a pressure slightly superior to the normal. This oxygen could not enter our compartment, where it met with a much superior pressure.

Deferring my expedition, therefore, we had to seek the precious gas, not now from the apparatus, but from the compartment we had quitted with the gas escaping there. Armed with a bit and brace, my companion, after freeing me from my helmet, attacked the partition near the door. The work was harder than we had thought. Not until a good hour had gone by did we succeed, relieving each other, in boring a hole, rather larger indeed than was required, through which the gas at once made its presence felt. Another hour passed, during which we allowed the gas to enter; then Yvonnec renewed his experiment with the trap-door.

This time no water fell. The equilibrium was re-established, and by means of a big nail driven into the hole, the quartermaster stopped further ingress of the oxygen. I was enervated by the delay. Again Yvonnec put my helmet on me, examined the dress, turned me round and round, and finally pronounced I was all right.

The dress weighed me down. I found all movement tiring, and, on reaching the third rung of the ladder, was compelled to pause an instant, with the perspiration pouring off my forehead. The leaden soles seemed to be dragging me backwards. I realized at present to what an extent I had been weakened by my five days' privations. I sat down on a step and called to Yvonnec to rid me of this useless weight, for, once in the water, I should know how to maintain a vertical position by the aid of what I might meet with in my progress. To my surprise I saw Yvonnec go further away and pick up the end of the gutta-percha tube which he had unrolled beforehand, drawing it out to the opposite extremity of the engine-room. He placed the tube to his mouth and spoke to me, and I heard him as distinctly as if he had been speaking in my ear.

"We have a real telephone in this tube, friend. I had not thought of it at first. What is it you were saying?"

I repeated my request, and the Breton came and took off the leather straps binding these novel buskins to my feet. I then continued my climb. The top of my helmet knocked against the liquid vault. My situation was a queer one. It was the first time a diver had entered the water head foremost, and certainly the first time he had climbed up to enter. Everything in this boat was upside down, on account of the extraordinary intervention of the compressed air.

I experienced some difficulty in forcing my way into the liquid mass. It was as though I were pushing into jelly. I felt the water run over my hands and feet, the only portions of my body which were bare. There was again a fall of a volume of water equal to that of my body which displaced it. My feet at length reached the trap. I stepped inside, and now I was entirely immersed. But here I was seized with a further attack of intense fatigue, and I stopped for a moment close to the trap-door staggering like a drunken man, and incapable of advancing.

"Are you all right, friend?"

Yvonnec's voice gave me fresh nerve, and the thought that it would accompany me throughout my exploration cheered me to go on.

"Speak to me often, friend," the voice added. "I shall be less anxious. What do you see?"

"I see nothing yet but the trap-door," I answered. "The rest is all dark, quite dark… I want to get accustomed to the change."

"Don't hurry," came the reply. "You will soon get used to the water."

I was about to say something back, but my hand, as I groped about, touched an object of peculiar shape. I ran my fingers along it and suddenly started with an energy I had not deemed myself capable of showing. Without suspecting anything, I had sat down on one of the corpses we had put away in this compartment the day before. The impression was a disagreeable one, and it needed all my will-power to overcome my disinclination to continue my journey. At last I started forward once more, telling myself that, if I could reach the upper room, and could find the switch, everything would go well. In my haste now I knocked against the instrument table, but the shock was insignificant, since I felt myself quite light in the heavier medium.

I had lost in weight a number of pounds equal in volume to the water I had displaced. And this volume was considerable owing to the helmet, the gutta-percha dress, and the air they contained. I scarcely touched the floor. I floated rather. By merely pressing my foot against the floor I rose up to the ceiling, and began to understand the utility and necessity even of the leaden soles I had just taken off. If I had them now I should hardly perceive the weight, and they would have made it easier for me to keep my balance, which I found compromised at each moment.

I clung to the table, and there my hand came upon an instrument which I recognized on account of its peculiar shape. It was the gyroscope, which served instead of the compass by the invariability of its plane of rotation. Then a sort of lint tore to bits in my fingers, and I guessed it was the hydro-graphic chart on which I had read the depth figures.

"Well, friend, you don't speak; say something to me."

I tried to answer the good fellow. He would have played this role better than I, being less nervous.

"My eyes are becoming accustomed to the obscurity," I said. "I can see a little; I have found the staircase."

There it was, indeed. Its polished brass rail cast a gleam that guided me, and now I could vaguely make out on the wall along which I groped switch-boards for distributing the electricity, together with levers, galvanometers, and other instruments that had given their name to this compartment, presided over by the second engineer.

I put my hand on an electric bulb. It was broken. We were lucky enough to have in the engine-room bulbs of thick glass capable of resisting the pressure of the water. The darkness in which I was plunged caused me to appreciate our good fortune in that respect.

On reaching the staircase, I stumbled against a body extended on the floor. I stooped and touched a cloth garment, then a face. There was no beard, but a slight moustache, and short hair. It must be the third lieutenant, whom I had only seen once. A word from Yvonnec encouraged me to go on. I told him of what I had just discovered. Then I stepped over the corpse and began to climb the staircase. It was steeper than the one leading down into the engine-room, being more properly a ladder. But I mounted it quite easily, the only difficulty being in avoiding a somersault. I tried the ceiling with my hand. The trap was not closed. I could enter the conning-tower.

There the obscurity was absolute. As the two trap-doors were not exactly over each other, the rays of light from the engine-room were not able to penetrate. The lighted trap appeared like a flattened moon, with an opal, far-off gleam. The rays, entering the water through its circular aperture, formed a phosphorescent cone, the base of which lost itself in the shadow, and the whole of which was shaken at each of my movements. In the turret where I now stood, it seemed as though I were surrounded by ink.

I waited a moment to remark whether my eyes would grow accustomed also to the darkness here. But there was no change. Not a glimmer arrived. A fossil buried for centuries in a block of marble could not be overwhelmed by a thicker night. And I said to myself that Jacques was in this narrow space where two men had difficulty in moving about. He must be here, for he had left me to go up to the conning-tower. I still heard his last words:

"We will meet up there when you have seen enough down below."

Here in fact we were meeting again. Amid my most fantastic imaginings I could scarcely have invented this tragic scene, my return to this rendezvous, this lugubrious *tête-à-tête* between a dead man and one whom death threatened. Yet the threat was not now so dreadful, since I was close to the switch which, by releasing the safety leads, could restore me to the upper air. So once again, with all the force of my will, I struggled against my weakness and emotion. I tottered, although the weight of my body was scarcely appreciable. My nerves alone supported me, but they would support me to the end.

"Take care, friend; I have only two yards of tubing left. You must have caught it against something."

This warning from Yvonnec restored me all my lucidity, by showing me the danger that might result from any sharp or careless movement. I had no doubt gone round the instrument table, but was too near my goal to turn back and remedy the mistake. I tried to make out my position. The turret narrowed towards the fore part, and the aperture through which I had entered was against the vertical bulkhead terminated by the cap. Against the bulkhead were the rounds of the ladder leading up to the cap, which was not much more than a yard above my head. I could reach and touch if it I wished; and I did wish, for in my brain, weakened by all my bumpings against obstacles, there was the irresistible impulse to settle the foolish question: Was it closed?

The question was foolish, because had it been open, had Jacques, at the moment of the accident, been able to open it and escape with the bubbles of air rising to the surface, as happened to the commander of the *Farfadet* in the Lake of Bizerte, the machinery would be at present full of water, since the formidable pressure of the sea would have weighed down and prevented our compressed air from chasing the water into the neighboring compartment. But there are moments when one only reasons with the absurd by practical experiment.

I mounted the steps with precaution; I raised my arm, touched the cap, seized the heavy handles that were screwed tight. It was closed, firmly closed. But what was this? My right hand, with which I had made the experiment, was no longer in the water. It bathed in air; I could not be mistaken. The change of sensation was too great. The phenomenon was simple enough; and, if I had not been in such an exhausted state, I should have immediately understood what had happened. The water had invaded the chamber from underneath, since it communicated only with the instrument-room. The air had consequently gathered at the summit of the chamber, and I had just thrust my hand into it.

Then a dreadful vision rose before me. For Jacques had been able to live in this imprisoned air. But not for long, perhaps a few hours, during which time he would have clung to the bars of the ladder, with the water up to his waist, struggling until the lack of oxygen completed his exhaustion. In the dark, sinister night, what a death must his have been!

Whereas I, a few yards lower down, at the same moment, was clamoring, and crying! I had space in which to give vent to my frenzy! I had light! I had a companion in misfortune! The water was not there—an opened grave waiting to receive me!

While these thoughts chased each other confusedly in my brain, I had forgotten the object of my expedition. I stopped, at present, stretched out my arm, advanced a little, groping. The body was not on the floor. In rising I touched a leathern garment. I ran my fingers along it... and met with a face, a short, thick beard. It was he! He was lying on his controlling switchboard. He had died at the post of honor. At this instant Yvonnec's voice called me:

"I am getting anxious. The tubing is paid out. Don't advance any further... Where are you?"

"Wait, Yvonnec! I am praying for him," was my reply.

It was true. An irresistible force had bowed me in presence of my friend's corpse. I threw my arms round the body, and within my dark helmet prayers and sobs mingled.

CHAPTER X
WE BEGIN TO MOVE

"Be sure and make no sudden movement," begged Yvonnec again through the tube. "The end here is on the water's edge."

"I can't reach the switch," I answered." I must shift the Commander's body."

The effort would have been a trivial one in the water, where the corpse weighed so little, if Jacques had not been riveted to his table. Following the direction of his arm, I found his two hands grasping a wheel like that of a motorcar.

The conning-tower table was an oval, the two foci of which were occupied by the rough-ground glass discs on which were reproduced the images of the periscope. A vertical ledge about eighteen inches high bordered this table on one side only, and in the centre of the upright portion my hand came across several instruments, a straight lever, two dials, and the receiver of a telephone.

The wheel on which the Commander of the *Dragonfly* had spent his last effort was at one of the ends of the upright. The switches I was seeking were on the table itself, but on the opposite side, and consequently under the corpse of my friend, which was wedged in between the tubes of the periscope and the edge of the controlling switch-board. In order to raise the body it was first necessary to loosen its grip of the wheel.

In the Cimmerian darkness I was some time in finding all this out. Moreover, my action was a good deal limited, for at each of my movements I felt myself checked by Yvonnec, who continued his questions and recommendations. With great difficulty I succeeded in loosening my unfortunate friend's fingers. There had been the same difficulty in loosening those of the engineer from the handles of the trap-door. It would seem as though drowning people put forth in a supreme effort all the muscular energy contained in their body, and thus produce extraordinary effects. Today I know that I broke two of Jacques' fingers in attaining my object. Never had I had need of greater willpower. I was obliged to keep telling myself that the means of our deliverance were there within reach, and that the ghastly work I was performing was one impossible to shirk.

Stiffening myself in my rigid garment, I pronounced, I remember, the word "Forgive" several times, as if I had been committing a sacrilege in snatching the Commander of the submarine from the post in which death had fixed him. On one of his fingers I felt a ring, which could only be his wedding-ring. I drew it off and slipped it under the gutta-percha bracelet that was round my wrist.

"If I am saved," I murmured, "I promise you, Jacques, to take it myself to her who gave it to you, and I will love your children as if they were my own."

At last, I was able to draw my friend's body forward and to have the table free. When I had laid the corpse at my feet I groped for the vulcanite cap covering the knobs that allowed communication with the safety leads. I found it at once. It was raised. No other than Jacques could have done this, for usually the cap was maintained in its place by a spring sunk in the vulcanite, and incapable of being affected by any accidental blow. The Commander of the *Dragonfly* therefore had already attempted to save the boat by the means I had come to try myself.

And when, in a terrible agitation, I put my hand on the central knob, I was sure, even before pressing, that my last hope was gone. Since the weights had not been cast off at Jacques' bidding, there was no reason why they should be at mine. The contrivance had failed at the critical moment. It would not succeed now. I pressed the button; it did not yield, being already pressed down as far as it would go, the arrangement being for the one pressure to be final.

I pressed on the four other knobs; they were down also. Everything had been essayed. For a moment I waited, holding my breath, counting on a miracle, as people in desperation will. No stir of our living tomb was perceptible.

The ascensional thrust, which should have been effected and have brought about in the boat a displacement of equilibrium appreciable by the survivors and unmistakable, did not occur. And during a few instants I stood as it were annihilated by this last blow.

"Well?" questioned Yvonnec anxiously through the tube.

In a series of short, hoarse sentences I explained what I had discovered, and, echoing my disappointment, there came the ejaculation:

"My God! My God!"

The system for casting off the leads in the *Dragonfly* had refused to act, just as in the *Lutin*. There, rust was the cause. In our case it appeared, from the inquiry afterwards made, that the Commander had attempted to cast off the leads just when the boat was in a vertical position, plunging towards the bottom. This change of position wedged the lead crowns and prevented their unloosing. What evidently is required is a system which will work in any position of the boat.

Now, I lost my power to react any further, and had death come upon me, I should not have struggled one jot against it. I forgot even that, within the reach of my hand, was a switch that would unfasten and send to the surface the buoy with the telephone attached to it. Yet Jacques had told me it was the first switch to be thought of in case of an accident occurring. Later, I learnt that he had thought of it, but that the plunging of the boat had also prevented the buoy from mounting. Perhaps, if I had remembered the existence of the buoy switch and pressed on the knob communicating with it, I might have had better success than with the safety leads, the boat being now in a nearly horizontal position. But my forgetfulness was comprehensible. I was altogether incapable of further reflection.

Indeed, at this moment, I must have made some imprudent movement. What it was I have no recollection. But suddenly I felt myself dragged back by the gutta-percha tubing and gliding through the water towards the opening of the con-

165

ning-tower. I felt my helmet bump against the steps of the ladder, then touch the floor of the instrument-room. A few instants after I passed through the lower door and fell head-first into the arms of Yvonnec, who was standing on the top-most rungs of the lower ladder. Dazzled by the electric light that streamed in through the eyeholes of my head-covering, my eyes closed, my head swam, and I sank into a state of half-consciousness.

When Yvonnec managed to free me from the helmet, which had become intolerable to my shoulders, I was unable to rise, and lay helpless and almost lifeless. I was aware that my companion began to rub me energetically with some of the alcohol used for the engine. Then he tried to take my tongue, no doubt to practice the rhythmic tractions employed with the apparently drowned. I opened my eyes at this, and his cry of joy I shall never forget:

"Heavens! How frightened I was!"

As soon as he saw I was in a condition to listen to him, he related to me that the end of the tubing had suddenly slipped from his grasp and had disappeared in the water. By himself plunging upwards into the instrument-room he had been able to catch hold of it again; but, believing my helmet to be full of water already, he had dragged me hastily through the water just as a drowning person is dragged to land. He was very much astonished to find no water in the helmet when he took it off me. On my side I was scarcely recovered enough to explain to him that the air in the tube and water-tight garment sufficed to keep the water back, and had continued to be breathable for two or three minutes. In return, I related to him what I had discovered in the conning-tower and what I had done. He listened, seated on the frame of the engine, looking with his kindly eyes into mine.

"Poor Commander!" he exclaimed. "He was a good cap-tain."

At the end of my narrative he rose with the appearance of a man who had come to some decision.

166

"It's now my turn to go up there," he said. "Will you help me?"

"What is the use, Yvonnec?" I replied. "You won't do any better than I did. The knobs are pressed home."

"I might say it was just to bid farewell to the Commander," returned my companion. "But I can't deceive you; I have another idea in my head."

"What else is there to be hoped?" I asked dejectedly.

"I don't quite know, friend; or rather I know, but I don't want to raise your hopes uselessly. Let me have my way."

I had no reason for opposing the quartermaster's wish, and I aided him to put on the diving-dress. Remembering the inconvenience caused me by the absence of my leaden soles, I fixed them on his feet. Then I recommended him to avoid the loss of tubing I had incurred through going to the right of the table instead of to the left, and a few instants after he disappeared in the trap.

Being so cast down, I made no guesses as to what project might have suggested itself to him. His functions did not often require his presence in the conning-tower, and Jacques' explanations to me had given me a much better notion of the various appliances for guiding the boat than Yvonnec could possibly have. I was gazing forlornly at the gutta-percha tubing as it entered further and further into the viscous-looking liquid, when I heard my companion's voice calling me:

"Friend, friend!"

I replied, and then he continued:

"Will you just give a glance at the board on the wall, on the side of the fly-wheel?"

"There are several," I answered.

"It's the round board with a copper lever-handle."

"I've found it. There are some numbers on a circle: 200, 300, 400..."

"No; that board is for the revolutions of the engine. I mean the other one, with the words *Forwards, Backwards*."

"Yes, now I see: *Forwards, Backwards,* and *Stop* in the middle."

"Where is the lever-handle now?"

"On the *Stop.*"

"Well!" said Yvonnec, "will you alter it to *Backwards?*"

I pushed the handle to the left, as if I had been performing some tedious action. I was too tired altogether, and this double atmospheric pressure in which we had been living for the last 24 hours had become a burden.

"It is done," I called back into the tube.

A few more minutes passed; then I heard Yvonnec shout: "Now pay attention!"

Attention to what? With my eyes fixed on the lever and the board, I stepped back, and, listlessly, I leaned against the fly-wheel of the engine. All at once I was hurled towards the ladder. The heavy iron wheel had begun to move. And when, staggering like a drunken man, I turned round to seek an explanation, the whole engine appeared to be vibrating and alive, as I had remarked and admired it on first descending into the engine-room.

It was not, as in the case of huge steamers, a to-and-fro of pistons, a zig-zag of rods, a whirl of regulators. Of the work that was being done inside the twin groups of cylinders, where the motor explosions succeeded each other in quadruple time, nothing was perceptible outside except the numberless short jerks of the escape valve-rods, and the almost invisible rotation, so rapid was it, of the wheel that stored up the living force.

All the parts that vibrated, revolved and fitted into each other, were hermetically enclosed in an envelope of steel beneath the cylinders. They moved there in oil, and, since the dampers for deadening the noise of the motor explosions had their outlets under the keel, and conducted into the water nothing but soluble gases which the sea at once absorbed, the marvelous machine worked with scarcely any noise, and with the minimum of apparent movement.

But it progressed, or rather regressed; and, while itself remaining silent in the setting of its massive frame, it communicated to all the boat, along its driving-shaft, the characteristic vibration that caused the floor beneath my feet to tremble. It seemed to me as though life had come back to this tomb in which we had been stifled for more than five days. And such was my amazement and delight that I found nothing to say to Yvonnec through the tube. The engine was working. I beheld it working, yet could not believe my eyes. And not only was it working, but we were moving. For, in less than a minute after the change of the lever, I felt the metal floor oscillate and start beneath my feet.

And this movement, which in previous voyages I had never much enjoyed because it upset my inside, appeared now to be the most agreeable and lulling that could be imagined. Just as my thoughts were on him whose act of reflection had produced aloft this result of such capital importance, I saw two leaden soles successively descend through the liquid vault of the trap-door, and the Breton almost tumbled down the ladder. In my turn I caught him in my arms; and I remember this detail, comic if we had not been actors in a tragedy, to wit that I pressed and hugged him in my arms, in spite of his diving-dress, such was my gratitude.

When at last he had taken off his dress, and his radiant face and bright eyes could be seen, he said, as he seized my two hands:

"Well, friend, you see we are moving; we shall get out of this hole."

Standing together, we watched the engine—the dead monster buried in the depths of the Mediterranean, which he had galvanized to life again. Now it ran and glided rapidly along the bottom of the sea; and, in our fancy, the idea seemed certain that we were returning to the light of the upper air. It would carry us out of the black depths; it would go towards the shore; and there it would strand like a strayed whale, and someone would come and let us out. We refused to suppose that, after the *Dragonfly's* almost miraculous start, following on nearly a week's immobility, this vision of deliverance should end in another disappointment.

A few minutes thus passed, and then we tried to understand better what had occurred, and also what was likely to occur. Our progress, indeed, was strange enough, manifesting itself by a rise of the floor, with succeeding slight shocks about every minute. Each time the shock was produced we were pitched forward and the inclination of our flooring was increased, while the water which had accumulated in a corner of our compartment then formed a small wave that dashed against the bulkhead. The boat seemed to be moving by a series of jumps, and one might have thought it was forced every minute to leap over an invisible obstacle.

"Have you guessed, friend, why I got you to shift the lever to that position?" asked Yvonnec, pointing to the dial of the reversing gear.

"For us to move backwards, certainly. But why backwards?"

"For two reasons, friend, though one would suffice. If we had started forward we shouldn't have moved at all, since, our prow being stuck in the ground, the screws would have driven the boat further into the bottom and we should have remained there till eternity."

"I understand. And now, with our stern inclined upwards, we are moving and dragging our prow along the ground."

"That's so. But there is another reason, friend. By traveling backwards we are retracing our course, and are moving towards the coast, towards the west, from where we came."

I shook my head with disquietude.

"That is true only," I said, "if the rudder has kept straight."

"It must be straight. Why shouldn't it be?"

"I don't know. If the accident happened when the Commander was steering towards Bizerte, the rudder will be turned."

"No, for I heard the second lieutenant, in the room above, repeat: 'North, 85 degrees east,' just when you came down to join me."

"You are right. I remember my friend had given up at that moment his plan of trying a deep dive. He did not suspect that we should dive all the same, poor fellow. He said to me: 'I should like to start from Cape Ras-al-Fortas; we will catch up a few miles in the east.'"

"So, by moving backwards, we are moving westwards?"

"That is towards the coast we hugged when setting out, and unless we are going towards Bizerte; it needs such a tiny angular difference in the boat's position, or that of the rudder, to make us miss the coast!"

I tried to remember what I had seen on the chart, the half-circle formed by the shores of the Gulf, the capes—Carthage to the west, Kas-Durdas to the east. Beyond Cape Carthage there was Cape Kamart. If we missed the coast of Carthage we might run on to that of La Marsa, lying between the two capes, always supposing that Jacques had not altered the direction of the rudder.

"Listen, friend," said Yvonnec, "this is what must have happened, as far as we can gather. When the Commander felt the shock, his first thought was to stop the boat, and he gave the order. So Renaut put the lever where you saw it, and the engine came to a standstill. Then the Commander must have pressed on the safety-lead knobs, and as he saw they didn't act, he tried to set the engine going again. Perhaps he placed the two horizontal rudders in the mounting position, but he had no reason for touching the direction rudder."

"You are right."

"While doing this, the water surprised him," continued Yvonnec. "He had no time to reflect that the lower starting-lever was at stop, and he turned his wheel full on for the forward movement. Nothing, of course, budged. He kept on trying until he was drowned, and that's why you found him clutching the wheel and making the efforts of a drowning man."

"Then he must have perished almost directly?"

"That's sure. How could he have lived even a few minutes?"

"In the pocket of air formed above in the conning-tower."

Yvonnec shook his head. He had not had experimental proof, as I had, of this pocket of air.

"The Commander did all he could," answered my companion; "and he must have been drowned directly, while trying to set the boat going again."

The idea that my friend had not suffered the long agony I had at first supposed was a relief to my mind. Yvonnec prowled about in the machinery. From the bench table he took a metal box containing nuts and bolts, emptied it, and bending under the case of the engine-motor, turned the tap emptying the radiator.

"Here," he said, holding me the box full of water, "make haste and drink as much as you can; in a few minutes the water will be boiling."

He was right. It was already pretty warm, and the temperature of the engine-room itself was rising.

"Ah!" cried the quartermaster, as he continued his inspection, "…and our dynamo?"

He geared on a strap by means of a lever in the axis of the cylinders, and, in the middle of the fluted wheel bearing the induction electro-magnets, the bobbin of the dynamo began to revolve.

"Our accumulators will get charged afresh," he observed, "and we no longer risk being without light. That was my chief fear."

"Mine, too, Yvonnec. But just now I have another. Where are we going?"

"Where Providence wills, friend," my companion replied.

He crossed his arms, and, standing with his legs apart, went on.

"Just imagine. We have here the only machine capable of working like that with closed circuit. Renaut explained it to me one day. It receives the carburetion air direct from the compressed air tubes of the hold, and exhausts the burnt gases

172

into the water without borrowing anything from the compartment we are in. Such a machine would work if submerged."

"That's true. Only, at the depth at which we are, part of its force must be employed in thrusting the spent gases into the sea.

"No doubt; but enough remains to carry us on."

Carry us on where? Towards what shore?

This was the great question. For the second time I asked: "Where are we going?"

"That," said Yvonnec, "we cannot tell."

"If the *Dragonfly* was being steered with its stern towards Sardinia when it stopped, we must be now moving towards one of the deepest portions of the Mediterranean," I suggested.

The quartermaster's brow contracted.

"There must be a depth of from 250 to 300 fathoms there," he said anxiously.

"You are far from the truth, my poor Yvonnec. When I saw I was about to embark on the *Dragonfly* I had the curiosity to consult a sea-chart, and found that to the west of Sardinia there is a depression of more than 1600 fathoms, and, off the coast of Crete, another of 2000 fathoms—real abysses!"

Yvonnec looked pensively at me with his chin resting on his hand, an attitude unusual with him.

"A depth of two and a half miles!" he exclaimed. "If we should be going there!..."

He did not finish his sentence, but his look was eloquent.

"Anyway," I added, "we should be crushed, smashed, before reaching a depth of 50 fathoms. The *Dragonfly's* hull cannot be made to support a pressure of 150 pounds to the square inch..."

"Then we shall be warned by the invasion of the water," said Yvonnec. "Meanwhile we had better close the trap..."

"What's the use?"

He was about to mount the ladder to close the lid all the same, when a shock made him lurch towards the table bench.

It seemed at certain moments that the *Dragonfly* was bumping on rocks or wreckage, and this impression recalled my night-dream. The fore part of the submarine must be delving in the sand the furrow which my fever had shown me as phosphorescent in the darkness of untrodden depths. This fantastic backward progress of the boat would cease only with the exhaustion of the alcohol, since its screw, remaining several yards above the ground, would escape the seaweed and other plants with trailing leaves that grow on certain bottoms.

Several yards! How high, then, was the stern raised above the prow? This question tormented me just as a while before that of the volume of our compartment. I drew my notebook from my pocket. The Breton bent towards me.

"Are you going to calculate again, friend? Let Providence see to that."

"Listen, Yvonnec," I replied. "Do you know the length of the *Dragonfly?*"

"Of course; 177 feet."

I drew on the white page a line that I divided into five equal portions; and I subdivided one of the latter into ten, which I called yards. Prolonging the entire line of four divisions equal to these last, I had therefore represented, on a scale that mattered but little, the total length of the boat. What was its inclination with the bottom? Such was the problem I set myself. I had before my eyes the means of graphically figuring this inclination.

Tearing another sheet of paper, I knelt down beside the pool of water in the fore part of our cabin. Slipping the sheet vertically into the water, while keeping one of its edges in contact with the floor, I profited by a moment's pause in the leaps of the boat to trace with a pencil the water-level on the sheet. I thus had the angle formed by the water's surface with our flooring, and, consequently, the angle formed by the boat with the plane of the bottom supposed parallel to the level of the sea.

This angle I transferred below my line of 177 feet, and, on the new undetermined line, I let drop from the 177 foot extremity a perpendicular whose length I measured. It intercepted about fifteen of my divisions. Therefore our screw was more than fifteen yards below the level of the sea. I announced the result to my companion.

"I understand," he replied quickly. "If we should come into depths of 15 yards the stern of the *Dragon-fly* would emerge from the water."

"And we should be saved," I added, "for as such shallow depths are only met with in the Gulf, our whereabouts would soon be discovered."

"And discovered by others, perhaps, before being discovered by ourselves, friend; for the stern might emerge without our knowing."

This thought of our possible proximity to the surface within a short time made our hearts beat so violently that we were unable to speak for a minute or two, and could only watch the engine continuing its regular vibration. Putting back the notebook into my pocket, I felt something I did not recognize. I drew it out; it was the mariner's compass found in the master-mechanic's coat. I had forgotten all about it.

"Perhaps with this," I said, "we might calculate our bearings."

And at once, bending over the dial on which the needle oscillated and trembled, we waited and gazed. The oscillations did not last long. The needle's blue point pointed in the same direction as that of our movement. It made with the boat's axis a slight angle towards the left, and this angle, nearly equal to the magnetic inclination, might be regarded as compensating it.

We were going straight towards the north!

To the north! That meant towards the region of deep bottoms, the abyss off Sardinia, towards annihilation!

CHAPTER XI
THE RACE TOWARDS THE ABYSS

The moment after our discovery was a horrible one. I do not think any we had passed through previously were worse. All our efforts to finish with this race to the abyss! It was some time, how long I cannot say, before we were able to speak or even to think. When at last Yvonnec broke the silence, it was to propose putting on the diving-dress and going into the conning-tower for the purpose of stopping the engine. So agitated was he that he forgot we had only to raise the lever before us in order to produce this result. No sooner had I made the remark to him than he stepped forward to cut off the light feeding the explosion-motor. I checked him.

"Never mind, Yvonnec," I said. "Let it go on. We will trust to Providence, as you put the matter just now."

To tell the truth, I preferred the noise of the engine, even with the risk we were running, to the sepulchral calm which had hitherto weighed our spirits down. I no longer had force enough to quarrel with destiny. All my fighting instinct, my hope and desire to live had been quenched. Destiny was the stronger. I abandoned myself to its will. At least, there would be one alleviation of our condition; we should have no longer to fear starvation, with its horrors; and the exhaustion of our provisions at present close at hand would be anticipated by the other event.

I watched the engine-room continually; and, as we went on, it seemed to me the sides began to contract. Yet I did not trouble. I was in the state of a man who, feeling his end approaching, should analyze his vital manifestations with tranquility. Yet, in spite of myself, my thoughts returned to the question of the atmospheric pressure. Since it must be increasing as we moved, why did not the water in the instrument-room overwhelm us? Was it possible that the *Dragonfly* could be moving along a horizontal plane, and would only, on reaching the end of it, descend suddenly into the 1600 fathom depth? Such might be the case, and still I was puzzled to conceive how the inside pressure of relatively feeble density, since we were able to live in it, continued to balance the outside pressure of the sea. This outside pressure must, however, be constantly making itself felt through the breach in front. And, if we were at more than 24 fathoms depth, as had been indicated by the experiment of the sluice, we ought to have been overwhelmed long since. Unable to suspect the truth with regard to this matter, I grew tired of thinking of it at last, and turned my mind, in what seemed to be my final moments, towards the dear ones of whom I had often had visions during my suffering and despair.

Nine days had gone by since I had left them, promising to be absent not longer than ten or 12 days. They must have already wondered why no telegram had arrived to tell them of my whereabouts and when I should return; and more than one childish voice would have asked:

"When will papa be back?"

"He won't come back at all, poor little ones," I said sadly to myself, "and you will never know where he is buried."

The tears ran down my cheeks while the engine went on working, lulling me with its hollow, monotonous throb, hypnotizing me with its jerking valve-springs and the glinting of its blue polished wheel. In the palm of my hand I held still the compass which had so brutally announced to us our fate. I looked at it again, taking care to keep it as horizontal as possible. More implacable than the first time, it oscillated for hardly a second, and the needle's point repeated: To the north! To the north!

I dropped it, flung it rather on the floor, in a last fit of exasperation, and it rolled towards my companion.

Yvonnec had been praying again, and had then squatted down near me with his elbows on his knees and his hands under his chin, as was usual with him. He picked up the instrument, looked at the needle himself, shook his head, and, leaning towards me, said:

"Friend, shall we bid each other good-bye?"

I embraced him with an affectionate, regretful tenderness. What a consolation it was to me to have had the society of this humbler mind, yet better tempered to endure trial than mine! If I had been alone, I should have succumbed in my weak despair.

Yvonnec rose, made the sign of the cross; then, urged by the irresistible need of movement, he began to stagger rather than walk round our compartment, pausing from time to time to look at the engine, and starting again on his restless course. Meanwhile I was sunk in my dreamy reflections and paid but listless attention to his doings. But suddenly he aroused me by a cry.

I turned my eyes and saw him steadying himself with one hand that clutched the ladder. In his other hand he held the compass, and was gazing at it with a look of amazement.

"Come and see, friend," he said. "The needle has turned; we are running towards the south... the south!"

The word electrified me. The south was Tunis, the Gulf, the coast. In one stride I was at the quartermaster's side. It was true; the needle's blue point, the north point, was now pointing in the direction of the boat's prow. And, as we were running backwards, we were going towards the south. I tapped on the glass of the compass to oblige the needle to turn freely. There was, however, no mistake. It kept its direction. We were undoubtedly running south.

"The rudder isn't straight," exclaimed Yvonnec brusquely. "We are acting like a snail and turning round and round."

Such might be the explanation. If so, strange adventures were in store.

Suddenly the truth broke in upon me. I took the compass and carried it successively into the other two corners of the compartment. In these two places it turned constantly towards one point; and this point was the dynamo.

Under any other circumstances Yvonnec and I should have at once thought of the influence the dynamo must exercise on the compass, which was now no use to us as far as telling us the direction of the boat was concerned. Even if we were to ungear the dynamo, the magnetic influence created in the room was too great to allow of any calculation being effected. The only thing we could say was that we were not necessarily travelling north, and we could, therefore, still hope.

Just at this moment, when we had made the discovery which again left our future uncertain, a shock occurred that stopped our under-sea wanderings. So violent was it that all the boat cracked and groaned, and I thought the hull had given way. Both of the lamps were extinguished; and as for me, I was flung against the door of the engine-room, where I fell on Yvonnec, whom the shock had treated similarly. The floor on which I came down had just been tilted considerably and an avalanche of water deluged us from head to foot.

I believed the sea had forced its entrance. We seemed to have arrived at the end of our troubles; and my companion, against whom I lay huddled, murmured a name and a prayer.

Darkness enveloped us thickly around; a second, then a third shock, less violent than the first, occurred at a few seconds' interval; and these were followed by fresh avalanches of water, while the floor of the compartment tilted up more. Next a strange, shrill noise mingled with the dull buzzing of the engine, which continued to work; and, quivering and cowering, with wide-open eyes, I clung to Yvonnec's body. It was limp and inert. Apparently he had been killed by the impact, from which his corpse had preserved me. And I found myself alone in the Stygian darkness, awaiting my own doom.

I tried at length to speak, to cry out, but my tongue refused its office. I shook Yvonnec, but he did not respond. And the strange noise, something like that of a siren, went on, with what seemed to be a more rapid movement of the engine. In our compartment the pistons worked at double speed, as though the motor had gone mad. I wondered whether the driving-shaft had broken, and was thus responsible for the din.

"Yvonnec! Yvonnec!" I succeeded in calling at last.

No answer came. I felt convinced he was dead, and gropingly I passed my hand over his face. A something warm and liquid remained on my fingers. It was blood; his head, face, and beard were covered. The poor Breton had had his head split open.

Again I called to him repeatedly; and, after about five minutes or so, which seemed to me centuries, a moan came from his throat, while a faint pressure of his hand replied to that of mine. Once more I spoke to him, and another pressure of his hand told me that he understood what I said, though he could not utter anything.

My prayer went up that he might live, and that, if deliverance were near for me, he might also share in it; but that, if death were near for both of us, I might not long survive him.

My own injuries were slight; a few bruises only. And as my brain grew clearer I endeavored to imagine what could have happened. My first thought was that we had struck on a fringe of rocks situated on the eastern coast of the Gulf. This granite wall, with summits of from 600 to 1200 feet, descends sheer down 25 to 30 feet in the sea.

The *Dragonfly* had probably dashed against this wall in a slanting direction, which accounted for its not being smashed; but the two screws were no doubt broken, and now, with the prow fixed in the sea-bottom, the hull was buttressed against the rock, checked for good and all in its vagabond course.

One thing was certain; we no longer advanced. We felt neither the pitching nor the swinging that had previously shaken us. I was just wondering whether this place we had reached was any more likely to be visited by those sent in search of us than the place in which the accident had occurred, when Yvonnec recovered fuller consciousness and his power to speak.

"Friend," he said.

"Are you much hurt?" I asked.

Instead of satisfying my anxiety, he raised himself up as if an electric current had passed through him. His hand again pressed mine, but this time as if it had been a vice. And his voice, harsh and spasmodic, asked:

"Do you hear the screws? Listen!"

"Yes," I said, "but keep quiet until I have washed your wound. Have you any matches?"

"Just listen to me," he answered impatiently, almost imperiously. "My wound does not matter."

"Anyway, it is bleeding a good deal."

"It's nothing, friend, I tell you, since I have heard and have understood. Can't you hear?"

"Yes."

"Well, don't you understand that the noise… is… is the noise of the screws revolving in the upper air?"

In the upper air?

I was on my feet in an instant. And I listened, panting, listened as I had not listened before, trying in vain to quiet the beatings of my heart. The outside whizzing appeared to me to be then the sweetest, most divine music, for now I recognized its significance. In many a rough voyage between Marseilles and Tunis I had heard the same whizzing of sinister sound during a tempest. When the ship dipped her prow beneath the waves, the stern rose out of the water, the screw revolved for a few seconds madly in the air, and a plaintive moan like that of a siren with one note only accompanied its whirl in the air. The noise was similar now.

But, if the screws were out of the water, the *Dragonfly* must have reached the surface, must be close to the coast, and our deliverance must be near also. My resignation had quitted me. I wanted again to live. A mad, surging joy invaded me. I hugged Yvonnec in my arms, smearing myself with blood, transported with an irresistible desire to shout my exultation to the four winds.

There was something too we had not thought of yet. The screws must be attracting attention by the noise they were making; and, even supposing we were on the rocky coast of the east, where colonists were not numerous and the natives lived in *douars* far from the shore, such a noise could not fail to be heard by someone. Everybody would have heard of the accident to the submarine, Arabs as well as Europeans. The Gulf was frequented by fishermen; boats from Malta sailed near the coast; custom-house officers were on the watch at the summits of the cliffs. It was not possible for our plight to remain undiscovered. These thoughts produced in me emotions I cannot translate into words. After despairing so long of deliverance, the almost certainty of it was bliss.

Now the essential thing was to hold on until someone came; and especially we must take care to do nothing that might lead to our sinking and sliding back into the depths.

"Have you any matches, Yvonnec?" I asked.

He handed me his box in silence. Joy had deprived him of his speech once more. The box had just two matches left in it, and luckily they were not wet. With infinite precaution I lighted one of them, and for a few instants our compartment became dimly visible.

My first look was directed to my poor companion. His head was all over blood, and a broad gash showed above his left temple. Next I glanced around us. The water, which was formerly a puddle only, covering the bottom end of the room, towards the front, hid at present nearly all the base of the engine and the lowest rung of the ladder. Part of the contents of the guard-room had been forced down upon us under the influence of the shock.

The sight of the water suggested to me the thought of washing Yvonnec's wound; but I reflected that the liquid, being dirty, might do more harm than good. This I told him.

"Yes," he replied, "let us wait. I feel better, and the bleeding has stopped."

We began to talk, forming one hypothesis after another. Was it likely that, after six days' useless search and fathoming, the engineers would have ceased looking for us? If so we should have to trust to chance. We wondered how much of the stern was out of the water, whether it were the screws only, or the compartment also in which we were originally confined. If the latter supposition was correct, the outside aperture of the

183

torpedo-launching apparatus must be also out of the water, and escape through it would be possible. Nothing but the difference of pressure prevented us from penetrating into our late dungeon. However, we could equalize these pressures by allowing the high-pressure oxygen in the other compartment to come into our own. We had already bored a hole through which this could be effected, and had made use of it twice.

Still, if we were to permit the oxygenated atmosphere to prevail where we were, we should have to get out of it quickly. Indeed, being so near to deliverance, we doubted whether we should be wise, in our weak state, to risk the experiment. To one or two of my last remarks Yvonnec made hardly any reply.

"Are you suffering, friend?" I asked, adopting the appellation which he used in speaking to me, since I wished to manifest my affection towards this valiant companion of my misfortunes.

"No," he answered. "I had forgotten my hurt... Just look there!"

"How can I look in this darkness, Yvonnec?"

"Perhaps it is my eyes then," he continued, " but I seem to see a faint light over there by the ladder."

I rubbed my own eyes. He might be right. If the stern was out of the water, the conning-tower could not be more than a few feet beneath the surface; and the light of the upper air entering through the windows could find its way through the instrument-room, causing the water there to have a semi-transparent appearance. But we had no idea whether it was night or day above us. I gazed and gazed, and ultimately I fancied there was some sort of light visible through the trapdoor.

Immediately I was seized with the desire to return to the conning-tower, and to test whether it was the sun's light which was there—the light celebrated by poets of antiquity, the light over which the gentle Iphigenia wept at the hour of her sacrifice.

But in order to go I must put on the diver's dress. And I forthwith began groping around to find it. The hum of the dynamo, which I almost touched as I passed it by, warned me that I might get a finger or an arm torn off if I were caught in the machinery. I therefore struck our last match, and was able thus to put my hand on the various portions of the dress, which were lying scattered where we had thrown them down in our joy on discovering that the boat was moving. Standing by the foot of the ladder, with water halfway up our legs, we gathered the pieces up; and Yvonnec aided me to get into the dress, after an expenditure of much patience and effort.

"In case the hood of the turret should be out of the water," he said as he screwed on the helmet.

"Oh! That's impossible, Yvonnec."

"Who knows? Anyway, if it should be, could you open it?"

On my reply in the negative he explained to me what I must do. There were four hand-screws to unfasten and a lever to be raised. More than an hour was taken up before I had the dress on all right. The expectation of seeing daylight made me nervous.

"Be quick, Yvonnec," I said. "It seems as though you would never finish."

"Commit no imprudence, friend; you would pay for it too dearly. Think of those you are going to see again," was his answer.

The leaden soles appeared light to my feet. My weakness of a while since had vanished. I felt as if I had wings. We were near the coast. I could fancy I heard knockings on the turret and voices! Perhaps the telephone would call me when I got up there.

"Quick, friend!" I said once more.

"I will follow you," exclaimed Yvonnec, "and will plunge my head in the water. Up yonder it is clean. A funny way, all the same, to wash one's self."

This was his first joke. We neither of us remembered at the moment the three corpses which were rotting above us. Everything is relative.

Now I was ready. I climbed the ladder and thrust my hand into the soup-like liquid before immersing my helmet. The surface of the water appeared to be more concave. Soon I was in the wardroom, to me, at present, the antechamber of daylight—the blessed light towards which I aspired with all the force of my being. Yet I had patience to wait until I had made sure that the water did not enter through my diver's dress.

Before me, on the ceiling, I could discern through the glass of the helmet a white gleaming circle, something milky and soft, a translucency in the darkness of our tomb. It was like a huge opal fallen upon us from the ethereal vault, a bit of heaven reappearing to my ravished eyes.

I stretched out my arms at the sight; I stumbled over corpses; I knocked against the table, the ladder. I hurried forward. I slipped along, still in ecstasy, my hands assuming a bluish tint as if tinged by the Moon's rays.

At length I reached the conning-tower. There an ineffable happiness took possession of me. The light, iridescent and so soft that no painter's brush could render it, was penetrating through the four windows with differing intensities. We had undoubtedly issued from the mysterious depths of eternal night; and, after six days' torment, I saw again daylight and its sweet radiance to which I had bidden adieu.

From the height of the profoundly blue sky the Sun's fiery disc darted its rays into the waves, and through the thin layer of water that separated us from the surface these same rays reached into our dungeon, like the caresses of a recovered friend.

Delirious with joy, I gazed around me. Jacques' switchboard loomed out vaguely with its lever-handles, its dials, and knobs. I saw the places where I had pressed in vain, trying to cast off the safety leads. There were the tubes of the two periscopes with their different diameters. They seemed to me to zig-zag towards the top of the turret through the water, which my movements agitated.

I walked towards the window that received most light, the one facing the surface. I touched the glass. A miracle! there was no water on it. The three others, on the contrary, were still covered. That was the effect of the general inclination of the submarine, and also of the invasion of our engine-room by a certain quantity of water. This water, coming from the instrument-room and also from the conning-tower, had been replaced by air, and the gaseous mass occupying the top part of the turret was consequently increased.

But I did not stay long at this best-lighted window. Certain weird-looking forms, long in shape, called my attention on the right. I peered out from-the glass of my helmet. I stared. At first I failed to understand. Soon, however, my eyes, sharpened by their experience of some hours' darkness, made out details in the receding, slender objects, apparently arranged in parallel lines and gradually fading away in the watery distance. I guessed it must be a colonnade. Indeed, quite near me rose a huge pillar; whether in stone or marble I could not tell, as it was covered with madrepores, actiniæ, infusoria, and petrified gorgons. Nevertheless, the shape was preserved, and I was able to distinguish its lotus-leaf capital bulging at the base.

Tremendously big masses of seaweed hung round it like a head of hair rising from the depths. Their supple filaments waved idly with eel-like wrigglings beneath the action of invisible currents. Rapid shapes flitted through them, sported in and out of the colonnade, disappeared, came back again, glided by the window—fishes with barbed backs, hippocampi that clung to an oscillating stem with their tails, and quitted it for another, like birds that hop from branch to branch, tunnies shooting up from the somber depths and diving down again immediately after.

My attention was more especially drawn to the remains of the entablature that overhung the lotus-leaf capital, and projected towards my window. Its truncated extremity was hardly more than a yard away from me. In its upper portion multicolored coral and polypi, flabelliform oculines, calcareous millepores were incrusted and stood up with the appearance of a nosegay. In reality they were sea-flowers set in an antique vase; but no museum would ever know their precious wealth.

The vertical wall of the entablature had been respected by the sea vegetation; and in the substance of the stone I could make out a series of engraved letters. There was an inscription carved by the chisel of a Punic workman, dictated perhaps by a suffetes,[28] and dedicated to a divinity contemporary with Belial or Moloch.

A few years ago I saw the inscription of the Reaper brought from the ruins of a town in the ancient kingdom of Bocchus by my companion Letaille, an indefatigable investigator. The characters composing it have the cuneiform appearance of those I now looked upon. To interpret this inscription, revealed for the first time since its burial, would require the science of someone like Father Delattre, the celebrated archpriest of the cathedral of Byrsa, and Superior of the White Fathers.

But my eyes sought to penetrate further, right into the mass of seaweed and debris whence rose the mutilated portico. For there, beside the base of the Punic pillars, I seemed to see truncated masts, prows lifted up in the shape of conches, hulks of triremes covered with a mosaic of shells. Was it a hallucination of my brain, fevered by the hope of approaching deliverance, and idly lingering over these visions of the abyss, like the Alpinist who cannot tear his gaze from the precipice down which he has nearly fallen? Was it the riot of imagination lending to this submarine flora the substance of antique things? I do not know. But I thought I beheld emerging from a thicket of saxifrage and parietary a massive stele supporting a horse overhung by a palm trunk—a horse, emblem of Carthage.

I felt myself transported into a world of unreality. My dazzled eyes, intoxicated with light, were unable to cease gazing at this engulfed temple, these vestiges of history, these

---

[28] Official of Carthage. Ed.

mysteries that no human eye might ever look upon again perhaps. An almost sacred emotion seized upon me, and I pressed
my fingers upon the glass of the window, dreading that the
spectacle should suddenly vanish, and that I might find I was
only dreaming.

While I looked, a shadow flitted across the entablature
bearing the Punic inscription. It came from above, passed and
returned, then remained still. My ecstasy immediately gave
way to the practical. This shadow was a proof to me that the
shore must be close; I no longer mused of orders given by
suffetes or of Salammbô's invocations. I calculated instead
that the *Dragonfly* must have stranded on the left coast, the
inhabited coast, and not on the girdle of rocks surrounding the
wild promontory of Cape Bon.

The ruin could only belong to the ancient Carthage. We
had come back to the quays of the city of Dido, and our im-
provised siren was calling for help at a short distance from La
Goulette, the Kram, Sidi-Bou-Said, and La Marsa. Definitely
rescued from the depths of the Mediterranean, we were lying
on the track of big ships, fishing boats, and pleasure barges.
Our deliverance was certain. Once more, and now across the
window turned towards the surface, I saw shadows flit. They
were small craft that had discovered our screws and were now
rowing round the spot; and in them were acquaintances wondering how our engine was thus able to work.

They would send for a diver; he would knock at the turret, he would stick the glass eyes of his helmet against the
window through which I was peering. He would not see me,
because I was in the dark; but I should see him, and would
knock excitedly on the heavy steel wall of the conning-tower
in order to answer his call. Somebody would soon come.

But, just as I was repeating these last words for the tenth
time, my excitement growing more intense the while, I all at
once felt the floor of the conning-tower sink beneath me; the
window through which I looked turned green and was covered
again with water; an eddy swept right up to the top of the
chamber, and Jacques' corpse rolled between my legs, as if

reproaching me for my selfishness in entering his private domain and thinking only of light and life whilst he was swathed with eternal shadow.

CHAPTER XII
TOWARDS THE LIGHT

What had happened? Was it a fresh catastrophe that overwhelmed us just as we were on the eve of escape? The *Dragonfly* had unexpectedly gone see-saw! Its screws, which a moment before were turning in the upper air, had sunk into the water again. The siren-like noise had ceased, and with it the call for help on which I had been counting so much. The submarine was still in a sloping position, but slanted now in the other direction. Its stern was at the bottom and the window through which most light came at present was the one that a few minutes before had been deepest under water.

The colonnade of the Punic temple showed only-very vaguely, and its capitals were several yards above the conning-tower. A huge tunny was swimming about not far from the window, and jelly-fish of enormous size floated near the tunny as if escorting it.

Something that especially struck me was the sinking of the water in the chamber where I was. All the upper portion of my body now emerged above the surface of the liquid, which was only just up to the controlling switch-board. I feared the instrument-room had been flooded, and shouted to Yvonnec. No reply came. At short intervals I repeated my appeal, but still no answer reached me. At present I reproached myself for allowing myself to be absorbed by the grandeur of what I had seen and for returning such brief response to the questions my companion had put to me on my arrival up here. I tried to keep my wits clear, feeling that, if I were to make any error, it might be paid for with my life. However, my position was a perilous one; my breathing began to grow painful; a cold sweat broke out on my forehead, and my head was oppressed as if by a weight upon it.

Evidently the air was no longer being renewed in the helmet, and the end of the tube through which fresh air had come was stopped up. To stay longer in the conning-tower would be asphyxia in a very short time. Summoning up, therefore, all my coolness, I stepped over Jacques' body and made my way to the trap-door; but, as I was about to descend, I reflected that I was going to return into the darkness, that I should risk knocking myself against the engine at work, against the fly-wheel whirling at full speed; and this thought caused me to pause for the purpose of switching off the motor. I turned the small wheel in the opposite direction, and immediately all vibration ceased in the *Dragonfly*. The silence that followed served to increase my uneasiness as I plunged into the darkness. Soon I had traversed the instrument-room and arrived at the bottom of the ladder leading into the engine-room below; but once there I staggered under the weight of my dress, the lack of fresh air having rendered my helmet intolerable.

Without waiting to look for my companion, I hastily undid the screw that fastened the tube to my headpiece. It yielded easily because Yvonnec had only tightened it with his fingers. As soon as the tube fell, I felt what seemed to be a violent blow on the nape of my neck, and my lungs and stomach contracted as though something were flattening them. My ears buzzed and strange noises assailed my brain. My eyes looked through a film in which danced myriads of violet-tinted jets of light.

Like a man that has been douched with icy water on quitting a steam bath, I sank down helplessly; but slowly my breathing returned to me and I began to experience the same sensations as when I had opened the Jaubert apparatus and drunk in the oxygen. Yet now I paid no attention to this, but groped about with but one wish animating me—that of finding Yvonnec. The first thing I touched was the big fly-wheel. And I said to myself that he had probably been caught by it when it was revolving 600 times a minute. Dreading I might discover him crushed against the wall, I bent down; and there, a foot or so away from the ladder, I came upon him lying. I touched his hand; it was wet and cold. A cry escaped me. It seemed there could be no doubt of the accident. When the boat had turned see-saw, he must have been swept off his feet by the water.

I broke into violent sobbing. Yvonnec had become such a friend to me during our hours of suffering together that my conviction of his being dead afflicted me more than anything I had previously gone through. I remained in a sort of stupefaction of grief, caring nought for the painful constraint of my diver's dress, nought for the pangs of hunger, which were keen enough, for, in our anticipation of deliverance, we had forgotten to partake of the meager remains of our provisions. I still held the Breton's hand in my own, and, clasping it, I lay down on the floor.

How long I remained in this prostration I cannot say. In the semi-darkness my notions of time had been lost. Perhaps I slept, and perhaps I dreamt; but if so, I did not remember. My returning consciousness surprised me raising myself against the steel partition. With throbbing temples I listened. *Someone had knocked.* At first I wondered whether the noise in my ears had come back. Indeed, whatever had struck my attention came only through the tube-hole of my helmet, and seemed necessarily more distant. But, as I leaned the helmet itself against the wall, the metal was also set vibrating, so that I soon had the certainty that regular blows were being dealt with some heavy instrument on the hull of the boat.

The blows were repeated, first in one place, and then in another; the person who was striking was apparently trying the various parts of the submarine in order to discover if there were survivors in any of its compartments. Now he came close to the place where I was. I had no instrument ready to hand; but, instinctively, I answered in the only way possible to me. I butted the side of the wall with my helmet, reckless of the shocks it produced in my head. I butted again and again with frenzy. One after the other the small glass windows in the sides of the helmet broke. Then the knocking of the outside diver ceased. So he must have heard me. I was the more persuaded of the fact when the knocks began again. On my side I recommenced the painful exercise of the bull who butts with his head against the thick palisade of the Plaza; and now the front window of my helmet cracked, but fortunately did not break; otherwise it would have cut my eyes badly, as my head was already cut by the bits of broken glass at the side openings. I could feel blood trickle on to my chest and arms, but paid no attention, and went on knocking until I fell exhausted close to Yvonnec, whose icy cold hand chilled mine.

I remained in a comatose state for some time, when the entrance of some water in my helmet revived me sufficiently for me to understand that, by staying where I was with my diver's dress on, I should incur a danger of being drowned. So I dragged myself near to the door of our first place of confinement. It was lucky I moved in this direction, for, if I had gone towards the ladder down which the water was just now flowing back into our compartment, I could not have well escaped being overwhelmed, weighted as I was. Poor Yvonnec! He rolled into the pool formed by the wave that swept from one end of the engine-room to the other. The *Dragonfly* was going see-saw once more, and was assuming the position again which it had when its screws revolved in the upper air. But this time the change was not caused by the boat's unstable equilibrium. There was some outside traction being exercised upon the craft by the saviors, who had at length discovered us.

The salvage had commenced. Gradually the floor tilted and I felt myself slipping. We were being hauled from the stern. The vibration of the chains dragging us intermittently was quite perceptible. How I hoped the chains would not break! My slipping continued. If I were to roll on the opposite side, where the water was deep, I should certainly perish. My fingers clutched at the ironwork, seeking something to hold by. There was the engine, and I could grip the dynamo and lean against it. But I feared to approach it, just as if it had been in motion. As I still groped, my hand encountered the edge of the door of the tube-compartment. The door itself was open. There I stood while the tilting of the boat yet increased. As the minutes went by my brain grew heavier and heavier. The helmet seemed to be a mass of lead. However, my desire to live, the ascending movement, and the encouragement afforded me by the unfastening of the torpedo-room door prevented me from giving way altogether. The slant of the boat was now very considerable; I could scarcely maintain my hold; my fingers grew stiff. My leaden soles seemed to be demons that were pulling me down. Finding my position untenable, I made a supreme effort and scrambled over the raised door-sill. Now I was in the torpedo-room itself. If only I could keep against the wall, I should be saved—saved on condition help was forthcoming soon, for I was breathing in an atmosphere that felt like fire, and I thought of the oxygen and Jaubert's saying: Death and Life.

Another scramble and I was sheltered behind the partition. I sank down with outstretched arms, and my hand touched a bare, moist skin. Quickly I withdrew from the contact; what I had touched was alive, and who besides myself would be alive in this sepulcher? It could not be Yvonnec; I had left him yonder, and, since the *Dragonfly* had accentuated its slant, he must be at the bottom of the water. I touched the skin again. It was warm, though wet. The sensation I experienced was utterly different from that produced by the icy cold hand I had held a while before.

I doubted so little then that it was the hand of a corpse that the thought did not occur to me to feel the face and ascertain the identity of the corpse. Indeed, I was convinced it could only be that of my companion. At present a glimmer of hope loomed in my mind. I must make sure. I advanced a little further. Now I could reach the face. The face and beard were those of a living man; and they belonged to Yvonnec. I could not be mistaken. The heart was beating too. So I was not alone to be saved after all. The discovery electrified me.

Soon I was doubly sure of my joy, for on the little finger of my faithful companion's hand I came across the ring— Annaïc's ring of which he had so often spoken to me. I called him by his name, but my voice did not carry. Its sound was scarcely perceptible to me. Gladly I would have pressed him to my heart, but we were separated by the heavy diving-dress, and all I could do was to press his hand, and the wrist, beneath which I could distinguish the pulse beating, though feebly.

And whose was the icy cold hand? It must have been that of Niclaus or of Renaut. In the see-saw of the boat one of the two bodies had evidently fallen through the trap, with the water, and remained at the foot of the ladder. Which of the two it was I have never been able to learn.

I was content from this moment to await the end of the salvage operations. Yvonnec was only in a swoon, and would probably not be too seriously affected by a little longer delay.

Ah! Now some one was knocking at the extremity of our compartment, near the orifice of the torpedo-tube. The noise of the blows was different from that made by the diver previously. The steel quivered, and those who were striking must be in the upper air. So the stern of the *Dragonfly* was out of the water. I replied to the knocks with my helmet again, but feebly, for I was too sore to do much.

Distinctly I could hear chains creaking, files sawing, hammers smiting. I even thought I heard voices, like a far-off murmur, and an unspeakable emotion took possession of me. I pressed Yvonnec's hand more firmly. I yearned for him to recover consciousness, so that he might share this happiness.

Suddenly there was an explosion close to us, not that of firing reverberating and dying away in the distance, but the lashing, whip-like detonation of a melinite cartridge breaking something on the spot. The whole compartment shook. How I dreaded the chains might snap and let us fall down below the surface once more!

At last a human voice pierced our obscurity—the first voice from the outside world since our disappearance beneath the sea six days before. A message fell into the silence of our funereal abode. Ah! It was sweet to listen to.

"*Courage! Who are you? How many are there of you?*"

It was the loud-speaking telephone working. A diver had found the telephone buoy still hanging on the turret and fastened, although the Commander had tried to switch it off. And to the buoy the diver had attached the wires of the apparatus, so that I was able to communicate with the outside world. If only the buoy had gone up to the surface six days sooner, and we could have spoken to someone above, what anguish would have been spared us! We should have known where the engine was driving us, and indications might have been given us as to the steering and other particulars.

"*Courage!*" repeated the voice. Echoed by all the receivers in the boat, and addressing thus so many corpses, the word seemed almost ironical. The dead ones could not hear it, and I, who heard, strove in vain to speak loud enough to send my message back. I wanted to say: "We are two. Make haste!"

I articulated the words. I turned my head as far as I could in the helmet so that my words might issue through the broken windows. But, as I afterwards learnt, no one caught what I said. The voice went on:

"*Can you open the shutter of the torpedo-tube?*"

I understood. The explosion had blown off the outside cap, and the only thing needed now was to undo the inside lid. We alone could perform this task.

At the same moment blows were struck on the inside of the tube; then on the shutter itself. A man was there waiting. We were separated from him, and from the light of Heaven, from our friends, and from all those dear to us, by the thickness of this inside lid. Immediately I recovered an energy I should have deemed myself, an instant before, incapable of manifesting. I forced myself to the tube, guided by the blows, and seized the handle of the shutter. Happily I knew what was required. I had to turn the lever a sixth round after raising it. It was seeing Yvonnec that taught me. Several tries were necessary, for my arms refused to bend. I was lying on my stomach. So placed, I buttressed myself between the Jaubert cylinders and thus completed the task.

The shutter was open—open to this extent, that the screws and grooved parts were disengaged from their bed; but it did not come away and could not come away, because an enormous force pressed it against the hind or outer portion of the tube—the same force of pressure which had intruded itself everywhere during our confinement.

I know now what happened while I was up there in the conning-tower, and an explanation will not be out of place here.

At the moment when the shutter refused to come away from its bed we were subjected to a pressure not merely of 37 pounds, as in the engine-room, but of 52 pounds. This was caused by the re-establishment of communications between the engine-room and the torpedo compartment. The communication had become possible through a piece of forgetfulness on the part of Yvonnec, who, wishing to renew our oxygen when breathing had become difficult, had opened the hole in the wall and neglected to plug it again. Absorbed by my second visit to the conning-tower, and also puzzled by my silence, he had not thought to put in the plug-screw again.

When the quickening of his breathing revealed to him the danger, the poor fellow tried to repair his mistake; but, being caught by the fly-wheel, he was flung violently against the door of the compartment and lost the end of the tube that sent air into my helmet. But, just when this accident occurred, a balance of pressure existed between the two rooms, and the door, not being fastened by the nuts and bolts, opened of itself, which circumstance saved my companion, for, if the door had resisted, he would have been killed by the impact. Happily, too, his head did not strike the metal; but the violence of the shock reopened the wound in his forehead, and the loss of blood that ensued was the cause of his prolonged swoon.

However, the brusque transference of the Breton from one compartment to the other had consequences much more serious. The weight thus displaced, though not in itself very considerable, caused the see-saw from stern to prow which threatened our chances of deliverance. It appears from the diver's reports that the *Dragonfly* had got wedged in between two upright pillars of stonework joined at their base by a narrow wall. After three successive jolts the boat came to a standstill, almost amidships, on this wall, with a slant that required very little to alter the balance. When Yvonnec was projected into the torpedo-room, the screws that were revolving in the upper air close to the surface re-entered the water, and, the equilibrium being modified, the stein began to sink, slowly at first, then more quickly as the water rushed from the engine-room into the torpedo-room, deluging my poor companion, but yet not covering him.

Notwithstanding the turning of the screws in the water after this change, the *Dragonfly* was not able to quit the spot, being held by the bulging portion of the boat's sides where the safety leads were fastened. So these leads, which had failed to do their duty at the moment of the initial accident, played, nevertheless, a very important part at the time of the salvage, for, if the boat had left the spot where it was perceived by those above the water, who knows whether we should have been saved alive!

On discovering that the shutter did not come away, my anxiety was great, as may be imagined. The oxygen was burning our lungs, and I feared Yvonnec might never recover consciousness. Our chances of survival depended largely on the rapidity with which we were conveyed to the upper air. The rescuers of the boat must be aware of someone's being alive, since I had replied to their signals by knocking; and I wondered, as the time slipped away, why no further attempt was made from the outside to communicate with me. Perhaps, as they did not dare to blow the shutter in with melinite, on account of the danger to us inside, they had sent for other instruments and tools to La Goulette, their nearest station.

My impatience increased. I bent over Yvonnec, I called him, felt his pulse, the temperature of his body, and my helplessness affected me keenly. Meanwhile the telephone had spoken several times, and I had replied with slight taps on the wall with my helmet. Once or twice I tried to raise my voice, but evidently the sound did not carry far enough, for the same questions were repeated each time.

The resumption of operations was revealed to me by sharp and powerful blows struck from the interior of the tube on the shutter. They were dealt, as I learnt afterwards, by a heavy piece of wood worked by ropes, which had been fetched from La Goulette, and was being used as a battering ram. The blows followed each other regularly, and their force was augmented continually. Evidently before long the shutter would yield beneath the attack. As I was thinking of what would happen when the successful blow should be struck, a reminiscence of what I had read in the naval lieutenant Delpeuth's book, *The History of Submarines,* flashed across my mind.

Bauer, the inventor of the first submarine, was experimenting with his *Diabolus* in the Cronstadt roads in 1856, when he ventured to let out his compressed air suddenly, after forcing it up to the highest pressure. The consequences were serious. So great a change without gradual preparation prostrated his sailors, and two of them nearly died.

I asked myself what would be the result for us, and for poor Yvonnec especially in his condition, if we should be as unexpectedly changed from our present pressure to one that was very much lower. The high pressure in our lungs would dilate our chests when there was no corresponding pressure outside and around us, and a rupture might ensue.

At any cost I must prevent such an accident; I must speak, I must make myself heard.

With a fresh knock against the shutter I broke the front piece of glass in my helmet, cutting myself on the lip and cheek, but not feeling the wounds. I shouted again and again: "Stop!" No one heard.

Then I seized one of the ear-nuts that fixed the helmet to the neck-piece of my dress. It yielded, and I unscrewed it. Necessity multiplied my strength; I undid three more screws in the same way. Afterwards I thrust my fingers into the joinings of the neck-piece, used them as levers, and the back-nuts came loose in their turn.

Throwing off the helmet, I called in a loud, hoarse tone:
"Stop!"

This time I was heard; the blows ceased, and through the telephone the question was asked:

"Who are you?"

"An officer, the only survivor, with a sailor who is in a swoon."

"Courage I we shall soon be with you through the torpedo-tube."

"Yes, I understand. But the pressure of air is here so great that there must be no sudden transition. We should not be able to support it."

There was a pause. I heard voices. The leaders were discussing. Ultimately the same voice continued:

"You are right. We will first of all bore a hole in the hull, so that the two pressures may be equalized a little."

"Shall you be long? My companion's condition is critical."

"A few minutes only; we have the necessary tools. Have you any light?"

"No."

"Courage!"

"Have you got the boat safely? Can it fall back again?"

"You need not be afraid. It cannot fall back; the stern is resting on a dock which has just arrived."

"Who is speaking to me?"

"Admiral Boehme, of Bizerte, who sends you his heartiest greetings, and has thought only of you for the last six days."

"Thank you, Admiral. Our hopes are all in you."

"A naval lieutenant who is by my side and hears you speak does not recognize your voice as belonging to any officer of the *Dragonfly*... Are you an officer?"

"Yes, but an officer in the army, a captain, professor at Saint-Cyr!"

An exclamation was the only reply I received this time. I could conceive every one's astonishment. No one knew of my escapade. At Tunis my presence with Commander d'Elbée might have been noticed, since I had dined with him at the Grand Hotel; but, as I was not in uniform, no one had paid attention to me. It was a revelation, therefore, to everyone to hear of my being on board, and especially to hear of a soldier being practically the sole survivor.

The conversation had exhausted me. I leaned against the Jaubert apparatus, determined to wait for the decisive moment without stirring. Above my head I heard the sawing of a file, then violent blows that shook the iron. In order to save time a chisel was being used. At last the opening was made and the chisel was withdrawn. The oxygenated air rushed out and a ray of light entered our prison. How welcome it was! It streamed across our darkness, was reflected from the polished steel of the tube, and struck on the opposite wall. Our dungeon was rendered light enough to see in. Yvonnec's body appeared to me doubled up, with smears of blood and dirt; but his chest heaved; he was alive. I called him again.

"Yvonnec. Wake up. Look, my friend. Awake!"

But the poor fellow lay motionless, unable to enjoy, like me, the first vision of sunlight, the life-giving sunlight of the globe. I had never till then appreciated the significance of sun-worship. At present I forgot my fatigue, my hunger and thirst, my sufferings. I wanted to sing, to dance; I was mad with joy.

But a strange sensation diverted my thoughts. I seemed to be swelling all over. The blood rushed to my feet, hands, and face. I tingled in all my limbs. I was experiencing what Bonvalot the explorer, who has climbed to heights of 20,000 feet, once described to me as the mountain malady; only now it was increased by the difference of pressure. I did not know what was the matter with me. My eyes grew heavy and dim; I wanted to close them.

At this moment the shutter opened quite, and I saw a hand with an electric bulb which lighted up the compartment. Following the hand came the head of a naval lieutenant, his face, beneath the cap, exhibiting resolution mingled with anxiety. His first words were:

"Where is the Commander ?"

"Dead... in the conning-tower! Be quick and take us out of here."

"Dead! Are you sure?"

"I have seen him!"

"Excuse me! He was my nearest friend!"

And his faltering voice revealed to me his profound grief. At once, however, he busied himself with the task of freeing me from the remainder of the diver's dress. He cut it down from the top with a knife so as to be the quicker, and uttered an exclamation of astonishment when he saw more than 30 liters of water drop from it. A sailor came and helped to take off the pieces. He had just entered by the tube, and carried ropes with him.

An exclamation escaped him at the spectacle I presented with my blood-stained head and body.

"Are you suffering much?" asked the lieutenant.

My brain was in a whirl, but, amid the chaos, one thought dominated me. I pointed to Yvonnec.

"Him first!" I cried.

His life hung on a thread; the swoon persisting frightened me.

"Him first, I beg," was my repeated recommendation.

A rope was passed under the quartermaster's arms, and the sailor introduced him head-first into the tube. There was some difficulty in straightening his legs, which were stiff and bent. At last Yvonnec disappeared... *towards the light*... the light which now flooded our prison through the tube.

Ah! This torpedo-tube! It was just six days since my companion had said to me:

"If you like, Captain, I will send you off through there."

Six days before, I had imagined the mad plan of escaping through the tube; mad because of the insurmountable obstacles which I did not realize until later. And yet it was through this tube that we issued from our tomb. And Yvonnec went out first.

Now it was my turn. The blinding light made me close my eyes. I felt my senses leaving me. My emotions were too overwhelming. I was conscious of being pushed and pulled, conscious of the open air, the sea breeze caressing me, an admiral's cap bent over me, sympathetic faces crowding round the ambulance on which I was placed. I heard also someone say:

"Poor fellow! He has turned white!"

And everything turned round, everything grew misty, and I went to rejoin Yvonnec in the world of insensibility and unconsciousness.

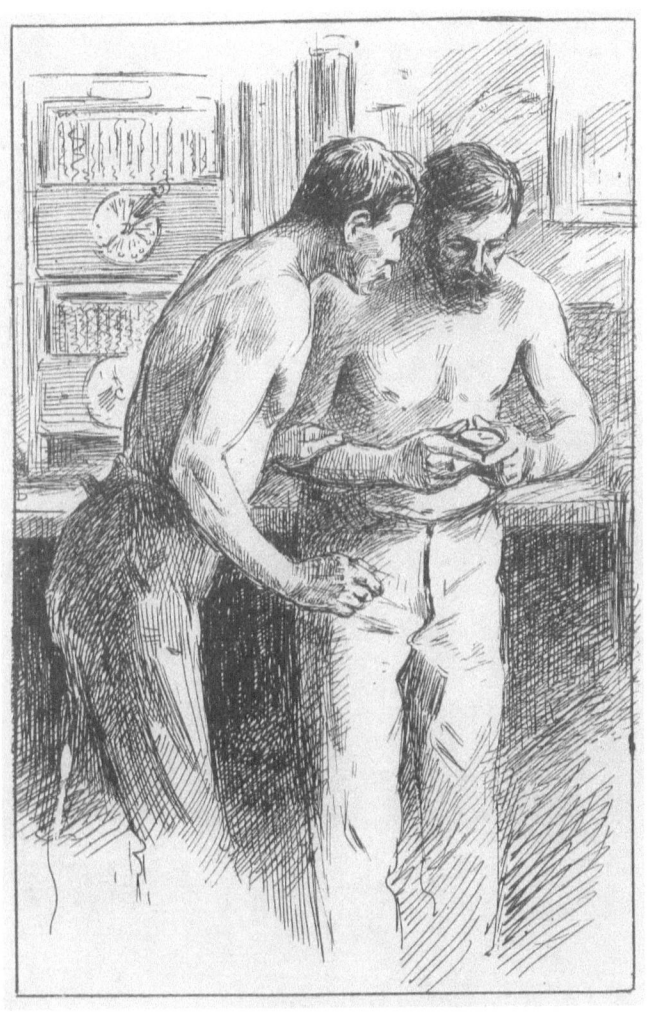

EPILOGUE
AT THE VILLA MARIE-THÉRÈSE

I opened my eyes in a pretty room papered blue, where the light was shaded so as not to hurt the sight, and flowers were in abundance. I closed my eyes again almost immediately, wondering for a few seconds whether I were not the victim of an hallucination.

But soon the thick mental fog which for two days and a night had kept me in an almost lethargic slumber, was rent. I remembered my coming out of the *Dragonfly,* the dazzling light as I issued from the tube, and I ventured to look out once more on the place where I was, with sensations as sweet as any I had ever experienced. The moment after, I had a shock. A glance in a mirror informed me of the truth of what I had heard said as I was carried out of the boat. My hair had become white during the long submarine night.

I had often accused novelists of exaggerating when they related that their heroes, under the influence of extraordinary emotions, had suffered this bleaching of the hair. I had to acknowledge now that in asserting this they were not going beyond fact.

Just as I raised myself on my pillow, restored to my full senses, the door was quietly pushed ajar, and I perceived a girl's graceful figure. She was not more than 16, and had large, brown, expressive eyes with long lashes, a well-formed forehead, over which hung a few stray threads of her mass of brown hair, a fairy shape, and charm in each of her movements. At once I guessed she must be the same that I had seen from the deck of the submarine. Behind her was the wide-awake, inquisitive face of a boy between 14 and 15, as blond as his sister was brown. He was clad in a sailor costume. Both had certainly been watching for my awakening, for they uttered a cry of joy and disappeared. A military doctor came in a minute later.

"Well, my dear comrade, you must have had arrears of sleep to pay off. Now I dare say your stomach is crying out. We will try to satisfy your hunger first; and then there will be your lungs to see to, for you have had an overdose of oxygen. Ah! There's no fever, I'm glad to find. And your tongue is not bad... You will get of easily. You are the more fortunate of the two."

Squeezing my hand, he walked to another bed, where I had as yet remarked no one, the head on the pillow there being swathed up. It was Yvonnec. My dearest wish had been anticipated in their not separating us. Anxiously I questioned the doctor with my gaze.

"He will pull through also," replied the doctor. "But if he had remained two hours longer without aid he would not have recovered. He has lost a good deal of blood; but at his age wounds are easy to cure, especially those in the head. He will have to wait a fortnight before being able to go off home on sick-leave. As for you, you will be on your legs tomorrow."

"Shall I find a boat starting for France?"

"Not tomorrow, but on Saturday."

"What day is it today?"

"Wednesday."

"And on what day were we taken out of the *Dragonfly?*"

"On Monday, at 10 a.m."

"Have I been asleep since then?"

"Yes; I was even thinking I should have a communication to make on your case to the Academy of Medicine."

We had embarked on the Tuesday of the preceding week at 6 p.m. We had, therefore, spent six days and 16 hours in the shipwrecked submarine. This, it appears, is a record. All I can say is, I hope no one will beat it.

I shall not try to describe the hours that followed between Yvonnec and myself, nor yet the manifestations of sympathy that reached us from everywhere, the attention of our host and hostess and their kindly solicitude about us.

Captain D***, the owner of the Villa, happened to belong to my old regiment, the 4th Zouaves. His wife was a delightful woman, who showed herself the most devoted of nurses. Both insisted on our being carried to their house on the day the boat was salved, since they wished to spare us the long journey from Carthage to the Belvedere infirmary. Their hospitality during the few days I stayed in the Villa Marie-Therese is one of my most precious memories.

My first care was to send news to my wife. Ignorant of what she might have heard about my adventure in the heart of the country, where she was living and awaiting my return, I simply telegraphed that I should be with her soon, and I reserved my explanations until I should see her.

Within a couple of days I had got back my strength and appetite; and all that remained with me of the past was the recurrence of its experiences in dreams and nightmares of which I did not get rid for some time. As for Yvonnec, he too mended rapidly. On the Friday he was carried on an invalid chair, at the time of the sea breeze, to a small pillared belvedere which I had noticed when we were out at sea as being a prolongation of the Villa colonnade.

On that day Lieutenant Duval had come from Bizerte. Deputed by the Minister of Marine to inquire into the causes of the accident, he had spent two hours with us, taking notes, setting down our replies, and reconstituting all the phases of the accident and the salvage.

In the evening, before dinner, we were all together on the very terrace where Marie-Therese had appeared to me. It was the hour when, ten days before, we had exchanged the farewell greeting which had played such an important role in our lives, and I had induced the young lady to promise that, in front of the Gulf spread out before us, she would tell us the story of the share which, it appeared, she had had in our deliverance.

The air was pure and calm, the sky of a deep blue, the sea shimmering and azure-tinted. At our feet the Cothon and merchant Port of Dido's city looked like two small pools that

211

the Mediterranean had left there in forgetfulness. From the excavations of the Forum studding the stony soil at the bottom of the hill, my gaze wandered to the ruins of the Quay, then beyond, as far as the buried temple whose ruins were visible only to my mind's eye and whose mysterious apparition had awaked in me, in spite of my critical circumstances, such powerful emotions. The others present instinctively turned their faces in the same direction as my own, and, for a few moments, a profound silence hovered over this evocation of our submarine tragedy.

The daughter of the house at last broke it at a sign from her mother. She began to relate what she had to say simply, but grew more animated as her story took possession of her.

She had been much impressed by the sight of our boat. Its turret alone visible above the surface and gliding on the waves; the good-bye exchanged with an unknown person just about to descend into the depths over which the shades of night were settling; the lugubrious accidents that had happened to the *Farfadet* and *Lutin,* of which she had heard a good deal, since they had occurred off Tunis; and then the boat's disappearance, which she had watched through a pair of opera-glasses, all these things had excited her youthful mind and prevented her from sleeping.

"So you may judge," she said with her big eyes still exhibiting traces of dread, "what a blow I received when the first rumors of your disappearance reached us from Bizerte, and especially when the news of the shipwreck was confirmed."

"When was it known, mademoiselle?"

"On the Wednesday evening. It was no longer possible to have any doubt, for the *Dragonfly* had not returned to Bizerte, and the worst of all was that nobody knew where to search for you. I could only say to the naval officers who came to the Villa that I had seen you pass by and go down over there. Throughout the night lights traversed the Gulf in every part; and, during the days that followed, crowds of small boats and a number of torpedo boats with them continued to scour the sea."

"My daughter remained on the look-out all the time," interrupted Madame D***. "Every day she came here at dawn, fancying that, if the submarine came up to the surface, she should be the first to perceive it, as she had been the last to see it disappear.

"It was a presentiment," I murmured.

"On the fifth day," said the Captain in his turn, "she came to us in tears. The search had ceased, or rather had been transferred to Bizerte. The soundings had been abandoned here, and not a boat remained in the Gulf."

"Yet we were over there on the Sunday," I replied, looking away towards the steep promontory of Ras-Durdas, which seemed in the misty distance like the step of a gigantic staircase.

"They went there," said the naval lieutenant. "But it would have been a miraculous piece of luck to hit just on that small point buried more than 50 fathoms deep."

So the search had been abandoned; and if, thanks to Yvonnec's happy thought, we had not set the engine going again, there would have been no deliverance; we should have been still over there, and the *Dragonfly*, buried with two extra corpses, would have been entered on the list of vessels lost with all on board, like the *Semillante* and the *Vienne*.

"The recovery of the *Dragonfly*," I said to the Lieutenant, "France owes to this brave fellow here, for I went up into the conning-tower before he did, yet I did not think of turning the handle controlling the engine."

"It's a gift of more than a couple of million francs you have made to the country, my brave comrade," said the Lieutenant to the Breton. "In England, you would receive a tenth or even a fifth of this sum as a present in return."

"Which would help on the marriage with Annaïc finely," I whispered to my friend as I leaned over to him.

He smiled and his pale cheeks flushed slightly.

"And what reward is he likely to have from us?" asked Madame D***.

"The military medal with a pension of 100 francs, or, at most, the cross of the Legion of Honor with 250 francs."

"About as much as is given to reward services in an election."

The conversation was drifting, so Madame D*** nodded to her daughter to continue.

"I was wretched all day on Sunday," resumed Marie-Therese, "on account of the search being abandoned; and on Monday morning I had come up here, after hardly sleeping all night. The Sun had just risen above the cliffs. It was about 4 p.m., and the sea was as smooth as glass. There was not a sail on the Gulf, nor the least noise on the ruins of Carthage. I was gazing at the place where the turret had disappeared when a peculiar noise, something like what you hear on board a liner when she is going to start, made me suddenly turn. Looking in the direction where this noise seemed to be coming out of the sea, I remarked, somewhat to the right, nearly opposite the ports, two black specks which were certainly not there a minute before."

She rose and pointed with her finger.

"It was there!"

Her voice was choked with emotion. And I myself passed once more through the hopes and fears of that moment when the noise of the screw struck on our ears.

"I was sure," continued Marie-Therese, "that what I saw was the *Dragonfly* showing its wings above the water. I went and waked up my parents; and, while my father posted off on his bicycle to tell them at La Goulette, for the telephone was not working at that early hour, I got my brother to jump with me into our little dinghy that you see over there moored by the ports."

"Without telling me," interrupted Madame D*** in tones of tender reproach.

"Yes, mother, I was afraid of being forbidden, though often enough George and I go a row as far as Bou-Said, when the sea is calm. How excited we were when we came near! It was certainly the *Dragonfly*. There could be no doubt about the matter. But how it came there was a mystery. We wondered whether it had been wandering about for the last six days, and whether it might not again disappear on its vagabond course. Especially, we wondered if there were people alive in the boat! We approached still nearer. The screws were turning at a terrific speed, not more than half a yard out of the water. Twenty yards away we could feel their whirling in the air. George was afraid that, if we went closer, we should be caught by one of the screws. But I had just seen something like a ring or hook on the surface of the sea. I had an idea in my head. I induced my brother to row nearer, and, as he rows very well, to keep the stern of our little boat so as to allow me to reach this hook."

"How far was the hook from the screws, mademoiselle?" I asked.

"About a yard."

"It was very imprudent," said Madame D***.

"A slip of the oar, and the boat would have been caught and smashed, and no one there to save them."

"I had brought a ball of string belonging to the kite of my little brothers Ralph and Robert," continued Marie-Therese. "I tied the end of the string to this hook, and then George rowed us away, with the string unwinding as we went. When we were at the other end of the string, a distance of about 50 yards, I fixed one of the seats of the boat in a noose of the last foot or two of string and threw the seat into the water."

"An hour after, when I came back from La Goulette," interrupted Captain D***, "there was no trace of the screws to be seen; but the motor-launch of the harbor captain, which arrived at the same time as myself, found the boat-seat floating at the place where the screws had emerged. Owing to my daughter's lucky thought, the diver who had come on the launch found the *Dragonfly* without needing to make a long search."

"By this means also, mademoiselle," I said, taking her hand, which she held out to me, "you saved us some hours, perhaps a night's longer waiting; and, in fact, you saved

Yvonnec's life. We owe you a debt of gratitude difficult to repay."

"I should like to offer you something, mademoiselle," said the quartermaster. And he held out his chaplet.

"You could not offer me anything I should prize more," she answered, accepting the present. "I will never part with it."

The next day was fixed for my departure and return to France. In the morning I had renewed my wardrobe, received visits from some comrades of the 4th Zouaves, and replied to further questions put to me by the naval lieutenant sent from the Admiralty.

Another visitor was Father Delattre, the Superior of Saint-Louis of Carthage. We were old acquaintances, and our greeting was a warm one. However, the archaeologist insisted on a hearing after the friend.

"I am told you saw some ruins, some pillars under the water," he said.

"As clearly as I see you," I replied.

"Columns of what order?"

"That I should want to ask you... Look, here is pretty much the form they had."

And I sketched a capital as nearly as I could like the one I had seen outside the conning-tower.

"Why, it's a mixture of Egyptian and Hindu," he cried. "That tells me nothing. What sort of inscription was there? Try to give me some idea on this piece of paper."

I attempted to draw, but in vain. My designs were a jumble of Egyptian, Arabic, and Chaldean hieroglyphics.

"What was about the depth?" asked the Father.

"Three or four fathoms."

"Ah! If only I had been in your place!"

I looked at my visitor, half astonished, half amused. He was quite serious.

"Could you see clearly at that depth?" he inquired.

"Yes, when the sea is calm and the Sun up, anybody can see as low down."

216

"Well! I will borrow a diver's dress and will make the descent myself."

The reverend father said this deliberately and quite in earnest, and I knew he meant to carry out his intention.

At 2 p.m., just as I was about to quit the Villa, and to embark, after cordially thanking our hosts and insisting for the tenth time on Yvonnec's promising that he would come and visit me at Saint-Cyr as soon as he had been home, I was delayed by the arrival of Admiral Boehme, who had come over from Bizerte in company with a naval captain and his own aide-de-camp. All three were in full uniform.

"I am glad to find you still here, Captain," he said; "first, because it affords me an opportunity of renewing to you my expression of affectionate esteem, and next because your presence will add to the value of what I have brought for this brave quartermaster. The telegram from the Ministry awarding him his cross of the Legion of Honor reached me only this morning, and I posted off in my motor-car so as not to lose a minute."

"The reward will help to put him on his legs again," added the naval captain.

When, after the ceremony had been performed in the midst of the hosts and guests of the Villa, and the cross had been pinned on the new coat of the invalid as he lay, I saw Yvonnec's tears roll down his cheeks, I felt myself overcome by an emotion which I neither was able nor wished to restrain.

"As for you, Captain," continued the Admiral, as he finished the ceremony by kissing the new chevalier on the two cheeks, "the Minister for War will decide. My report starts with Duval, who will travel by the same boat as yourself, and I need hardly tell you that I especially mention the share you have had in this extraordinary salvage."

"Oh! Admiral, I expect I shall get 30 days' confinement from my Minister, as soon as I return to Saint-Cyr."

The Port Admiral smiled.

"In reality you have done something to deserve them," he said; "but I fancy, all the same, the Minister will overlook the disobedience connected with your clandestine trip in the *Dragonfly*, and will remember only the circumstances connected with your leaving the submarine."

"And our poor *Dragonfly*, Admiral?"

"Has received no other damage than the breach which caused the catastrophe, so that she will be able to go to sea again within a month. I accompanied the tug which took her back to Bizerte the day before yesterday, and she is at present in the docks. What an affecting sight was the opening of the flooded compartments!"

I pass over the lugubrious details given us by Admiral Boehme, as also over the description of the ghastly spectacle presented by the crew's quarters, where 23 men were assembled for their evening meal when the accident occurred. There is one detail, however, which has its importance for the reader of this narrative; it refers to the sounds we heard on the third day, and which ceased on the fourth.

Who was the survivor that had escaped drowning at first, and how had he ultimately succumbed?

The results furnished by the inquiry, and more especially by certain post-mortem examinations carried out by the naval authorities, cleared up these points. The other survivor was the master cook. He also had taken the precaution to shut out the invading sea-water, and was alone in his compartment with plenty of fresh water, provisions in abundance, and had very little sea-water on the floor of his cabin. It was the oxylith which had caused his death, whereas it ought to have saved his life. He was familiar with the handling of the Jaubert apparatus; but he was ignorant of the danger run in breathing oxygen in too large doses. He must have allowed the oxylith to escape carelessly, for his lungs were shriveled and dried up, just as if they had been exposed to the action of fire.

"None the less, Admiral," I said by way of conclusion, "but for the Jaubert apparatus Yvonnec and I should have been asphyxiated on the third or fourth day, and then the *Dragonfly* would never have been recovered."

"And you may be sure, my young comrade," answered the Admiral, "that your hard experiment will not have been made in vain. It is a final one, and will settle once for all the question submitted to the naval committee of inquiry."

On board the *Ville-de-Rome,* as we were steaming towards Marseilles, Lieutenant Duval gave me the solution of the important problem which had several times engaged my attention during my submarine confinement. What I had not been able to explain was that we had succeeded in unconsciously driving the water out of the engine-room, although the depth of the submarine's immersion was 30 fathoms, and the outside pressure of the boat must have consequently been between 75 and 90 pounds.

The reason was the following. The *Dragonfly* had been struck by the keel of some passing vessel, and the front compartment, which had been pierced, was one of those padded with cellulose. The hole made was a triangular one about four feet long and two feet wide. As the cellulose did not act immediately, the water at once flooded the fore part of the submarine and some compartments in the stern. When at last the swelling of the cellulose stopped the breach, it was too late; the boat had sunk to the bottom of the sea. But this obstruction did allow the automatic door of the damaged compartment to close, thus cutting off communication between the outside pressure of the sea and the pressure we had the means of using inside, through the oxygen and compressed air.

To the closing of this door, therefore, we were partly indebted for our preservation. Among all the life-saving instruments on board, this one alone did its own work.

When I reached the Hermitage, a small country residence, quiet and surrounded with verdure, where my family were expecting me, my wife had just been informed by some friends that I had been in the *Dragonfly* and was one of the two survivors from the accident. Already she had learnt the details of the catastrophe, and had been painfully affected by them, but she had, of course, no idea that her husband was concerned in them, so that she had not to suffer any anxiety about me, being apprised at once of my share in the tragedy and of my deliverance. I may be excused for not dwelling on the joy of our meeting, all the keener on my side as I had abandoned the hope of ever seeing my dear ones again.

The cross of the Legion of Honor, which was conferred on me a few days later, showed me in what eulogistic terms the Port Admiral of Bizerte must have spoken of my conduct. Better than anyone I knew that I had not altogether deserved this distinction, since at first I had failed in courage and energy when brought face to face with death. Anyway, I had escaped, and unfortunately only those that escape can be rewarded. The motive of the award was set down as "my helping to save one of the country's vessels." "A premium offered to disobedience," wrote Admiral Boehme jokingly, when sending me his congratulations. "But," he added, "don't try the thing again. Your description has been given to all the commanders of submarine and submersible boats." Try the thing again! Indeed I have no wish to!

Sometime after these events, I made a pilgrimage to Carthage with my family, and my daughter and Marie-Therese became great friends. On our return to France, we stopped at Larmor in order to be present at Yvonnec's wedding. Indeed, I was his best man.

From all parts of Brittany people came to the little church venerated by fishermen to rejoice at the happiness of him who had returned from the depths of the sea. Annaïc was just the sort of naive, fresh-looking Breton girl that would make a suitable wife for this fine but still delicate husband. He wore proudly the gold stripe given to him in presence of all his sailor comrades on his return from his sick-leave, and proudly also the red ribbon of the Legion of Honor, a rare decoration on a simple sailor's jacket. But the admiration he excited among all the spectators reached its maximum when it was known that he was to re-embark on the *Dragonfly,* now seaworthy again, as assistant sailing-master.

I congratulated my friend on this fresh proof of his courage; for in the boat everything must at each instant remind him of the possibility of an accident. Before I left him it was settled that, if he had a boy as his first child, the little one should be called Jack, in souvenir of the late commander of the *Dragonfly,* and that I and Marie-Therese were to be godfather and godmother.

When Jacques d'Elbée's young wife had the news of her husband's having perished broken to her, she was seized with a brain fever which kept her for a month between life and death. I was therefore compelled to delay my visit to her for the purpose of acquitting myself of the vow that I had made. Nor did I go until I was summoned by a message from her, for I feared that something or other I might say would cause a relapse.

In her mourning garments, rendered all the more striking by her blond hair, and, with her two little boys of eight and five by her side, she looked like a veritable *Mater Dolorosa.* She was aware of my reasons for hesitating to call on her, and reassured me, as she offered me her thin hand.

"The first shock nearly killed me," she said. "I loved him so much. But today, having reflected, I feel stronger. If Jacques had died in battle I should have been proud of him. I should have held out his example to my boys, and should have wished to rear them with thoughts of a like readiness to sacrifice themselves. And I ask myself if his death is not, after all, a death in battle."

"You are right, Madame," I replied. "The struggle of the submarine with the sea is a real battle, more terrible than any fought under the open sky and Sun. And in this battle your husband died as a hero, having done everything required of him by his duty."

"I was told... you found him... in his conning-tower... before the salvage," she said, sobbing.

I paused before answering.

"Speak, I beg of you," she continued. "Speak of him, and do not be afraid for the children. They bear his name, and can hear all."

With a voice that quivered in spite of myself, I went through the painful story; then, presenting to the young widow the gold ring I had taken from Jacques' finger at the dread moment when I stumbled against his corpse in the darkness, I said:

"His spirit should be near us at this instant, Madame. I promised him that, if I were saved, I would hand you this sacred souvenir and would love his children as my own."

She thanked me amidst her grief, and pushed her two boys into my arms.

"Sir," said the elder one, with a movement of his fingers that thrust back his long brown curls, "I intend to be a sailor like father."

Life of the sailor, life of discipline, devotion, danger and self-denial! How many times I have admired it, envied those that engage in it! Today, after fathoming the experiences it reserves for men of the sea, I regard it as the finest that exists in the world!

CAPITAINE DANRIT

ROBINSONS
SOUS-MARINS

FLAMMARION

50 Ces le volume illustré.

LA GUERRE
DE DEMAIN
OUVRAGE COURONNÉ
PAR L'ACADÉMIE FRANÇAISE

PAR LE
Capitaine
DANRIT
(Commandant DRIANT)

E. FLAMMARION, Éditeur, 26, Rue Racine, PARIS.

Bibliography

La Guerre de Demain (*The War of Tomorrow*) (4 vols.) (Flammarion)
1. La Guerre de Forteresse (*The War of Fortresses*) (1889-90)
2. La Guerre en Rase Campagne (*War on Open Land*) (1890-91)
3. La Guerre en Ballon (*War in Balloons*) (1891-92)
4. Le Journal de Guerre du Lt. Von Piefke (*Lt. Von Piefke's War Diary*) (1896)

L'Invasion Noire (*The Black Invasion*) (3 vols.) (Flammarion)
1. La Mobilisation Africaine (*The African Mobilization*) (1894)
2. Le Grand Pélerinage à La Mecque (*The Great Pilgrimage to Mecca*) (1895)
3. Fin de l'Islam Devant Paris (*The End of Islam Before Paris*) (1896)'

Histoire d'une Famille de Soldats (*History of a Family of Soldiers*) (3 vols.) (Delagrave) (*non-genre*)
1. Jean Tapin (1898)
2. Filleuls de Napoléon (*Napoleon's Godsons*) (1899)
3. Petit Marsouin (1901)

Ordre du Tzar (*Orders from the Czar*) (Flammarion, 1900) (*non-genre*)

La Guerre Fatale; France-Angleterre (*The Fatal War: France vs. England*) (3 vols.) (Flammarion)
1. À Bizerte (*To Bizerte*) (1901)
2. En Sous-Marin (*On A Sub-Marine*) (1902)
3. En Angleterre (*In England*) (1902)

Le Drapeau des chasseurs à pied (*The Flag of the Infantry*) (Matot, 1902) (*non-genre*)

Évasion d'Empereur (*The Emperor Escapes*) (*Journal des Voyages*, 1903; Delagrave, 1904; revised Flammarion, 1911)

Si Nous Avions Eu la Guerre (*If We Had A War*) (*Je Sais Tout*, 1905)

L'Invasion Jaune (*The Yellow Invasion*) (3 vols.) (Flammarion)
1. La Mobilisation Sino-Japonaise (*The Sino-Japanese Mobilization*) (1905)
2. Haine de Jaunes (*Yellow Hatred*) (1905)
3. À Travers l'Europe (*Across Europe*) (1906)

Vers un Nouveau Sedan (*Towards a New Sedan*) (Juven, 1906) (*essay*)

Robinsons de l'Air (*Robinsons of the Air*) (Flammarion, 1907; revised as Un Dirigeable au Pôle Nord (*A Dirigible at the North Pole*), Flammarion, 1910)

Robinsons Sous-Marins (*Robinsons Under the Sea*) (Flammarion, 1908)

La Grève de Demain (*The Strike of Tomorrow*) (Tallandier, 1909)

L'Aviateur du Pacifique (*The Aviator of the Pacific*) (Flammarion, 1909)

La Révolution de Demain (*The Revolution of Tomorrow*) (co-written with Arnould Galopin) (Tallandier, 1909)

Les Deux Drapeaux (The Two Flags) (1910) (*poetry*)

L'Alerte (*The Alert*) (Flammarion, 1910)

Au-Dessus du Continent Noir (*Above the Black Continent*) (Flammarion, 1912)

Robinsons Souterrains (*Underground Robinsons*) (Flamma-rion, 1913; revised as La Guerre Souterraine (*The Underground War*), Flammarion, 1915)

Essays on Captain Danrit (in French):

"Le Capitaine Danrit, L'Utopiste de la Guerre" by Jean-Jacques Bridenne in *Fiction* No.25, 1955

Capitaine Danrit on the website *Le Roman d'Aventures* by Matthieu Letourneux:
http://mletourneux.free.fr/auteurs/france/danrit/danrit.htm

Capitaine Danrit entry in Pierre Versins' *Encyclopédie de l'utopie, des voyages extraordinaires et de la science-fiction* (1972).

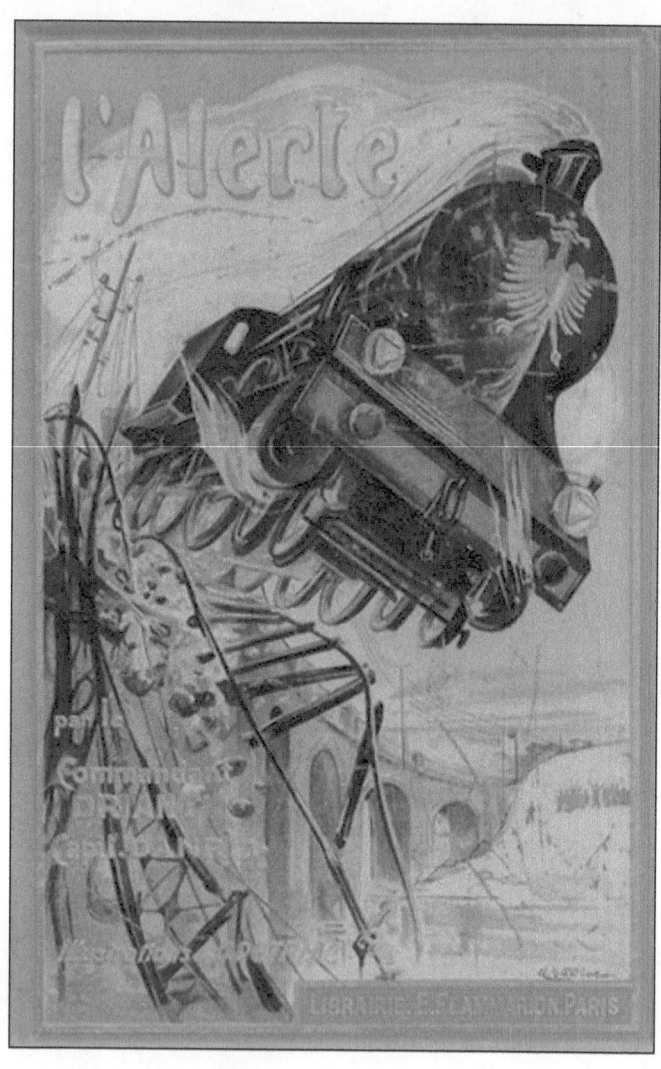

SF & FANTASY

Guy d'Armen. *Doc Ardan: The City of Gold and Lepers*
G.-J. Arnaud. *The Ice Company*
Aloysius Bertrand. *Gaspard de la Nuit*
Richard Bessière. *The Gardens of the Apocalypse*
Félix Bodin. *The Novel of the Future*
André Caroff. *The Terror of Madame Atomos*
Didier de Chousy. *Ignis*
Captain Danrit. *Undersea Odyssey*
C. I. Defontenay. *Star (Psi Cassiopeia)*
Charles Derennes. *The People of the Pole*
Georges Dodds/Paul Wessels (anthologists). *The Missing Link*
Harry Dickson. *The Heir of Dracula*
Jules Dornay. *Lord Ruthven Begins*
Sâr Dubnotal *vs. Jack the Ripper*
Alexandre Dumas. *The Return of Lord Ruthven*
J.-C. Dunyach. *The Night Orchid; The Thieves of Silence*
Henri Duvernois. *The Man Who Found Himself*
Henri Falk. *The Age of Lead*
Paul Féval. *Anne of the Isles; Knightshade; Revenants; Vampire City;
The Vampire Countess; The Wandering Jew's Daughter*
Paul Féval, *fils. Felifax, the Tiger-Man*
Arnould Galopin. *Doctor Omega*
G.L. Gick. *Harry Dickson: The Werewolf of Rutherford Grange*
Nathalie Henneberg. *The Green Gods*
V. Hugo, P. Foucher & P. Meurice. *The Hunchback of Notre-Dame*
Michel Jeury. *Chronolysis*
Octave Joncquel & Theo Varlet. *The Martian Epic*
Gérard Klein. *The Mote in Time's Eye*
Jean de La Hire. *Enter the Nyctalope; The Nyctalope on Mars; The
Nyctalope vs. Lucifer*
André Laurie. *Spiridon*
Georges Le Faure & Henri de Graffigny. *The Extraordinary Adventures of a Russian Scientist Across the Solar System* (2 vols.)
Gustave Le Rouge. *The Vampires of Mars*
Jules Lermina. *Mysteryville; Panic in Paris; To-Ho and the Gold
Destroyers*

Jean-Marc & Randy Lofficier. *Edgar Allan Poe on Mars; The Katrina Protocol; Pacifica; Robonocchio; Tales of the Shadowmen* (anthologists; 7 vols.)
Xavier Mauméjean. *The League of Heroes*
John-Antoine Nau. *Enemy Force*
Marie Nizet. *Captain Vampire*
C. Nodier, A. Beraud & Toussaint-Merle. *Frankenstein*
Henri de Parville. *An Inhabitant of the Planet Mars*
J. Polidori, C. Nodier, E. Scribe. *Lord Ruthven the Vampire*
P.-A. Ponson du Terrail. *The Vampire and the Devil's Son*
Maurice Renard. *The Blue Peril; Doctor Lerne; The Doctored Man;. A Man Among the Microbes; The Master of Light*
Albert Robida. *The Adventures of Saturnin Farandoul; The Clock of the Centuries.*
J.-H. Rosny Aîné. *Helgvor of the Blue River; The Givreuse Enigma; The Mysterious Force; The Navigators of Space; Vamireh; The World of the Variants; The Young Vampire*
Han Ryner. *The Superhumans*
Brian Stableford. *The New Faust at the Tragicomique;The Empire of the Necromancers (The Shadow of Frankenstein; Frankenstein and the Vampire Countess; Frankenstein in London); Sherlock Holmes & The Vampires of Eternity; The Stones of Camelot; The Wayward Muse.* (anthologist) *The Germans on Venus; News from the Moon; The Supreme Progress*
Jacques Spitz. *The Eye of Purgatory*
Kurt Steiner. *Ortog*
Villiers de l'Isle-Adam. *The Scaffold; The Vampire Soul*
Philippe Ward. *Artahe*
Philippe Ward & Sylvie Miller. *The Song of Montségur*

MYSTERIES & THRILLERS

M. Allain & P. Souvestre. *The Daughter of Fantômas*
A. Anicet-Bourgeois, Lucien Dabril. *Rocambole*
A. Bisson & G. Livet. *Nick Carter vs. Fantômas*
V. Darlay & H. de Gorsse. *Lupin vs. Holmes: The Stage Play*
Paul Féval. *Gentlemen of the Night; John Devil; The Black Coats ('Salem Street; The Invisible Weapon; The Parisian Jungle; The Companions of the Treasure; Heart of Steel; The Cadet Gang)*
Emile Gaboriau. *Monsieur Lecoq*
Steve Leadley. *Sherlock Holmes: The Circle of Blood*

Maurice Leblanc. *Arsène Lupin vs. Countess Cagliostro; Lupin vs. Holmes (The Blonde Phantom; The Hollow Needle)*
Gaston Leroux. *Chéri-Bibi; The Phantom of the Opera; Rouletabille & the Mystery of the Yellow Room*
William Patrick Maynard. *The Terror of Fu Manchu*
Frank J. Morlock. *Sherlock Holmes: The Grand Horizontals*
P. de Wattyne & Y. Walter. *Sherlock Holmes vs. Fantômas*
David White. *Fantômas in America*

SCREENPLAYS

Mike Baron. *The Iron Triangle*
Emma Bull & Will Shetterly. *Nightspeeder; War for the Oaks*
Gerry Conway & Roy Thomas. *Doc Dynamo*
Steve Englehart. *Majorca*
James Hudnall. *The Devastator*
Jean-Marc & Randy Lofficier. *Royal Flush*
J.-M. & R. Lofficier & Marc Agapit. *Despair*
Andrew Paquette. *Peripheral Vision*
R. Thomas, J. Hendler & L. Sprague de Camp. *Rivers of Time*

NON-FICTION

Stephen R. Bissette. *Blur 1-5. Green Mountain Cinema 1*
Win Scott Eckert. *Crossovers* (2 vols.)
Jean-Marc & Randy Lofficier. *Shadowmen* (2 vols.)
Randy Lofficier. *Over Here*

HEXAGON COMICS

Franco Frescura & Luciano Bernasconi. *Wampus*
Franco Frescura & Giorgio Trevisan. *CLASH*
L. Bernasconi, J.-M. Lofficier & Juan Roncagliolo Berger. *Phenix*
Claude Legrand, J.-M. Lofficier & L. Bernasconi. *Kabur*
Franco Oneta. *Zembla*
L. Buffolente, Lofficier & J.-J. Dzialowski. *Strangers: Homicron*
Danilo Grossi. *Strangers: Jaydee*
Claude Legrand & Luciano Bernasconi. *Strangers: Starlock*

ART BOOKS

Jean-Pierre Normand. *Science Fiction Illustrations*
Raven Okeefe. *Raven's L'il Critters*
Randy Lofficier & Raven OKeefe. *If Your Possum Go Daylight...*
Daniele Serra. *Illusions*